DOG
TAGS

By Alexis Jude

New Victoria Publishers Inc.

Published by New Victoria Publishers, Inc., a non-profit, feminist, literary and cultural organization.
PO Box 27, Norwich, Vermont 05055

Printed on recycled paper
Cover Design by Ginger Brown

Library of Congress Cataloging-in-Publication Data

Jude, Alexis, 1954-
    Dog tags / by Alexis Jude.
        p.   cm.
    ISBN 0-934678-50-2 : $9.95
    1. United State -- Armed forces -- Gays -- Fiction. 2 Lesbians -
- Korea -- Fiction. I. Title.
PS3560. U36D64   1993
813' .54 -- dc20   93-11798
                                                        CIP

This book is dedicated to all the lesbians in the Armed Forces, both past and present, who have suffered and still suffer from harassment, indignation and discrimination. I salute you for your perseverance and determination.

Chapter One

Kneeling before the foot-high table, Mamasan rested back on her heels, beaming over the many paper wrappings and boxes scattered around her. Before her new friend with round eyes, Myra Sturdivan, had come along, Mamasan did not believe she could befriend GIs, only work for them. They seemed so different, lazy and soft and undisciplined and always angry, ordering her about, looking down their noses at her, acting as if her job was less important than theirs. It almost seemed they were angry at *her* for their being in her country.

But now she had an American friend sitting on a pillow across the table, accepting, as if it were nothing, that her cup of tea had to be set on the floor because the white frosted cake with red trimming and thirty-eight half-melted candles marking her age took up the entire table space.

Chong-kil, Mamasan's sister, ten years younger and dim-witted, knelt at the side of the table, bright-eyed and more excited than herself. Just as her friend didn't mind her tea on the floor she also treated Chong-kil as if there was nothing wrong. "Mamasan," she remembered her U.S. friend explain one day, "not all Americans are the same. Many are angry because they have to be here. It's just that they're lonely and want to be with their families and friends."

She understood that. "Yes," she had answered, "but I no to blame."

"No, you're not," her friend had agreed but said nothing more. Mamasan had seen in her eyes that she didn't want to say that nearly all the Americans felt they were better than Koreans and were here protecting people they considered

1

unable to protect themselves.

Sipping her tea, Myra waited for Mamasan to recuperate from the surprise of all the gifts, especially the kerosene heater. Myra smiled to herself. Mamasan wouldn't have to burn charcoal briquettes under the floor for heat anymore. This method of heating was common to Koreans but the briquettes brought with them a risk—death by carbon monoxide poisoning—if not properly ventilated. Myra wanted to give something that would heat safely. Korean winters themselves could be killers.

Mamasan bent to the side and hugged her new heater, smiling at Myra. "Thank you, thank you, Stuuuurdi." Then she straightened and spread her arms wide, gesturing to all the boxes and wrappings. "So happy! Happy, happy birthday me."

Myra laughed, delighted as always with Mamasan's clipped English. Mamasan understood English well, but speaking it was harder. She had no formal education in English, but had picked words up here and there where she could.

Mamasan's house, or hooche as GIs called it, was about twice the size of an average U.S. living room, with no sofas or chairs but pillows for kneeling or sitting. A thick curtain of multi-colored beads separated this living and eating area from a deep sink and double burning hot plate set on the floor. Open shelves above the sink held pots, bowls, rice, kimchi, ramyon and other foods. A sky-blue cloth curtain separated the sleeping area where Mamasan and Chong-kil slept on mats, called yos, on the floor. Mamasan could have an U.S.-style bed, but she preferred the custom of her parents. An inside bathroom was a luxury for hotels and restaurants and the like. Here they shared a community toilet about twenty feet out back called a byon-so. The entrance door to the hooche was like a sliding patio door but made only of thick paper. These living conditions seemed scanty to GIs, but to Mamasan and her people they were simple, practical and good.

Mamasan reached over the cake. Myra extended her hand and Mamasan took it in her two and held it to her cheek, saying, "Mamasan so happy." Speaking English might stump her, but she knew how to get her message across. Myra squeezed Mamasan's hand in return. Besides the heater Myra had wrapped a number of different-sized boxes containing what she knew Mamasan wanted most—ones, fives, tens, and twenty dollar bills. Mamasan wouldn't spend them. No, she was too smart for that. She would squirrel them away for retirement or sickness. Not one of the empty boxes or wrappings would touch the trash can either. Mamasan would carefully fold them and sell them to a shopkeeper to be used again. And the big cake on the table? Well, Mamasan would make sure her sister enjoyed a piece, and she herself might dip a finger into the frosting just to taste the sweetness, but most of that cake would be sold to a restaurant. Smart.

"Come," Mamasan said, pulling Myra toward the sleeping area. "I give."

"No, Mamasan. I came for your birthday, not a massage."

"Come. I give free."

This Myra hated. Koreans in general tended to want to repay anything given. They were raised on hard work, discipline, doing without, humility, respect, honor, duty. All the things Myra herself valued. Myra pulled her back down without effort. Mamasan stood four foot seven inches on a thin frame. Her hair, black with bangs and cut straight at the shoulders, seemed as if it might weigh more than her entire body.

"No, Mamasan. This is your day."

Mamasan looked as if she had been rejected, then hissed in regret when she caught the time on Myra's watch. She tapped at it. "Bali bali," she said, pulling Myra to her feet.

Myra checked her watch, eleven-forty-five, as Chong-kil hurriedly retrieved Myra's jacket from the sleeping area.

Flicking her wrists, Mamasan shooed Myra out the door of her hooche, saying, "Bali bali back to room."

"'Night, Mamasan. Yes, I'll hurry. I know it's almost midnight."

Smiling wide, Mamasan bowed, then waved, closing her door.

Myra bowed in return, zipping her jacket up against the cool October air, and turned toward camp, still smiling. The

3

area was dark. There were no street lights—no streets, for that matter—in this back area off the main road. There were no sidewalks or grass or trees. It was just a circular area of connected hooches on hard-packed dirt. Alleyways, just wide enough to let two people walk side by side, provided they walked very close together, led deep into a maze of more hooches. Anyone not familiar with them could get lost.

Myra visited Mamasan often and knew the place well. Her First Sergeant had told her, "Now, girl, you be careful. That's Thousand Won Alley. It ain't the best of areas." Thousand Won Alley translated into two dollar blow jobs for GIs. Many of the Korean women were aged well beyond their years from trying to survive here.

It wasn't the best of areas but it was the cheapest place for Mamasan to live. Her mother had died of pneumonia at a young age and her father had followed within six months. The doctor had said it was a heart attack, but Mamasan swore it was from a broken heart. Just the same, Mamasan was left with Chong-kil to care for and a deep-rooted fear that tragedy would hit again when she least suspected. Knowing she would never marry, she knew she would have only herself to rely on. She could afford a better place but chose to save her money.

Mamasan lived in Thousand Won Alley but she didn't sell pleasure. She worked in Myra's barracks cleaning soldiers' rooms, clothes, boots. The work offered less backache than planting and harvesting in the rice paddies and she had gotten the job on her own with no favor from anyone. She was so proud of herself that she refused to be called by any other name but her job title, 'Mamasan,' Mother, a title of reverence, caretaker to the troops. Myra grinned in self-satisfied mischief. On Mamasan's cake she had put Chung-ja, Mamasan's real name. Mamasan had pointed at it, then wagged her finger in teasing reproach at Myra. In mock irreverence Myra had indignantly stuck her tongue out at her and said, "Blame Chong-kil. She gave your identity away."

Three months ago, in July, Myra had met Mamasan. One day that month Myra had returned to her room tired, sore and filthy from a three day bivouac. Her door was open and she found Mamasan with a towel wrapped around her wet head, fresh as if she had stepped out of the shower, which she had. It was something she could be fired for. Guilt had reddened Mamasan's face and fear erupted in her eyes while non-stop apologies in Korean gushed from her lips.

Grinning in amusement, Myra had let Mamasan carry on as she pulled her field gear off her back, made a pot of coffee, then headed for the shower herself. She had stopped next to Mamasan before passing and said in Mamasan's language, "Easy, Mamasan. Shower any time. My turn now. Stay. We share coffee."

Mamasan had been flabbergasted that Myra knew some Korean, not well, but spoke it and understood it a bit, too. She had been shocked that even though Myra knew she had broken a rule and had caught her, yet didn't seem to mind. In fact, to show that she didn't mind Myra had invited her to break the rule again, and had offered her coffee. Too stunned to move and needing to know the fate of her employment, Mamasan had agreed stay to and have coffee. Later Mamasan had told her that she had been even more surprised that she enjoyed, actually enjoyed an American's company. Before she left that day Mamasan had thanked Myra by giving her tired shoulders a massage.

Now Myra shook her head and grinned with the memory. So many times she had tried to get Mamasan's name out of her. "Mamasan, your name? You know mine. What is yours?" Mamasan would pat her chest with a closed proud fist, saying, "Mamasan." Just the same, Mamasan was soon helping Myra decorate her room and going shopping with her. She showed Myra's, too, how she cleaned clothes by stomping on them in a large bucket.

Myra had made sure Mamasan had the biggest cake in South Korea and enough gifts to unwrap all night. Because? Myra wasn't sure why exactly. Some of the other soldiers had asked why she liked to be around 'filthy Koreans' that didn't have flushing toilets or showers and liked to urinate in their rice paddies. Myra had answered, "I've seen GIs piss on the sidewalk and some won't take showers even though they have the facilities. And who here uses a flushing toilet when we're out in the field?" They didn't like what she said and some of them started shunning her company. But Mamasan offered her genuine friendship, and more. When she ate dinner with Mamasan and Chong-kil, she felt the warmth of the family she had lost years before. Then, too, there were Mamasan's impish jokes. Like the time Myra had returned to her room cranky after work. Mamasan said nothing but as soon as Myra's back was turned she drew a frowning smiley face with agitated brows on her mirror, making Myra laugh. The biggest reason though was that Mamasan accepted her love for women. "Love good," Mamasan had said. "No matter who."

"What about you, Mamasan? You have no man or woman."

Mamasan had shrugged and rolled her eyes, smiling coyly. "One day one will come." Smart as Mamasan was though, Myra hadn't been sure if 'one' meant a man or a woman.

Still smiling with the memories, Myra headed for one of the alleys. It was deathly quiet and she assumed it was due to the late hour. After all, she'd never been out this late before, not in this area anyway. Usually there were lots of Korean women out peddling their flesh. It was uncomfortably quiet and she quickened her pace, but froze when she heard a muffled cry coming from the alley.

Her heart started beating hard in her chest. She considered running to the Korean National Police station by the gate, but she thought by the time she fetched them it might be too late for whoever was crying out. Then she reminded herself she was a U.S. soldier, committed to defend. Feeling around on the ground, she found a fist-sized rock and palmed it.

Cautiously she approached the alley. There was little light but there was no mistaking—a rape was going on in there. The muffled cries and sobbing were painful to hear. Despite her own heart pounding in her ears, Myra took aim at the humping black shadow and whipped her rock with wounding accuracy.

She hit him between the shoulder blades just short of the head she had aimed for. Just the same, she saw him stiffen with the impact. Then he kneed himself up to his feet where he paused, rotating his shoulders to dislodge the pain. The small dark shadow of the victim jumped up and ran. No doubt it was a Korean woman. Keeping an eye on the man, Myra crouched, searching frantically for another rock. This rapist was not Korean; his shadow was too big. Whoever he was, Myra wasn't going to stick around to find out. She grabbed the rock she had fingered and bolted.

She got maybe five yards, then was jerked to a halt by a big hand on the back of her jacket. She was pulled into the same alley the Korean woman had just fled. Before she could release a scream she was slammed against the alley's stone wall and silenced by another big hand across her mouth. She just managed to hide the rock in her hand behind her back.

"You scream, bitch, and I'll bust your head wide open."

His breath was sour with the stench of whiskey. She could barely see his face but the sound of his voice brought him into clear focus. It was Craft, the file clerk specialist for her company who had arrived in the country the first of this month.

He grabbed a fistful of hair and pulled her head back. "You assaulted me, Sturdivan." He let her mouth go but nabbed her throat.

"You were raping that woman."

"That Korean hole? That was my lay for the night. She put me on her credit plan. You know," he smirked, "buy now, pay later?"

"You raped her. She was crying."

"Cries of joy, sweet thing. Besides, you're to blame for that."

"What!?"

"You should've gone out with me tonight instead of coming here to see your Mamasan. You made me follow you, and that hole came along, and you weren't coming out of that hooche and, well, a man has to do something."

The hammering of her heart in her ears was making it difficult to hear.

"Jesus! Oh, God! Craft, you don't really expect to get away with that?"

He pushed the back of her head to the stone wall. "You feel that, bitch? That hurts, doesn't it?"

Myra didn't answer.

"And think, I ain't even tried to really hurt you yet. All you

7

know is that hole was a bought whore. You can't rape the willing. You got that?" He pushed her head into the wall.

The grains of the rough stone cut into her scalp. She nodded and he eased up.

"And what is a pretty little girl like you doing in Thousand Won Alley, anyway?"

"You followed me. You tell me."

He yanked her hair. "Don't play with me."

"Visiting Mamasan," she cried. "And you know it."

"Yeah," he said smugly. "But for what?"

"She's a friend."

"Friend, huh? Your Mamasan is a friend who lives in Thousand Won Alley, huh? You won't go out with me but you come out to Thousand Won Alley to be with a Mamasan?"

"What the fuck are you trying to say?"

"A little girl like you won't go out with me. You wear combat boots. You keep short hair and you visit your Mamasan. Know what I think? I think you and Mamasan buck together on a double-headed dildo."

Myra clenched her teeth and squeezed her rock. This accusation didn't surprise her. In the Army if a woman wasn't with a man she was accused of having sex with a woman whether or not it was true. They didn't seem to believe there was any such thing as just friendship. It hadn't helped to avoid the temptation of love relationships either. As if it was anybody's business who she slept with. At her last post she had been suspected and managed to survive only by her own silence and a request for transfer back to Korea.

"You nasty bastard."

He laughed. "Me, nasty? You're the one deprived me of some normal recreation. I wasn't quite finished if you know what I mean. Now you're going to help me finish. You're going to help me finish and you're going to enjoy it and you're not going to say a word about tonight. It'll be our little secret. And after tonight you'll see me on a regular basis. In fact, you won't go out with anyone but me. After all, you don't want word to get out that you're a dyke and have been buying pussy on Thousand Won Alley, do you?"

Myra could only stare into the dark, wide-eyed.

He laughed at the fear on her face.

"To tell you the truth, that sounds pretty good. I think I'll spread it around to keep the other guys away. Double my insurance." He hardened cold blue eyes on her. "You won't go out with me? I'll turn everybody against you. In the end you'll come begging to me for comfort. And if you don't keep your mouth shut I'll just pay a visit on your sweet Mamasan. She's like all the rest. They love U.S. meat."

Myra's head was burning and swimming. This guy was nuts. This guy was dangerous. This guy she had to get away from. "I'll see you in hell," she growled through clenched teeth and banged him on the head with her rock.

It stunned him long enough for her to escape into the maze of alleys.

Chapter Two

Myra Sturdivan stood with her back to her supply room door. The top half of the door was open and the lower half was closed and locked from the inside. Atop the lower half was a metal shelf she used as a counter. All around her were fans, linen, pillows, gas masks, canteens, MREs, field gear, toilet tissue, ponchos, helmets, insect repellent, mosquito nets, office supplies and a myriad of other items for her company. She kept everything neat and orderly from her throne.

Her throne was a roller, a black cushioned chair with armrests, tucked close to her old but solid wooden desk squatting in the middle of her queendom. Behind her were two more desks for her assistants. She felt as one with her throne. It was well-worn and abused with the cushion ripped along the sides. She felt she understood what it had gone through before she arrived nine months ago. Reigning in her queendom, she felt calm and in control and powerful.

Only she knew the contents of this room. Her two helpers she had let loose earlier this afternoon would keep their mouths shut. She was viewed as a good supervisor and they knew the importance of supply where items were sometimes fought over. Only she, despite her monthly reports to the company commander, could say whether she had more of an item in big demand, like fans in the summer. And anyone wanting anything must talk nicely to her—at least while he was trying to get it.

This room was the knot at the end of her rope. In this room she could convince herself that no, she was not dead, not in hell—she was alive, albeit barely. Keeping this room neat and tidy not only reflected her competence in her field but also kept her mind neat and tidy

Doing her monthly report, Myra stood with a pencil in one hand and pad in the other, checking and counting gas masks when her ears alerted her to a laughing, unfamiliar female voice. Seven women besides herself and two hundred and two men made up Admin Company, Seoul, South Korea. Having good ears, she could identify every woman's and nearly every man's voice. Since she maintained impeccable records on everyone's supply issue, she knew when everyone had come to the company and when their tours in Korea would end.

"You're kidding!?" Myra heard the unfamiliar voice remark, astonished, from down the hall. "She'll shine my boots, make my bed and clean my room!?"

This woman had to be new to Korea, since she didn't know yet about Mamasan.

"That's right," Spec 4 Craft's voice confirmed. At the sound of his voice Myra's body stiffened and the familiar feeling of panic began to creep up her spine. He continued, "She even sets you up for inspections. All for only thirty dollars a month. More if you want to tip her, but I wouldn't advise it."

Myra's brow cocked as she twisted her lips and mouthed a mocking "I wouldn't advise it" to the gas masks. She kept a countdown calendar of Spec 4 Craft's departure date, exactly four months from today, April 29. She should know. Daily he took a copy of his orders for Stateside duty out of his fatigue shirt pocket and, with a carnivorous grin, waved it at her, saying, "Not much time left to have me."

"Why not? Doesn't she do a good job?" the woman asked. Both she and Craft sounded close now. She liked the woman's voice, husky and firm.

"She's only a half-head."

Myra's neck tensed into tight cords over Craft's label for Koreans. She didn't turn around to them even though, by the sound, he and the woman had stopped on the other side of her half-door. She could picture Craft leaning a muscular arm on the counter, completely convinced he was impressing the woman with his knowledge as he continued, "She'll only steal from you if you start tipping." Craft boasted as if he knew about every Korean on post. The sad fact was that many of her fellow GIs agreed with him.

Then Myra heard IT. The pencil poised above her pad suddenly bore down, the point snapping. She was used to IT, had heard IT countless times. She knew IT was born from jealousy and anger and vengeance and hurt. She didn't know exactly when IT had begun. One day IT wasn't and the next IT...

"Miiiiikeeeey!"

There IT was again. By reflex her hand clamped onto the dog tags that hung from her neck. They were two simple, two-inch rectangular pieces of aluminum on a long, beaded silver chain. Name, social security number, blood type and religion were indented on each piece. Beige rubber casings prevented them from clanking together. Soldiers wore their dog tags tucked unseen inside their shirts. But not Myra. Hers dangled conspicuously outside her shirt. Her hand clamped onto them and squeezed. Her knuckles turned white as she labored to regain her composure while trying to ignore Craft's lilting, mocking call. "Oh, Miiiiiikeeeeey!"

Again, but this time IT was longer, more intense, nauseatingly sweeter. She would not answer or even turn around. A psychology course had taught her that if she didn't respond to inappropriate behavior, IT would go away. But IT refused to quit. She held on to her tags and herself. Waves of prickly goose bumps raced up and down her spine. Her stomach somersaulted, tying itself into a tight kink as she remembered, could never forget, Craft's humping shadow in the alley six months ago. Alternating hot and cold flashes launched an assault on her head. IT was cruel enough that IT showed ITself at all, but to do so in front of a woman with such a pleasant voice seemed akin to slicing her nipples off with a jagged, rusty razor.

When Craft called the name the first time and the Specialist behind the counter didn't turn around, the new woman smiled with him, thinking it was a pet name. With no response to the second calling, she grew concerned, considering that maybe there was a lover's silent quarrel going on. As he crooned the name the third time, the woman saw that his blue eyes danced more with malice than mischief and his thin lips curved into a sneer rather than a smile. There was something seriously wrong here. Her gut suggested it was something she had run into before, but not on such a blatant level.

"Oh..." Craft started again.

The woman silenced him with a touch of her hand to his chest. One more croon and she wasn't sure she'd be able to stop herself from backhanding him. Craning her neck, she addressed the silent woman's rank. "Specialist."

The tone of the new woman's voice acted like a giant, warm hand soothing away Myra's tension, comforting, loosening a memory of long ago love. As soon as she recognized the thought she hastily smacked it back.

"Specialist, are you all right?"

This time the woman's voice commanded, jolting Myra. Thinking the woman had to be an officer, she clicked her heels to attention. As she whirled about, executing a precise about-face, she knew it was not the possibility of officer rank but rather the woman's voice she was responding to. She now stood at perfect attention, but for the hand that still clutched her dog tags, braving the woman and Craft.

"Yes, Ma—" Eyeing the woman's rank, three stripes and two rockers, Myra stopped. This was no officer but a Sergeant First Class (E-7), two steps above a simple Sergeant (E-5). "Yes, Sergeant," she corrected herself.

Myra was embarrassed over the incident and found herself only able to glare at Craft. He was snickering, turning his head away as if embarrassed for her, and stealing glances at the Sergeant First Class. Myra's sole comfort was in remembering the cut and bruise her rock had left on his now healed head. Though only a second had lapsed since she about-faced, it felt like an eternity to her. She braced and forced her eyes to the Sergeant's.

The Sergeant had already taken in the Specialist from her glossy, black combat boots up the petite body clad in green jungle fatigues, or BDUs as they were called, Battle Dress Uniform, to the heart-shaped face. A mass of thick chestnut hair twirled and pinned into a loose bun crowned her. She was an attractive woman with a sharp military appearance. So why was she wearing her dog tags outside her uniform? Why was she pulling on them so hard that the chain seemed to be cutting into the back of her neck? Those questions were wiped completely out of her mind when her eyes were entrapped by the Specialist's.

Years of discipline had taught the Sergeant to keep herself in check, regardless of the situation. And this situation demanded the use of all her discipline. She felt herself being drawn into the Specialist's doe eyes. It seemed as if this Specialist was physically reaching out to her, calling while tenderly gathering her hands in her own and gently bringing their bodies together. The Sergeant blinked and this time saw creases on the sides of her fetching lips, on her forehead and by those beautiful eyes. Age hadn't created those creases. The harrowed eyes and careworn face translated into confusion and weary hopelessness. Shocking. Still, they exuded a gentleness and love that whatever this Specialist had gone through could not destroy.

Myra couldn't pull her eyes away although she felt almost insubordinate maintaining eye contact. The Sergeant had charcoal eyes, round and deep and rich. They were soft and understanding but firm. Her face was handsome but stern with a no-nonsense expression. Her short tapered hair shone with the same dark color and richness as her eyes. Realizing she wanted to touch that face with its smooth olive complexion, she forced her eyes away.

Now able to clearly see the black, pin-on rank on her collar, the Sergeant could see that this Specialist was not a first-step Spec 4 like Craft but a Specialist 7th Class, equal to her own Sergeant First Class. The difference was that she, as a Sergeant, commanded groups of soldiers while this Specialist commanded only expertise in her field. Though technically equal, the Sergeant held authority over the Specialist. The sight of the Spec 7 pins gave the Sergeant an ear-to-ear grinning advantage. "At ease, Specialist."

Myra separated her boots but not by much.

"Specialist, is your first name Mikey?" The Sergeant watched the face pale and the knuckles over the dog tags stretch shockingly whiter.

"No, Sergeant. It's Myra."

"Is Mikey a nickname of yours? Or do you prefer to be called Mikey?"

Craft sobered. His brows furrowed in uncertainty.

Myra hesitated, glancing at Craft.

"*I* am addressing you, Specialist, not him."

Myra's eyes dutifully darted back to the Sergeant. "Uh, no, Sergeant." She released the dog tags and brought her hand down.

The Sergeant turned to Craft. "Specialist, take a good look at her rank and tell me what it is."

"Oh, come on, Sarge. I was just—"

"*Answer* my question."

Craft didn't look. He shamefully admitted, "Specialist 7th Class."

"Does that outrank you, Specialist?"

Craft tucked his head and mumbled, "Yeah."

"Stand at attention, soldier, and speak up."

Craft jumped to attention and stared straight ahead, humiliation reddening his cheeks. "Yes, Sergeant."

"Who is your new Admin NCO, Specialist?"

"You are, Sergeant."

Myra's brow arched. So, this Sergeant would be replacing Gallo as the new Non-Commissioned Officer in Charge of the Admin office. Craft was not making a good first impression.

The Sergeant continued, "Very good, soldier. Now I will say this only once so I advise you to listen up. That Specialist," the Sergeant pointed at Myra who reared back, "and any other Specialist E-5 and above may not be able to command you, but they outrank you and you will, I repeat, you will respect that rank. If there is a personal problem between you, you will not show it. You will act like a professional. You will not call any soldier by a name by which she does not wish to be addressed. You will adhere to military courtesies at all times. Being on a hardship tour does not give you liberty to regress to a barbaric level. Do I make myself clear?"

"But, Sarge, you don't know about her. You don't wan...."

"Specialist!" the Sergeant silenced what she felt certain he was about to imply, judging by the cynical "Mikey." This Specialist was a lesbian and therefore not worthy of living freely

15

as a human being, let alone worthy of respect by rank. She had run into this attitude a lot at other duty stations and already this one was proving itself to be no different. "If you ever try to tell me what I want or don't want again, I will make your remaining four months here so damn miserable that brown fuzz you call hair will turn white. Your own mother won't recognize you after I'm through with you." She paused, inhaling and, anchoring angry eyes on Myra, vowed to herself that if he was responsible for so much as one crease on that face... She returned her attention to Craft, willing to bet he was. "Your charge of assisting me through in-processing has ended. Dismissed."

"Thank you, Sergeant." Craft did a clumsy about-face and fled.

* * *

As soon as Craft squealed around the corner out of sight, the Sergeant turned to Myra, but carefully. If the Sergeant didn't, she was sure she'd lose herself in Myra's heart-melting brown eyes.

Myra held her stance but now fear showed in those eyes. After all, the Sergeant was Myra's new superior, not just Craft's. But fear was the last thing the Sergeant wanted this Specialist to feel toward her. The Sergeant grinned. "Well, I'd say that was a good beginning to my new duty."

The Specialist lowered her eyes and smiled shyly. The Sergeant could see that something or someone had beaten this woman down, yet she stood erect on two, shoulder-width apart, firm boots. Something in that face spoke of greater strength, she was sure, than this Specialist might be willing to admit. Just the same, the Sergeant's gut advised her to tread very carefully.

"Are you going to let me in?" The Sergeant turned her back, hoisted herself onto the counter, swung her legs over and landed gracefully on the floor inside the supply room. "Or do I let myself in?"

Stunned, Myra could only gawk. In dress greens and skirt this woman had done a hurdle. "Oh, uh, whichever you prefer, Sergeant."

The Sergeant threw her head back and laughed. Surprise

16

was better than fear.

"Sit." She motioned Myra to her throne. "I perform only for the chosen few." Once Myra was seated, the Sergeant reached a hand over the desk. "I'm Victoria Barrett. Tory."

The hand the Sergeant offered looked capable and strong and as olive-toned as the rest of her. Myra took the firm, warm hand, hoping her own was just as pleasing. "Myra Sturdivan, Sergeant, Specialist in charge of Supply."

Tory held onto Myra's hand and with her left grabbed hold of Myra's collar rank and shook it. "Yes. I've been told. But this." She shook Myra's Spec 7 collar rank again. "This says we're equal in rank. Call me Tory."

Myra felt uneasy yet almost giddy with delight. She was staring at the woman's hand and thinking how finely sculpted it was when a "Hmm?" as if Tory were clearing her throat caught her attention. She looked up to what later she'd identify as The Look. Tory was tucking her head and throwing her charcoal eyes up at her. The Look would come to mean a number of different things, depending on the circumstances, but The Look always meant Tory would win. And because The Look always had Myra's best interest at heart, Myra would grow not only to not care that The Look won, but love it. The Look at the moment said, I'm waiting.

"Yes. Tory. Thank you." Myra wondered when Tory was going to release her hand while wishing she'd hang on forever.

"May I call you Myra?"

"Myra would be pleasant." She smiled and confirmed herself with a squeeze to Tory's hand, but didn't release it.

Yes, pleasant and gentle, Tory said to herself. Her voice was so gentle. The squeeze pulled Tory deeper into Myra's eyes. Discipline, she told herself. Not responding to it, her mind screamed, REMEMBER?! Releasing Myra's hand, she backed up to lean against the half-door and crossed her ankles and arms comfortably.

"I want to take action against Craft. Since he was insubordinate to you I'll consider your suggestion."

Myra paled. Wouldn't that be great! "Mikey" crooning all over a report in black and white. The Army gladly hunted people like herself out for discharge. She wasn't about to draw an arrow and wave it for them.

"I'd prefer you let it slide."

"Is it a lover's quarrel?"

"In *his* mind," she said, half concentrating on what Tory was saying and half on how Tory looked with her slender ankles and shapely legs, the hem of her skirt precisely at mid-kneecap, the rest of her uniform fitting as if tailor-made, all brass highly shined. Obviously, she took pride in her uniform and filled it with a body that wasn't slim or stout but strong, looking as though it could handle just about anything.

Tory was encouraged. "He asked you out and you refused."

"More than once."

"Is that the only reason?"

"No, but I'd rather not go into it."

Piss on that. "No action at all?"

"The guillotine would be good," Myra mumbled, thinking about the Korean woman in the alley and his threats on Mamasan and herself.

"Excuse me?" Tory had heard but wanted Myra to expound.

Myra shook her head. "You've already taken appropriate action."

"I've talked with Top. He's given me the basics on my duties and my troops. He speaks highly of you and your work. I hear you're also a bull's eye with the M16." She said it teasingly and got what she had hoped for. A wide smile stretched Myra's cheeks. Such beautiful white teeth.

Myra liked Top, the company's First Sergeant. He was gruff yet sweet and often won his way with the Captain. She quickly began to pull forms out of her desk drawer. The compliment both unnerved and delighted her. Finally she said, "I'm flattered but I'm not that good."

"Supply was the only section that didn't have to work overtime to prepare for the last Battalion Inspection and passed with flying colors."

"That's true," Myra said in dismissal. As of late she wasn't used to such kind treatment. "I have all the forms. We can either begin your issue now and you can carry your things with you or you can just sign the forms and I'll bring them to your room later."

Tory smiled. "I take it I won't have to watch over your shoulder to ensure this section is run well?"

Myra squared on Tory. "You can bet your paycheck on it, Sergeant."

Myra's assertion sent a familiar tingle to Tory's groin. She smiled again, then checked her watch. "Admin work hours run 0800 to 1600. It's 1545. Let's get the issue and we'll both take it up."

* * *

Toting heavy loads, Myra and Tory wobbled their way along the cement walk from the large Quonset hut that held the Admin, Supply and Arms offices to the three-story barracks building a hundred feet behind. Their arms struggled with field gear, bedding and suitcases that constantly threatened to slip.

"You're going to find out you should have listened to me," Myra warned, blowing a wisp of hair that had fallen from under Tory's helmet.

Tory had already found that out but refused to surrender. She giggled, "Come on, soldier. Back in Basic you did the impossible, remember?"

"Yes, but I was younger then. And you've probably forgotten what the barracks are like."

Tory backed the door of the building open for Myra to enter first. After all, Myra did have her duffel on her back as well as both arms loaded.

"Then tell me. What's life like here in the barracks?"

Myra shuddered, then quickly recovered. "There's hardly any noise. Most of the guys stay in the village outside the gate with their yobos."

Tory followed Myra, letting the door close by itself behind her. "I've heard that's called the ville. 'Yobos' I haven't heard of."

"It means husband or wife, but that's what the guys call their Korean girlfriends or, more accurately, their bedmates.

19

They're local women who have little one room hooches in the ville. Basically, these women rent themselves out by the month. The guys live with them in their hooches but still maintain rooms here. The women give them sex, feed them, do their laundry, anything. But mostly the guys have them for sex. The woman calls her 'renter' her husband and takes care of only him until he either doesn't pay his bill or transfers out. Then she finds another 'husband'."

Incredulous, Tory elbowed Myra, stopping her. "Why would—"

Myra cut her off with, "It's a different world here, Tory. Korean women still walk three steps behind their men. Their job options are limited and they have to survive, so they hire themselves out to GIs. They get no respect but they earn their living. Craft calls all Korean women 'holes' whether they sell themselves or not."

A bit hurt, but more confused, Tory said, "But I had heard prostitution is legal here."

"The guys think so because prostitutes here aren't arrested unless someone gets hurt. Mamasan says her government knows women have to survive so they turn their heads."

Myra looked into Tory's still confused eyes. "But to be fair, Craft's not the only one who calls them all 'holes'. There's at least one guy here who wants to marry his yobo but he won't until the last minute before he leaves because he doesn't want the other guys laughing at him, saying he's marrying a whore."

"Are you kidding?"

"I wouldn't kid about that. 'Half head' is another endearing term used to describe Koreans in general."

"I heard Craft say that but I didn't understand why."

"It's sick really. And many of the others share his sentiments. Even some of the women, but they're the ones hanging on guys, you know, needing to be liked. Anyway, I think the reason Koreans are called that is because they don't understand or speak English well. So we call them stupid."

"But that's ridiculous. We're the guests here. We should be learning Korean."

Myra looked seriously at Tory, nodding her approval.

"That's right."

Tory lowered her eyes, then raised them. "Let's not say 'we'. I'd rather not be included in that and I doubt you are." She watched Myra smile wanly, then said, "We better get moving or I'm going to drop right here."

Myra turned and started again but seemed lost in thought. Tory, concentrating on Myra, didn't notice the wide, green-tiled hall they were crossing or what they were heading towards, but she did notice that she didn't like Myra's silence. It brought home the saying "Truth is painful."

"Can I assume hooches are houses?"

Myra's head jerked as if awakened abruptly. "Oh, tiny apartments. Paper-thin walls. It's not a Korean word. I'm not sure where it came from but you don't want to live in one."

"Why not?"

"A few reasons, but mainly guys are almost expected to want or have one because, you know, it means they've hired a Korean woman."

"Ah! If I wanted one just for privacy I'd—"

"Yes," Myra said, abruptly stopping her.

Tory shut her mouth. She knew when to take a hint. God forbid a lesbian dare exist in *this* homophobic US Army.

Very few women lived in the ville for the same reason Myra herself didn't—fear of being labeled lesbian. She could remember one woman who had, however. Kraider. Kraider had been a Drill Sergeant at the school near the DMZ. The school trained soldiers for becoming Sergeants. She had been sick to death of having to ward off the men's crude advances, so she requested to live in the ville. When the guys made the same request they were automatically approved and slapped on the back with a 'Way to go', but Kraider had had to fight a couple of months for the same right. She'd finally gotten it after getting a Chaplain to state it would be best for her mental health. And it was. Kraider had hired a yobo. Last Myra had heard was that she was trying to get her yobo home to the States.

"If there's privacy and quiet here, what's wrong?" Tory asked.

"Well, I might as well warn you. You're going to be hit on

21

fast and in a very direct way. The word is that Korea is a lonely place and the boys feel that loneliness. To curb it they'll hit on anything that even looks like it might wear a skirt. There are plenty of prostitutes but they want American women."

Tory hooted. "I suppose that's because they don't see U.S. women as 'holes' like the Korean women, right?"

"Right," Myra affirmed.

"What about the military women? I know they get lonely."

"The women aren't seen as having that problem. After all, there are plenty of men to help pull them through. But, what's really wrong with the barracks?" Myra suddenly stopped, startling Tory. "Those."

Tory followed her eyes up stairs that seemed to go on forever. "Mama!"

"The first, second and part of the third floors are all for men, NCO as well as enlisted. Except NCOs get private rooms. Officers are housed in another building. To your right is the mail room and dayroom where there are beer, soda and munchie machines. We," Myra paused, lifting her eyes all the way up, stretching her neck, "females are on the third floor."

"Mama, mama!" Tory cried. Her back and arms were aching and she knew Myra's were, too. "Let's drop everything here. You go up with a load and I'll watch the rest. Then you can come back and…"

"No way." Myra stopped her, then tried to pat the rank on Tory's jacket sleeve but the bundles prevented her. "You are Tory," she teased, reminding her of their equal rank.

"Touché. But I've got two inches on you. I'll bring up the rear. In case you trip I can at least cushion the fall."

By the time they reached the second floor they were groaning about their aching legs. As they climbed to the third Myra heard an "Oops" behind her. Cautiously she turned. Tory was bent in a V with her ass in the air, leaning her bundles forward to stop her expected tumble backwards. Stifling a laugh, Myra lumbered down and shouldered Tory's behind.

Tory straightened herself with a grunt and twisted, looking down at Myra. Seeing Myra wasn't moving to take the front position again, she said, "One little oops and you caste all faith in me away?"

"Oh, no, Sergeant. It's only that I'm more familiar with these steps."

"Well," she said indignantly, "if you put it that way."

As soon as Tory turned Myra stifled another laugh.

At the third floor landing Tory halted. "Sturdivan, lead the way, and quickly. I'm about to give out."

Without hesitation, Myra willed her muscles to hang on and ran right to the door of room 306 and dropped the bundles and duffel. She ran back to Tory, grabbed a couple of her bags, ran back to the door, dropped them, ran...

At the door Tory stretched the kinks out of her muscles. Rubbing her neck, she squinted at Myra. "How old are you anyway?"

"Thirty-four."

"So that explains your greater stamina. I have not only two inches on you but two years as well."

Myra smiled with the attention. How long had it been since she felt so giddy and, she raised her eyes to Tory, so secure beside a person?

Tory saw Myra's eyes glimmer briefly with a life struggling to come out. She smiled knowingly, then unlocked the door. A musty closed up odor smacked her in the face. When Myra brought in all bags, Tory stood still, taking in her new home. Yellow cinder block walls, the same green tile on the floor, two bunks, two gray metal lockers, an old wooden desk and chair, a small bathroom or 'latrine' with a sink mirror, commode and shower.

Seeing the misgiving on Tory's face, Myra blurted, "It's really very nice for us higher-ups here." She opened the white venetian blind, then the window. Sunshine filled the room, exposing dust. The air gave it life. "We at least have private rooms. As you settle in you'll collect things from the ville and dress it up."

Tory was dazed, grappling with the reality that she was indeed here, in Korea, ten thousand miles from home.

Myra planted herself directly in front of her. "Sergeant?"

Tory blinked. "Sorry. I must have spaced out."

"This is your first time in Korea. You have a lot of adjusting to do." Myra's voice was soothing.

"You're right. And I haven't lived in barracks for years. I...I sold my house before coming here...reluctantly."

Myra nodded in sympathy. "I'm sure you want to freshen up. Dinner is sixteen-hundred to eighteen-thirty."

"I don't think I'm up to eating."

"I know, but you really should. I'm going to find Mamasan and send her to make your bed. I'm in 301 by the fire escape if you need anything."

Tory wanted her to stay but said, "I don't even know who Mamasan is."

Myra smiled softly, wishing she could hug Tory and make her feel easy. "Actually, 'mamasan' is a Japanese word, but our Mamasan is a very helpful Korean woman, a civilian. She is the one you'll be hiring for thirty a month to clean things and polish boots. She has a master key and will just let herself in. You'll be glad you have her."

Myra rushed out then, running from the feelings that had begun when she first heard Tory's voice. Very dangerous, she said to herself, remembering the sobbing woman in the alley and Craft's threats—at least for the next four months.

* * *

Within five minutes of her leaving, Tory heard the click of her door opening. She had removed her pumps and jacket and was sitting on the bunk by the inner wall. Turning, she watched a Korean woman in her thirties, with jet black hair and black almond eyes, come into the room and stand by the bed. She wore an ankle-length gray skirt, a simple blouse and a gray kerchief to hold her hair back. She was grinning wide, bowing, saying "Yoboseyo" to her. Tory had no idea 'Yoboseyo' meant hello, but to be respectful she returned the bow and greeting which made Mamasan smile wider.

Mamasan was eager to please this new American. Myra had never asked her to be especially kind to any other woman new to the company. For this one though, Myra had asked, offering a generous tip. Myra had asked but Mamasan had seen in her eyes a plea. It told her this new woman had to be good and special. Mamasan liked the way she returned her bow and greeting. Most Americans just laughed and nodded their heads as if bowing was beneath them instead of a cordial respect.

"I make bed? This one?" Mamasan pointed to the one by the window. "That one?" She pointed at the one Tory was sitting on.

With a jolt Tory realized what she was asking. "Oh. That one." She half-smiled, nodding at the bed by the window. Mamasan bowed and began removing bags and bundles from atop the bunk. Tory brought the heel of her hand to her forehead. "I can be so stupid," she said and got up to help.

"No, no, no," Mamasan insisted, shooing her back to the other bed. "Sit. Sit." She brought a hand to her own eye and motioned the wiping away of a tear. "You no feel good. Sit. I do."

"You're right there," Tory agreed and sat. In-processing, chewing out Craft and being with Myra had silenced the pain of being so far from home, of jet lag and of a stomach that wanted to regurgitate.

Determined to make Tory feel better, Mamasan smiled wide again but close and into Tory's face, startling her, demanding her attention. "Your friend, Stuuuurdi," she sang the name, "come get me. Say, bali bali. You no feel good."

"Bali bali?"

Mamasan ran in place, nodding, smiling to coax Tory into smiling with her. Tory couldn't help but laugh with the kind woman.

Gladdened, Mamasan turned to the bed, saw the condition of the linen Myra had issued, and turned back to Tory with a raised finger saying, "I be back." She went to Myra's room and let herself in. Myra was standing by her desk having already taken off her boots and fatigue shirt. In her hand was a cup of coffee she had raised to her lips about to drink.

"No, no," Mamasan said, wagging a chiding finger. She rushed to Myra and took the cup from her hand. In Korean she said, "If you don't know how to treat someone special special, then I will do it for you." She turned to rush out.

Surprised with her now empty hand, Myra answered in Korean, "Mamasan, no sure she special."

Mamasan went back to her. "Yes," she said, switching to

English. "You sure. I see what you give. This." She raised the cup in her hand. "I give her for you."

"No, Mamasan. That might be too much right now."

"I know," she said, reverting to Korean as she went toward the door. "I must be careful that you don't look like a woman lover until you know she's the same. Trust Mamasan."

"Trust you!? You haven't even told me whether you want a man or woman."

Mamasan grinned at her from the doorway. "Thanks to you I've found happiness. Soon you'll know."

Stunned, unsure of what that meant, Myra said to the empty room, "Well, all right. I'll just swig from the pot."

In Tory's room Mamasan bowed, grinning, offering the cup to Tory. "For you from Stuuuurdi."

"Really?" Tory asked, taking the cup. "I'll have to thank her."

Mamasan nodded and turned to the bed, finding the linen and pillow for it. Now somehow to tell this new American that Myra found her attractive. She picked up a pillow and said, "Ooooh," pressing her cheek to it while smiling at Tory. "So new!" She swept her hand along the folded white sheets and pillowcases and blankets, then pointed at another pillow. "*All* so new! *Two* pillows! Stuurdi nice lady. You, her?" She crossed her index and middle fingers together. "You, her?"

Surprised and uncertain, Tory could only shrug her shoulders.

"You, her," Mamasan stated firmly, nodding her head. "Stuurdi nice lady. Very." Mamasan made her face into a deep frown and used her middle finger and thumb to gesture a down movement from her eyes.

"Sad?" Tory asked.

"Sad, yes," Mamasan said. "Hurt." She tapped a loose fist to her heart. "You her friend. All new. No other get all new. You, her." She crossed her fingers in finality.

Tory smiled and Mamasan, satisfied, settled into her work.

Chapter Three

Sergeant First Class Victoria Barrett had been to many different posts in her military career. "But none like this one," she said aloud, peering through the venetian blind at the dark outside. Lights from other buildings told her there was life out there, but damned little and the night looked desolate. "Everything looks worse at night." She dropped the slat and flopped onto her bunk, fingers entwined behind her head.

Her gaze drifted about her new home. The lockers stood open, one containing her civilian clothes, the other her military issue. Tomorrow Mamasan would clean and press everything. Such wonderful service. But what did a soldier do with her free time? It was only eight o'clock in the evening. No TV, not even a radio. Couldn't bring a car here to at least go for a drive. She had showered and changed. Her stomach growled but her brain stamped a 'no go' even at the thought of food. No place that she knew of yet to go. No friend yet to go anywhere with, except—her mind paused as her eyes settled on the field gear in her locker—except for Myra.

Myra had issued her not only brand new bedding but also brand new field gear. Tory imagined that Mamasan's words were true when she said, "No other get all new." After all, she entered all rooms daily to do her work. Could Myra have been saying something intimate with the all brand new issue or had she just been catering to her rank?

"Well, hell," Tory said aloud, pushing herself up. Why not see what Myra did with her time? Maybe get a little closer now that they were off duty. Needing to return the cup anyway, she kicked off her slippers for white sneakers.

The fire exit door was propped open and a cool breeze flowed into the hallway. Tory tentatively knocked on Myra's door. With no answer she knocked again firmly, putting an ear to it. She heard no bunk springs creaking, no feet shuffling, no shower running. "Damn."

She studied the long hall. Not one body stirred along it. The faint sound of music drifted from one of the rooms at the opposite end. Myra hadn't exaggerated. These barracks were eerily quiet. Where did everyone go? Where should she go? Maybe getting some air would help.

After placing the cup by the door, she stepped out onto the fire escape landing. Steps led down through the dark to the ground. She took in a deep breath of air laced with an unidentifiable sour smell and leaned her elbows on the steel railing. For several minutes she stood, ingesting the foreign land around her. The night seemed darker here than in the States.

"You really should have a jacket on."

Tory jerked upright. She had thought she was alone.

"The breeze is very pleasant. Enjoy it but don't let it fool you. It'll bite when you least expect it. It still has a touch of winter."

Tory recognized the gentleness and patience of the voice. It came from below. She strained her eyes, but still...

"No. You can't see me, but if you're smart you'll see this as a learning experience. There are always eyes."

Hanging onto the rail, Tory cautiously moved down the stairs. She'd be damned before she let this game continue. On the second landing Tory found her. "Myra!" she scolded. "No wonder I didn't see you sitting here. Black jeans, black socks, black sneakers, black jacket and black hood!? You look like the Grim Reaper."

Myra slowly pulled the hood off her head.

Tory cocked her head. "What's with the outfit?"

"Outfit?"

Crouching, Tory grabbed the jacket sleeve and shook it. "What's with the black get-up?"

"It makes me feel as one with the night."

Confused and a bit frightened, Tory searched Myra's eyes. They were the same as before with the glint of love shining through the despair.

"Being one with the night makes me feel invisible, peaceful."

Tory sat down on a step and surrendered to a shiver. Myra was right. Now the air chilled her.

Myra rose to her feet, unzipped her jacket and removed it. "Here," she said, spreading the jacket over Tory's shoulders.

"Oh, no..."

"Yes. I have a sweater on. And I'm used to the air. Tonight cool and breezy. The morning cool and calm. Tomorrow warm and breezy."

"That's why they call it the Land of the Morning Calm?" Tory looked up, uncertain. Myra wore a black pullover sweater. That didn't confound her so much as the swinging dog tags, still on the outside of her clothes.

Myra finished arranging the jacket and smiled. She gave Tory's shoulder a squeeze and retreated to her former seat. "Yes, the mornings are always calm."

"How long have you been here?"

"About a half hour. I can relax here. With the summer coming on though, I'll have to find another spot. Most everyone uses the inside steps during the cold, but tonight I've seen more than the usual number of people use these."

"What I really wanted to know was how long you've been in country."

"Oh, sorry." Myra blushed, embarrassed.

"Don't be sorry. I'm glad I found out about this hidey-hole of yours."

"I'd rather you don't spread it around."

"Guaranteed. How long in-country?"

"Years."

"But Korea's only a one year tour."

"Yes, but you can re-up for it, put in for an extension, or return to the States and immediately put in for Korea again. Most people don't like duty here so it's fairly easy to get. Heck, Top's been in service twenty-two years and spent seventeen here."

"What about you?"

"I've been in," Myra paused to think, "oh, about sixteen years now and spent nine here. Not here on this camp. All over. But here in Seoul is good. There's a fairly large shopping ville outside post."

"Damn!" Tory cried, running a hand through her hair. "I've been in eighteen and never thought I'd ever see Korea. Hell, I did a stint in 'Nam. I felt sure that was enough. I put in for Germany—they send me here." With that her stomach growled.

"Did you? I was in 'Nam, too. They sent me when I re-upped the first time back in '72. I was there only six months when I got this." Myra pulled up her left pant leg and pushed down her sock. There was a three inch scar on the left side of her calf. "Got intimate with a land mine. They dug a piece of metal out of my bone. Took quite a while to heal but it's almost as good as new."

"No purple heart, I bet."

Myra jerked her sock back up and her pant leg down. "I wasn't in actual combat. They sent me home right away."

"When I was there in '68 I saw men with hangnails getting them."

"I did get Spec 5 out of it."

Tory's stomach growled with greater anger.

"Have you eaten?"

Tory waved it off. "Not hungry."

Myra, used to the dark, saw tears swell in Tory's eyes. "Hey," she said, giving a squeeze to Tory's forearm, comforting, "you may not be hungry but your stomach is."

Tory shook her head. "No." She wiped away an escaping tear. "It's just that sometimes I wonder why I keep re-upping. Women never get thanked. And tonight, well, I guess it's just that I'm not yet comfortable here. Everything's strange. I miss my place, my friends."

"I know why you keep re-upping. You as well as I love being in uniform. We love being a part of the colossal, protective shield."

"Colossal, protective shield? With the way you were talking earlier about what the guys call Korean women and Koreans in general I don't see how we're protecting."

"I know, but I prefer to think of the main objectives of the Army being to protect and defend. Remember? Duty, honor, country, integrity, dedication? The quickening of your heart as you marched to the beat in parades, flaunting your purpose? We are colossal when we unite for a cause—and we would protect if any fighting broke out. As far as women not getting thanked, well, it doesn't matter. What does count is that we know we're worthy of being in Athena's Army. But enough of that." She stood. Offering her hands, she said, "Come."

Tory looked up at Myra's hands. Strangely enough she felt as if she were one with Myra. Both Myra and she had joined the Army when women joined not the Regular Army but the Women's Auxiliary Corps and were called WACs. The goddess Athena represented the WACs. She was independent, strong, compassionate, wise—the goddess of war, yet battled with peace and wisdom as her weapons. All WACs wore a brass bust of Athena on their dress uniform collars during Basic and Advanced Training. After training they wore the brass of their occupational specialty.

Tory looked from Myra's hands to her eyes. She herself had loved being part of the WACs, had loved flaunting Athena on her collar even if it had been for only the short periods of training. And she found the women who shared that special feeling for Athena were, in most cases, lesbians, proud of themselves, respecting other women. Was Myra a lesbian? Tory wasn't really sure yet. She laughed weakly. "We're not WACs any more."

The assertion didn't rock Myra. "Our queendom was abolished in '77, but I'm sure we both keep Athena's memory. I won't say it again. Come."

Tory's eyes darted from hands to eyes. Yes, the WACs were abolished in 1977. Women integrated into the Regular Army. "I'm sure we both keep Athena's memory." Tory wondered if Myra had been saying she was sure both of them were lesbians?

"Trust me," Myra urged.

Trust? Trust someone who liked being one with the night?

Trust someone who at the moment seemed a bit touched in the head?

Myra didn't say, come, again. She took Tory by the hands and pulled her to her feet.

* * *

"A chicken leg!" Tory hailed, waving the drumstick like a magic wand as they strutted along the nearly deserted road. Every so often a blue Korean taxi or a few other soldiers passed, breaking the quiet.

Myra grinned, glad her taking Tory to the snack bar had worked. "You going to dance with that all night or eat it?"

"Such a simple, little, deep-fried chicken leg, Myra. But right now I'd take it over sex if it were offered."

"I guess so, not eating since yesterday morning. You should be ashamed. You've been to 'Nam. You know it's a big change from the States, and you need to help yourself adjust."

Tory faked a pout, then bit into the meat. "Well," she said, chewing and grinning, "I never did adjust there. Wasn't in any fighting. Can't claim any post traumatic stress syndrome, but it still scared the hell out of me just being close. I know there's no fighting here but the possibility of it scares me."

The possibility was real. Only a weak truce protected the peace here, but Myra wasn't going to tell Tory that. Not now anyway. "Don't worry about that, Myra said. "We practice alerts once a month, sometimes more, but it's no big deal. Besides, even if you were still in the States, the possibility of being called into action is always present."

Tory cocked her head in thought, swallowing the last of the meat. "You're right. It's just my being new here. Once I settle in I'll be okay. Being new, plus the fact that I wanted Germany. I wanted to see Europe before retiring. But, you know." Tory stopped in her tracks and gave Myra all her attention. "I'm not so sure being sent here wasn't a blessing in disguise."

Myra was unsettled by Tory's sincerity. She felt split between wanting to encourage the closeness it implied and wanting to dissuade any such possibility. The message in Tory's eyes was filling her with a promise of intimacy, rousing sensations she hadn't felt in a long time, hinting the "I know" of mutual attraction, almost teasing. Myra hoped her return-

32

ing gaze wasn't betraying her heart. She lowered her eyes to Tory's lips, full and assertive, mesmerizing with their suggestion of satisfaction guaranteed. Then those lips tipped upward. Myra's gaze had betrayed her. She stepped back but learned too late her action only enticed Tory. Playful recognition was alight in those eyes, alarming Myra. It made her feel suddenly alive, but they were out in the open—close to the barracks fire escape steps. She snapped her head in its direction.

Confidently Tory stepped close as Myra's right hand shot up, capturing the ever-present dog tags. Tory said, "I'm so glad you took me to the snack bar tonight. I wouldn't have eaten if..."

Tory's words reached Myra's ears but her mind was focused on Craft and Tracer standing out on the third floor landing, smoking. She could see Craft's repulsive smirk behind his wave that said, "I see you BOTH!" And beside him stood his right hand man Tracer. Jesus! God! her mind screamed. No more! Please, no more.

"Hey," Tory called, then shook her by the shoulders. "Hey!" Myra's attention slowly steered back to Tory. Terror and dread discolored her face. The creases seemed to have deepened. Confused, Tory looked up to the top of the fire escape. Nothing. Just a fire escape. "What?" Myra didn't respond. She shook her again. "What?"

Myra shook her head. "Come on. I'll show you the dayroom. I'm sure you'll want to take a soda or something to your room." She released the dog tags and headed for the front entrance to the building.

Had Myra seen something? Did she perhaps suffer flashbacks of 'Nam or had she seen something real that scared the hell out of her? Or was she manic, teeter-tottering in and out of reality? Who else but a crazy person sat alone on fire escape steps, dressed all in black, being one with the night?

"Damn. Is it always this quiet?" Tory asked as they entered the dayroom. Four guys were playing a game of pool. Sitting on a cushioned chair in the corner, another guy was reading a western novel.

"Usually. Most come in, get their drinks and leave. A lot of guys are out either shopping or getting drunk or with their

Korean women. The rest enjoy their quieter rooms once their roomies leave." She dug into her pocket and pulled out quarters. "I'm going to have a Pepsi. What will you have?"

Tory checked out the room. Clean but old. It seemed neglected.

And while Tory was checking out the room Myra noted that the guys, though trying not to appear too obvious, were checking out Tory, the new woman. Thanks to Craft, Myra had stopped getting requests for dates months ago. That was good. She hated to have to refuse the guys time after time anyway, but they didn't need to know she was a lesbian. She had overheard Craft tell a guy one time, "You don't want her. She eats pussy." That was true and she hoped she did it very well, but it was none of anyone's business. What irked her to no end was that straights viewed lesbianism as something strictly sexual, that lesbians were low-life and cruised dirty bars, staking out the place for other low-life, looking for a night or an hour or two of sexual gratification. They didn't seem able to understand that lesbians formed friendships or committed themselves in relationships similar to marriages. Or maybe they just didn't want to understand because to understand would mean acceptance of lesbianism as something good and right and natural.

One guy in a white T-shirt and jeans was brazenly giving Tory the once over, clearly pleased. He took a drag on his cigarette. He had heard Myra ask Tory what she would have from the machine and since Tory hadn't answered, he said, "You can have me, pretty lady, if you don't want a drink."

Myra had warned her earlier in the day that the guys would hit on her and because of that warning she was able to find him amusing. "Thank you. I'll keep that in mind." She turned to the machines. "I'll have a Pepsi and some potato chips."

Or maybe deep down, way down at the base of this lesbianism-is-a-perversion myth, was the fear that if lesbianism was accepted then all women could be lesbians. Myra said, "This is Sergeant Victoria Barrett," to the guys while coining for the goods. The brazen fellow who had spoken, Miller, a mechanic in the motor pool, threw up a hand, saying, "Sorry, Sarge, no offense intended."

"None taken." Tory smiled and left with Myra.

As they climbed the stairs Myra said, "I don't care to say I told you so but... He was nice about it, but still—it's let's go somewhere and screw, not let's go somewhere and talk. I used to think they turned callous from being here in Korea where there are so many prostitutes and buying sex is like buying a cup of coffee."

"I'm not about to make excuses for them. I've had my ass pinched more than once in the States."

"Well, they're not all like that."

"No." Tory smirked. "Just the ones who think of us as sex objects."

Myra wasn't finding any humor in it. "Most are good guys. I mean most won't force themselves on you or anything. You'll learn who to avoid."

"Like Craft?"

Myra was silent for a moment and then she said, "Yes. But you can't avoid him."

At the top of the stairs Myra glanced down to the end of the hallway opposite their rooms. Craft and Tracer's heads jerked back behind the wall at the other fire escape. Her hand grabbed her dog tags.

Tory caught the movement and quickly checked the end of the hall. Nothing. "You, uh, want to talk about this 'Mikey' business?"

Myra stopped at Tory's door where she released her tags. "While we're on the topic of sex you should know—"

"Yes!" Tory didn't think she'd talk, but since Myra had brought up sex again, she repeated, "Yes," then opened her door and walked in. Myra wasn't following. "Come on in."

Myra knew exactly what Tory was thinking—she stayed put. "No, thank you." She looked down the hall. Craft and Tracer were watching. "You need to rest. Jet lag and all. But what I wanted to tell you is to be careful choosing guys. Most utilize the yobos' services. The yobos are supposed to keep their VD cards updated every two weeks, but even so they can have something worse within two hours after checking out well."

"In other words, there are long lines daily at the dispensary

35

for VD shots. Keep me company. Come in."

Myra smiled her beautiful smile. "Maybe another time. Good night, Sergeant. You know where I am if you need me."

Chapter Four

Looking for Myra, Tory went to breakfast early the next morning. She had slept well after having eaten and felt more comfortable now in her fatigues and boots. The mess hall, another Quonset hut, rested about twenty feet from the Admin hut and also served the 631st Infantry Company.

Entering the hut, she showed her meal pass to the private on chow duty, then got in line. Unlike large Stateside posts, Camp Bolden had only fifty-five hundred troops. Consequently, companies carried fewer soldiers and mess halls served fewer also. Only four others stood ahead of Tory.

When she reached the service area the Sergeant in charge of the mess hall reached between a couple of privates and over a vat of scrambled eggs. "Sergeant Hart, Sergeant. Jim. Just arrived?"

Tory shook his hand, noting the E-5 rank on the color of his white shirt. "Yes, Jim. Yesterday. Admin Company. Victoria Barrett."

"Well, Victoria, welcome to the mess of opportunity. What'll you have? We aim to please if you're willing to wait an extra minute."

After getting a ham and cheese omelet, Tory reviewed the dining area. Lots of troops. No Myra. She spotted Craft with others at a long table.

With some reservation she joined them. He needed to know her reprimanding him yesterday was nothing personal. She greeted the group and roosted at the head of the table where Top had sat five minutes before.

"Good morning, Sergeant." Craft spoke for the group who appeared half comatose, trying to wake up. "You come at a good time."

"Oh?" Tory mouthed a forkful of eggs.

"Payday. We labor only half a day. At noon the bell of freedom will ring." He smiled, waiting as if he expected a pat on the head for his wit.

"That's right. I had forgotten." His smile dropped. "Stateside was the same. I'm glad we practice that tradition here."

"Yeah. Only essentials have to work, like MPs and dispensary."

"Zip! Got to get silver bullets." A private who sat beside Craft, staring into his coffee cup, blurted the words suddenly and just as suddenly fell silent.

Tory checked out the private. He was skinny and over six feet tall. His eyes were green and surrounded by a complexion so pale he appeared anemic. His hands, holding his coffee cup as if holding the world, showed fingernails bitten painfully down to the quick. She said, "Craft, how do we get the checks and what are silver bullets?"

All at the table laughed. Craft puffed his already bull-like chest in self-importance.

"The mail clerk puts the checks in everyone's boxes by eleven. You can get a silver bullet any morning at the dispensary but you'll have to stand in line. The silver bullet is the medicinal power that combats the aftermath of exotic pleasures." He put an arm about the private's shoulders. "This is Private Tracer. The word—he mouthed 'dispensary'—sets the 'zip' off."

"I see," Tory smiled in uncertainty. "I'll be careful."

"Do," Craft continued. "Tracer works in your office as message and office-to-office carrier. He leaves in another two months. I maintain files. Private First Class Walker," he pointed to a black woman across from him, "types everything." Tory nodded with a smile to Walker. She was a pretty, small-boned woman, similar in size to the Korean women Tory had seen so far. Briefly her eyes met Tory's, then darted away. Tory felt she was hiding something.

"Spec 4 Henry there," Craft flipped his hand at the light-skinned black man seated by Walker.

Tory turned her smile to Henry who met her head-on with

clear, honest eyes. He appeared a mixture of Hispanic and black with an easy smile and sensitive face, his fingers long and delicate. He looked as if he knew more than he would tell and when he did he would be discreet.

"Hell," Craft continued, "we hope to find out one day what he does."

The others stifled laughter. Henry slung his biscuit at Craft who dodged it. "I oughta smack that smirk off ya face, mothah fuckah. You so eat up with the rot your pecker only hides between your legs."

Again Tory waited in uncertainty.

Craft laughed. "Okay, Henry oversees us for you, Sarge, and makes sure you sign everything you're supposed to."

Henry's face broke into a grin, giving away the play.

"Well," Tory said, wiping her mouth with a napkin, "this is certainly a novel way to begin the day." But she couldn't help wondering how much truth there was in his humor.

All laughed, accepting their new Admin NCO. Henry took over. "Those two at the end of the table, acting unsociable, belong to Supply."

Tory nodded to a female Spec 4, Johnson, with piercing ice-blue eyes and sandy hair cut in Dutch boy style. Her eyes were magnificent and boldly held her own as if trying to tell Tory something she couldn't say aloud. Even more startling than her eyes was her size. She was sitting, but Tory could tell she was much taller than Craft and maybe even taller than Tracer.

From Johnson Tory turned to a male private named Guiterrez who had black hair, smiling black eyes and a black scraggly mustache. He was small-boned and feisty like a lightweight boxer.

"Speaking of supply," Craft started, "here comes Mi..., uh, Sturdivan."

Tory turned and caught Myra's back disappearing into the line. Her spirits lifted considerably. "Good. She'll be joining us." She spotted eyes lowering as if hiding something. Tracer rose suddenly from the dead and excused himself from the table. Snickering, as if to tell Tory he tried to warn her, Craft followed.

As soon as Myra exited the line Tory waved for her to join the table. Myra lifted a no-thank-you hand and took a seat at a vacant smaller one. Disappointed, Tory asked, "Does she always eat alone?"

Walker neared her head to Tory's and whispered, "She's not exactly right, you know." She touched a finger to her own head.

At the end of the table Johnson hardened her ice-blues and slammed a spent cigarette into an ashtray, shaking the table. "She ain't no crazier than we are, Walker." With that she stood.

All the way up, Tory thought, her neck stretching to follow.

With contempt Johnson looked down at Tory's wide-eyed stare. "If you want to know, I'm six five."

Smiling in awe, Tory deliberately looked her up and down, checking the height she carried like a proud athlete and the solid forearms Tory was sure could do some serious damage.

"Mama!" she cried, laughing. "You're a whole lotta woman to love! Glad you're on my side."

"Eh!" Guiterrez cheered, bolting to his feet with a laugh and a fond slap to Johnson's back, then a thumbs-up to Tory. "Number ha-na, Sarge," he finished in a thick Hispanic accent and left.

"Number ha-na?" Tory asked to anyone.

Johnson's face broke into a shy grin, giving away her youth. She extended a massive but gentle hand to Tory who used both of hers to engulf it in friendship.

"It means number one, Sarge. The best." Then she left, clearly because she didn't want to hear what she knew Walker was going to say.

Guiltily Walker picked up her tray. "Well," she said, glancing at Henry as if for approval, "I don't want no part of Sturdivan." But she didn't look happy about it.

As Walker left, Henry looked sheepishly at Tory. "Sometimes I think some of us are so miserable here we need something or," he tilted his head at Myra, "someone to pick on. Some folks tend to blame the Koreans instead of themselves for their being here. Sturdivan there likes the people and the country so that's one reason she's seen as not right. She used to hang with Mamasan a lot. Lately, though, I don't think she has. Hangs by herself like she got something heavy on her mind she can't talk about. The other reason, well, the other reason I don't see got nothing to do with nothing. I don't know how to help, Sarge. See you at the office."

Tory sat at the now empty table, trying to collect her thoughts. More stunned than anything else, she turned and caught Myra sneaking a glance at her. Her watch said there was yet another hour before the work day began.

Sipping coffee, she shifted her eyes toward Myra and again caught Myra stealing a peek. One calls her Mikey, another says she's crazy, yet another says no crazier than anyone else, and all seem to ostracize her—Tory turned and looked square at her. Myra looked, darted her eyes away, looked again, but this time held contact—or was Myra ostracizing herself?

Such an attractive woman. Was she crazy or—her hand formed a loose fist and tapped at her heart—or was she hurt as Mamasan claimed? A voice inside her boomed, Attention! Have you forgotten how kindly Myra treated you yesterday and last night? No, she answered, and I remember some strange behavior, too. She got up.

* * *

Myra's heart drummed as she watched Tory dispose of her tray. Then she turned away. She was sure now that Tory knew what the others thought of her and would begin shunning her also. She picked up her coffee cup. It shook. She put it back down on the table, wishing she liked to drink. Better still, she wished she had a valium, something to make the jitters go away. Or a sleeping pill to ease her nightmares. Or a whole slew of sleeping pills to make everything, especially her guilt over not reporting the rape she had witnessed, go away. She tried her cup again. Again it shook. She put it back down and reached under her shirt to the belt on her fatigue pants. Fingering the slim black case attached to her belt but concealed from view, she calmed. The case was made of nylon and she could feel what it held. Touching it, being reminded that it carried a mother of pearl handled switch blade with a razor-sharp edge, relaxed her as well as the dog tags did.

41

"Mornin'!"

Myra jumped, her hand ejecting from under her shirt.

"Are our nerves already a bit frazzled this morning?"

Myra couldn't help but smile with Tory. "I saw you take your tray up. I thought you had gone."

"May I?" Tory asked, pulling out the extra chair.

"Yes, of course."

Tory took the seat, then studied her. How her serene voice masked the troubles confessed by the lines on her face baffled Tory. She watched the cup Myra raised to her lips shake and continued to watch as Myra used her other hand to stabilize it.

Under Tory's scrutiny Myra's eyes darted about. What was she staring at? Had the others told her? Was Tory trying to decide if she really was? Could she tell by looking? What's with all the questions? She had thought they understood each other last night. The silence tortured her.

"What does this mean?" she asked, tapping at her chest as Tory had.

Tory came out of her daze and flicked her wrist. "Just thinking out loud. I don't believe you heard me last night, so I came over to thank you again. You helped me through a very difficult evening."

Myra picked up her cup and sipped some coffee. Her hand no longer shook. "You might like to know coffee's always available here between zero-five-hundred when the doors open to eighteen-thirty when they close."

Tory raised her own cup. "My high-performance fuel."

"Everybody runs constantly back and forth with cups. It's amazing how a drink that stimulates the nervous system acts to calm it as well."

"It has to be the eighth wonder of the world. And speaking of wonders, I wonder if you'd help me out today?"

"Sure, I'd be glad to."

"You don't have to. I just heard today's only half a day."

"Payday. Yes."

"I don't know where anything is. The bank, the cleaners..."

"Easy duty. Camp Bolden like all US camps in Korea is

small. Everything's within walking distance. Korea itself is small. From Seoul to Pusan, its Southern most tip, is only about three hundred miles. There's only one highway that runs from North to South and it has only one stoplight." Myra took another sip of coffee, confident the tremors were gone. "Which is good since we can't have cars here. But buses run constantly, hitting stops every half hour. If you're in a real rush, just call a taxi. They don't cost much."

"You sound like just the kind of guide I need."

"It'd be my pleasure, Sergeant."

"Pleasure" twirled around in Tory's brain, zipped down through her stomach, stimulating her groin, and landed with a tingle in her toes. She squeezed Myra's hand. "I'm sure it'll be more mine." She stood.

"Sergeant, why don't we meet right here at thirteen hundred. That'll give us time to change and pick up our checks from our mailboxes."

"Sounds like you've got it all together, Specialist." Absentmindedly she fingered the E-7 black, metal rank on her fatigue cap. "You know, sooner or later you'll have to tell me what you have hidden under your shirt. Your hand wasn't high or low enough so I know you weren't playing with yourself." She grinned and left.

* * *

Right hands were always to be free to render salutes to officers, so Tory carried her coffee cup in her left as she walked to the front entrance of the barracks. She still had ten minutes before her duty began. She stood on the outside cement step, wishing she had a cigarette.

Three years ago she had dropped the habit for a woman. They had fought over it and she thought giving it up would end the problem. When she had kicked the habit Doreen kicked her out. Battling over smoke had only screened the true problem. Doreen had fallen in love with someone else and was trying to find another way out besides blaming herself. It had been a shock but Tory was grateful to Doreen for having helped her stop smoking.

But a cigarette would sure be good right now. In the distance an infantry company was doing their morning run,

43

chanting cadence. Other soldiers walked about, going to various duty stations. She spotted Myra exiting the mess, heading to the Admin hut.

Myra. Tory had had a few lovers before Doreen. Military life, moving from post to post, encouraged short love affairs. Husband and wife teams could request transfers to the same post. The government assisted them financially, allocating separate allowances for off-post housing. The military stamped them 'Sanctioned'. But lesbian couples? The military didn't just stamp a 'no go' on them, the military discredited their very existence in its fine institution. Tory sipped her coffee. She was glad she had only two years to retirement. She loved being a soldier, loved being a part of the colossal protective shield as Myra had put it, but the need to hide herself was becoming too much of a strain.

Did the others suspect Myra was a lesbian? Was that why they left the table? Johnson. Johnson with the ice-blues that seemed to want to tell her something. Johnson would be the one to talk—even more than Henry.

Myra. Since Doreen, Tory had had no lover. It wasn't that the breakup had been so traumatic that she swore off women. Heaven forbid! It wasn't for lack of women either. Very simply, no one had caught her interest or touched her heart—until Myra.

Her internal alarm sounded. She checked her watch and her eyes popped. "Myra, hell!" she blurted, seeing she had one minute to get to the office.

You idiot, she scolded, dashing the hundred feet. Your first day and you risk being late for daydreaming!?

Rushing into the hut, she spotted Top about to cross the threshold into his own office. "Oh, shit," she mumbled, praying her watch was right. "Good morning, Top," she said cheerfully. A visible display of innocence nearly always quashed trouble.

Top checked his watch, then cast an accusing eye on her. "I'll say one thing for you, Victoria. You are punctual. Come on in here."

Tory stepped in with all sorts of excuses running through her head except daydreaming. She took the seat opposite his desk. A long time ago she had learned to volunteer nothing. She waited.

"You know," Top began, tossing the papers in his hand onto his desk and picking up his coffee cup, "I'd prefer you call me Alan unless, of course, we're in mixed company."

Tory laughed more out of relief than his double meaning on "mixed company" which meant subordinates among higher-ups. "Thank you, Alan."

"You know," he continued, "there's really not a whole helluva lot of work around here. It's enough to keep us going at a turtle's pace, but otherwise we just fake it. We get really busy come Battalion Inspection, but that's ninety-five percent panic." He stuck a short, thick cigar in the corner of his mouth and reached behind him bringing out, front and center, a baseball bat that he proceeded to rub and scrutinize and generally play with.

"Now I know yesterday when we talked I was all professional and shit, but we fake that, too, when necessary." He threw a twinkling blue eye at her.

Tory caught it with a raised brow. He was a big man and hard looking. The cigar wagged in his mouth as he growled his words with a Texas drawl, but his eyes exposed him as a marshmallow. She judged him to be a fair man who would become an intimidating figure if crossed.

"What I'm trying to say is, Korea is a bitch of a place for a lot of troops. They're ten thousand miles away from mommy and daddy and get rice stuffed down their throats daily. We're in a different world here. A good century behind. Hell, they still use water buffalo to plow their rice paddies." He paused for a moment. "But I won't give no shit if I don't get no shit. Your office help there." He pointed his bat in the direction of the Admin office. "You keep them disciplined. Give them time off when work's caught up or when you want. Take as much time as you want yourself. Only thing I want is to be left alone with the work done right and on time. I report to the Captain daily. Only way I can keep him smiling is by you keeping me smiling. You follow what I mean?"

"Absolutely, Alan. Work holds top priority. If done right we can play. If not, there'll be hell to pay. Don't bother you with anything unless it's life threatening."

Top grinned around his cigar. "Yep, Victoria, I think we're going to be one helluva team. Now for the other thing on my mind. You just got in yesterday. I expect we tuckered you out with all that in-processing. We set aside two days for it. You done it in one. Hell, your tush is probably still sore from that giant gamma globulin shot we all gotta bite the bullet over. Now I know today's only half a day. You might feel a bit cheated, but you got it free. Take a long hot shower or sit on your pity pot. I don't give a damn. Report Monday morning ready to learn your job from Gallo."

"That's very kind of you, Alan. I don't have anything to do and I haven't been anywhere to know where to go. Would you mind if I call my people aside and talk with them one-on-one? Get to know them?"

"It's your time. But if you're going to do that," he twisted the neck of the bat as if contemplating homicide, "take special care with Myra."

"What do you mean?"

Top raised his bat and peered down it as if it were a rifle. "I've been here a year and expect to stay another. She's put in for a year's extension. She'll get it because I want her here." Sighing, he lowered the bat and let it rest on his legs. Staring out the window that gave a view of the mess hall, he chomped down on his cigar.

"When she came here she was alive, spry. That supply room was a mess. She straightened it all out. That's one area I have no diarrhea over."

Allowing herself time to respond, Tory took a sip of cold coffee. She knew she needed to sound objective. "So what's the problem?"

"The last four, five months she's grown old, tense. Like the life's been sucked out of her."

"What happened?"

"Don't know. I go around every so often. Try to mess with her, give her a chance to talk."

"Did she always wear her dog tags outside her uniform?"

"No." Top turned again to her. "I believe that started about three months ago. It ain't no big thing. But it's odd, I'd send

46

her to counseling but I got nothing to base it on. She's not bothering nobody. Her work's gotten better. She talks right. Can't help but think, though, that Craft's got something to do with it."

"Oh?"

"Yep. That boy's had the hots for her since he arrived, but she don't care diddly-squat for him. Fact is, he wanted her so bad he started a rumor she's a lesbian to keep the other boys away from her."

So that's what Henry meant when he said, "The other reason I don't see got nothing to do with nothing." They believed she was a lesbian. That, even more than her liking Koreans, was why they had left the table. Sammie came to mind. Sammie had been a mechanic in the Motor Pool at Fort Sumter, North Carolina. Everybody liked her. She could fix anything on the vehicles and made Soldier of the Month more than once. But then someone had connected lesbian to her name and the next time Tory saw her, Tory had been filling up her gas tank at a civilian garage. Sammie was one of the mechanics there and came out wiping her hands on a rag to say hello. She was making more money but missed the uniform. She had said, "...They wanted me to spill my guts and give names, Tory. They said they'd just send me to another post if I did. But I couldn't. Heck, my First Sergeant even came to bat for me but still..."

Tory's stomach twisted into a knot, the juices burning. She had to appear objective, distanced, to ward off even the possibility of suspicion. Two years, she prayed, just give me two more years. All lesbians in the military stayed on constant alert, always watching the way they walked and talked and even looked. Some went to extremes with make-up and jewelry and skirts to appear "more of a woman." All guarded themselves, suspicious of everyone, wondering who would be the one to turn them in. Some even married for a cover or, at the least, wore wedding bands on their left hands to deceive. Tory looked directly at her new First Sergeant and without so much as a flutter of her eyelids asked, "How do you know it's a rumor?"

Top grinned around his cigar, twisting his bat. "I got my

47

ways. He's got everybody believing it. She got wind of it and came to me to help her get a transfer. That gal was feeling so bad she was even willing to throw away her sixteen years and take a discharge. Course, it don't work that way here. Only thing screaming queer will get you here is harassed."

Korea was considered a combat zone. Many people didn't realize it but the Korean war that began some thirty plus years ago never ended. The two sides had a cease fire truce only. The border dividing the North and South Koreas, the 38th Parallel or Demilitarized Zone—the DMZ, was the most heavily guarded border in the world. A chain link fence marked it.

There were stories of both US and North Korean soldiers shouldering loaded weapons, eyeing each other through the fence, and constantly taunting each other, hoping they would start something. Before they pulled guard duty at the border, US soldiers were taught to expect jeers and taunts but to retaliate only if a North Korean pointed a weapon at them. It was rumored that the table at Panmunjon where North and South Korean dignitaries met for peace talks had to be constantly replaced. Bit by bit its legs were sawed off by whichever side was upset the most that day, creating a psychological advantage in the next round of talks.

Guards patrolled everywhere. ROK, Republic of Korea, soldiers carrying M14 rifles watched the civilian roads, airport, official buildings. US soldiers with M16 rifles walked the fence or stood vigilant in dugouts at the DMZ, and every US camp maintained tight security with guards in towers.

Beyond the DMZ in North Korea there were an estimated sixty-five thousand North Korean soldiers who stayed on constant alert status, ready to strike in seconds. Along the DMZ, US vehicles with drivers, whose only duty was to sit behind the wheel and wait twenty-four hours a day, were kept idling below the tower guards at the DMZ. If the guards spotted any combative activity their job was to radio headquarters then jump into the ready, waiting vehicles and get out—fast!

The Bridge of No Return crossed the border from South Korea into North Korea. Anyone was allowed to cross into North Korea and was even given a blessing as he went. But anyone attempting to cross that *Bridge of No Return* from

North to South was shot.

Duty for Americans in Korea could be fatally lonely, as well as depressing and demanding. Endurance was the key. There were reports of soldiers in the towers, unable to stand another long, cold, dark, silent night, saying good night, kissing the muzzles of their M16s and—pulling the trigger.

A combat zone wasn't the best place to pull duty so the only thing that mattered was having bodies capable of toting weapons, not the sexual orientation of those bodies. Later, after those bodies pulled their duty, the private lives of those bodies were once again very closely monitored.

"No," Top continued. "I wasn't willing to transfer her and I sure as hell wasn't about to discharge her. I guess, too, I was being selfish. I like that gal and I like her work. I couldn't see letting me or my company suffer because of a lovesick puppy. I told her that much."

Sammie's problem hadn't been a "lovesick puppy." It had been another mechanic, a male who resented her pointing out to him trouble spots in engines and then having the gall to be right. Tory shook her head, forcing her mind back to Top. "When did that happen?"

"About four, five months ago."

"That's when you said she started growing old."

"Yeah, well." Top tucked his head momentarily. "All I could do was talk to the boy. Told him to leave her alone. Didn't want to open no damn can of worms, making things worse for her, by charging him with defamation of character. Officers would start their bullshit of digging into every damn detail and the next you know she'd be the one at fault."

"And that's why he calls her Mikey," she said more to herself. Her initial gut feeling had been right.

"But you'll see nobody else does, not in front of me anyway. Yep, he's pissed. Thinks he can pressure her into going out with him that way. Stands her ground that one. I like that. Still, he's got everybody believing it and I'm willing to bet that's eatin' her up bad."

Tory cocked her head. "Suppose, Alan, she is a lesbian? Suppose that's exactly why she wanted me to let it slide yesterday instead of charging him with insubordination?" She didn't like direct confrontation like this. It was too risky. But she had to know his ground.

Top's jaw tightened. "I don't care diddly-squat as long as she keeps doing a good job and don't bother nobody. Fact is." Top turned again to staring out the window, appearing nervous. His face took on a wounded look. "Fact is, I threw my own daughter out when she wanted my blessing on her union with a woman. I regretted it the next damn day, but by then it was too late. Haven't seen her in four damn years and can't locate her."

Tory watched his chin quiver. "I'm sorry, Alan."

Lost in the memory, he nodded with the sympathy. Then, as if awakening to the present, he set his jaw, scowling. He stood up, placing his bat on his desk, and leaned on it and into her.

Wide-eyed, Tory reared back as far as her seat would allow.

With a snarl that would have frightened God he said, "I don't give a fuck what she does in the privacy of her own room. I don't give a fuck what *Your* personal feelings on the subject are. You *will* treat her as any other. You *will* come down hard on anyone who tries to harass her. You *will* respect her rank and her equality as a decent human being. Now, I can't *order* you to befriend her. That's your personal business. But I can tell you that it'd make me smile a mite more to see her with a friend, some companion, someone who holds equal rank with her. Maybe that *friend* could even bring some of her youth back. And all I've said here will stay here. Do I make myself clear?"

By now Tory was desperately searching for an exit. "Uh, yes, Sir, Top. Absolutely. Your orders will be followed to the tee."

"Good," he growled and then straightening himself, he resumed his seat. "I suppose that's enough." The twinkle in his eye was back. "Have a good day and weekend." He returned his bat to its spot behind him.

After a moment's rest Tory pushed herself to her feet. If there was a proper response to all this it was as Guiterrez had put it at breakfast just an hour ago, "Number ha-na! Number ha-na!" Number one, the best—yes! Tory wanted to clap her hands, whistle, tip her hat, offer him a drink, thank him. Tops to Top.

But, considering the uniform on her back as well as Top's clear directive that all he'd said here would remain here, Tory chose to be discreet. The sobering fact was that even Sammie's First Sergeant hadn't been able to help her.

She said simply, "You also, Alan. Thank you."

Knowing his personal feelings was uplifting, but she left feeling shaky. No doubt, she would neither fail nor cross Top.

Chapter Five

When thirteen-hundred was drawing near, Tory was enjoying coffee with Top in the mess. Henry, the Specialist directly under her, Walker, her office typist, and Pamela Johnson from Supply kept her and Top company.

"Payday," Top growled. "Goddamn kids get a couple of bucks in their pockets and got to rush out and buy rotten pussy." Top was referring to Craft and Tracer who had just gobbled their lunch and flew out of the mess, making a beeline for the ville with their pockets full of money.

Tory chuckled wondering if Craft and Tracer had any understanding of the part they personally played in creating and perpetuating the rotten pussy they would buy and later discard.

"Can't tell them a goddamn thing, though. They all get 'virgins,' then silver bullets," Top finished.

Tory laughed not so much over what Top said but the way he said it. His speech was simple and painfully blunt. He had just called Craft and Tracer idiots for paying a higher price to a prostitute who tells them she's a virgin, take their "goodies," then end up at the dispensary waiting in line for silver bullets, wondering how they could have possibly picked up VD.

At thirteen-hundred on the dot Tory spied Myra entering the chow line but didn't wave for her to join the table. After this morning when Myra clearly indicated she wished to eat alone, Tory felt another attempt would only push Myra further away.

Sitting at Top's right, Tory faced Myra who was now sitting down to her lunch at a vacant table. Tory was looking at Myra and trying to figure out how she was going to befriend her per

Top's orders from this morning when she sensed Top lean close.

Top was no more than six inches from Tory's left cheek when he asked, "Well, Sergeant? I expect you talked with everyone but Myra?"

Oh, yes. Her talks with her people one-on-one this morning. Tory glanced at Johnson who was glancing back at her. What a day this was turning into. Johnson with the ice-blues, no doubt, was a lesbian in the budding stage, but Tory couldn't say for certain. That was the damn problem in the Army. The threat of dishonorable discharge kept lesbians isolated by secrecy. Divide and conquer was the Army's way. But eventually lesbians identified one another and united. And what was conquered? The few unfortunates discharged were quickly replaced by droves more.

"Hey, Top," Johnson jumped in, "Sturdivan was too busy finishing up the monthly report." Johnson knew Top cared for his troops and was concerned about Sturdivan. He had called Johnson aside a couple of times to ask if she knew of anything bothering Myra. To Johnson's chagrin, she had been able to report only that Sturdivan wouldn't let her get close. And after talking with Barrett this morning, she hoped her response would protect both of them.

"Johnson," Top twitted, "did I ask you?"

One of the two things that emerged from Tory's talks with the others, especially Johnson, was that Top loved to fret and be fretted back. He believed this game boosted morale. The other point of interest was that everybody liked Myra. She was the 'best damn supervisor' Johnson and Guiterrez had ever had, and if she was a lesbian, they hoped to have another at their next duty station. Guiterrez appreciated Myra's high regard for Koreans since he was planning on marrying his yobo. He asked Tory to keep that confidential since he knew most others in the company would laugh at him. Henry respected Myra and her ability to keep a secret. She had sneaked a purchase of calamine lotion and slipped it to him one time when he had been too embarrassed to go to the dispensary for a poison ivy rash on a private part of his body. According to Henry, Walker had suffered from the same rash but she hadn't divulged that to Tory. But wasn't that funny? The Army claimed homosexuality was a threat to national security yet she and Myra were the best secret keepers.

Walker had said she was in love with Henry and was afraid she'd be risking his love if she openly showed friendliness toward Myra. After all, Myra was rumored to be one of 'them.' And besides, "Craft says she is one of them and he warned me. He said, 'You know how the Army is. If you're friends with one of "them" then you must be one.'" That was true. Who was it? Tory searched her memory to five years back. Ferguson. Terry Ferguson, straight as an arrow, stood up for Whitner who was under suspicion. The Army discharged both of them.

Tracer seemed a possible problem. A year ago he had married a woman within a week of her husband's death. Now she was filing for divorce and Tracer was bitter. "No disrespect intended, Sarge," he had said, "but women suck. They either don't want you or they use you. I don't like this place either. From here on I'm going to have fun in this goddamn armpit of the world and I don't care how." Tory sensed he did indeed intend disrespect and really didn't give a damn about anything but his anemic-looking, stuck-on-his-pity-pot self.

And Craft seemed, well, sneaky was all Tory could come up with for the moment. There was something hard or festering behind his eyes. "I want that little girl," he had said, referring to Myra. "And I'm going to get her. Little by little I'll get her." He smiled but it looked as if he was smirking. Tory warned him that one complaint from Myra would bring him disciplinary action. "No, no, Sarge. I wouldn't pester her or anything. I'm just going to be available when she comes around."

"Huh?" Top grumbled into Johnson, clamping down on his ever-present cigar.

Johnson reared back in exaggerated mock fear. Henry distracted him.

"Remember, Top? The monthly report you want right and on time or there'd be fingernails to pay? Sturdivan was working on that when Sarge wanted to talk with her."

Top popeyed him. "Son, I see I got to learn you some propers. You don't side with the women!"

"I don't know, Top," Tory played along, scrutinizing the

fingernails she preferred to keep. "There might be benefits to siding with the women."

"Oooh!" Henry intoned while Johnson snatched the cigar from Top's scowling lips, said, "Chew on that awhile, ya ole poot," then slammed it back into his mouth with a "HA!"

Top's pretentious evil eye spared no one while the twinkle in those blues tattled his pleasure. His troops had accepted and welcomed his new Admin NCOIC. He slapped his hands on the table and pushed himself to his feet. His grin was sly as he leaned into Tory's ear. "Since you don't have anything to do," he said, using her own earlier words, "I think now would be a fine time to have your chat with Myra."

Tory smiled but felt no pleasure. She took in Johnson, Walker and Henry's eyes. All were wide and on her and asking, "What's your move, Sarge?" What was her move? Wasn't it enough to have to contend with jet lag, nausea from the foreign food, discomfort from unfamiliarity? This was only her second day here for godsake. She wanted to get to know Myra but she hadn't expected this pressure. Then she answered herself—sternly. What kind of game are you playing? Myra had been busy when you asked Johnson to send her to the mess where you would talk. But she was free within the hour when you told Johnson to tell her you'd catch her another time. You had put her off with this exact scene in mind. At 1300 when you were to meet Myra, it would look like it was Top's wishes you were catering to, not your own.

Damn straight! she answered herself. She was playing the only kind of game the lesbian was allowed in the service. Top's feelings wouldn't amount to piss in a boot if she appeared too hungry or eager. The Army only gave a damn about duty, not feelings. She wouldn't risk her eighteen years by being open with this man. This man's daughter was a lesbian and he wanted his child back. His daughter's ultimatum to accept or forget forced his current sensitivity. Even so, he was an uncommon man. In fact, the first of his kind Tory had run across in her eighteen years. He at least came to accept. Just the same, as powerful as he was in his company, he was not powerful enough to stop the axe from coming down on her anymore than Sammie's First Sergeant had been able to. Not even a Captain or Colonel could stop it if implications by troops started sharpening the axe. Top had already admitted that much when he said, "...all I've said here will stay here." No, getting Myra to open up would not be seen as her desire but her duty, what any good NCO would do.

Sergeant First Class Victoria Barrett pushed her chair back and squared herself on the First Sergeant. "Exactly my thought, Top. I don't know where anything is either. Perhaps she'll be kind enough to escort me to the bank. You understand, of course, this may take some time."

Satisfaction bubbled not only in Top's eyes but Johnson's, Walker's and Henry's as well, though none were willing to voice that feeling to the others.

"You got twelve months, Sergeant."

* * *

"Later, guys. Duty calls." Tory rendered them a slack salute and left the long table for Myra's smaller one.

This time Tory didn't ask if she could sit. She pulled a chair out as if it were her right, elbowing herself on the table closer to Myra. With intentional exaggeration, Tory grinned wide and into her, as Mamasan had done to her, and intoned, "Stuuuuuurdi," again as Mamasan had done.

Myra reared back, smiling around a mouthful of cheeseburger. Her eyes squinted and shimmered with childlike delight. "Mamasan."

"You're right. She's very nice and thinks you are, too."

With a flip of her wrist and a grin, Myra said, "I pay her off."

"Speaking of paying, how do I pay for her?"

"By noon the day after payday bring the money to supply. We give you a receipt and send everyone's payments to Housing. They pay the Papasans and Mamasans directly. And I do mean by noon. Even if you pay later the money is automatically taken out of your next month's pay. It will not be returned, no matter how much you beg."

"That'll keep a soldier paying her bills on time."

"That's the idea. It's bad enough some of the guys treat them like slaves. Failure to pay will not be tolerated."

"What do you mean, they treat them like slaves? They work and get paid, don't they? Just like we work and get paid."

"Yes, but I've seen guys throw their boots at their Papasans and tell them to do them over because they didn't think the boots were shiny enough. Look at this boot." Myra stretched her leg out from under the table, displaying a boot glistening with a mirror shine. "Mamasan did this, not me. She sets the other females up for inspections better than they could do it themselves. And I've never had to search for a clean shirt."

"The women throw their boots at Mamasan, too?"

"No. At least I've never seen one. It's more like they expect Mamasan to do it all without complaint, without thanks and, sometimes I think, without being human. I mean, everybody needs an 'atta girl or 'atta boy. Even we get them in the Army."

"Maybe it's the language barrier."

"Maybe, but I doubt it. I think they think the thirty dollars a month they pay is all the Papasans and Mamasans get. The pay's cheap so they treat the Korean workers cheap. What they don't figure is there are two Papasans for each floor of the barracks except for the third that has Mamasan for the females and one Papasan for the males. Mamasan and the five Papasans all work together and split the money. There are two hundred and eleven of us, each putting thirty into the pot. If more troops are stuffed into rooms the Papasans and Mamasans decide for themselves whether or not they need to hire another hand. Usually they don't. Usually they just work harder and take the extra pay. Whatever, Mamasan and the Papasans are well paid."

"I was wondering how all that worked. So what do I owe for one day?"

Myra bit into a French fry. "Nothing. Sorry. I guess I spouted out at the mouth. It's not all the guys. It's not all the women."

"Just a lot of them, huh?"

Myra's face twisted in confusion. "It just that it gets sickening sometimes. Like on our last field exercise we shot off all our rounds so the Koreans in the area could have the brass. They make things like ashtrays, figurines and such to sell."

"So what was wrong with that?"

"Nothing with that. They picked it all up, then went through the trash. Koreans are very resourceful, you know. Very little gets wasted. One Korean man was going through the trash, minding his own business, when one of our guys grabbed him around the waist from behind, then slapped and rubbed the Korean's butt."

"What!?"

"Yes." Myra nodded to Tory's shock. "It's unreal. First he laughs at the man for sifting through the trash then pats his butt." Myra shook her head. "To this day I can't understand what was going through that guy's head. It's like they see Koreans as toys."

"Probably because of their smaller size."

"The Koreans are hardworking, smart people. They can take just about anything and make it into something you want....and they have feelings."

"Where were the others in the company when this happened?"

"Standing around. Watching. Laughing at the entertainment."

"The Captain, too?"

"Our wonderful Captain was the only one not wearing his helmet when we're all supposed to wear it in the field at all times. I went up to him and asked him to stop the guy." Myra stopped herself.

"And?" Tory urged.

"He said it was all just good-natured fun. Then he reminded me I'd been in service long enough to know I was supposed to salute officers."

"But you don't salute in the field. It's a rule to protect an officer from enemy eyes."

"I know that and you know that and now you know where our Captain's priorities lie. I clicked to attention, saluted, said thank you, Sir, and about-faced."

Tory raised both brows and puckered her lips as if to whistle but released an "Ooh" instead.

"Anyway, you owe nothing. It was taken care of. Henry may be second to you in your immediate office but I'm technically second to you in the hut. Just as you take care of me I'll take care of you."

Tory's eyes lit up. "Sounds like a great deal. Too bad it's not like that in the States."

"That's one of the reasons I like it in Korea. There're no outside friends or family to be able to go to so we have to depend on each other more. Dependence leads to kinder treatment."

"Except when you're dealing with someone like Craft."

Myra's hand bolted for her dog tags as she stuffed the last bit of burger into her mouth.

Like an automatic reflex, Tory thought. Mention Craft and the ever present dog tags get mugged. She wondered if Myra was even aware of it.

"Was Craft the guy in the field?" She watched Myra drop the tags and shake her head no but wearily. Tory decided to change the subject. She pulled her ID holder out of her front pants pocket. It was black, made of plastic and bulging with more than the military ID it was intended to hold. She pointed out the torn edges. "I need a new one of these. Would you show me where the PX is?"

Glimpsing the flashed ID, Myra reached for it. "May I see?"

Tory handed it to her. "I'm sure it wasn't meant to be stuffed with money and other things. That's probably why I go through them so fast."

Myra pulled her own out of her jeans pocket. "I do the same," she said, flipping it open, closed, then whisking it back into her pocket.

"Not so fast there, Stuuuuuurdi. If I let you see my nasty picture, the least you can do is let me see yours."

Ignoring the remark, Myra studied the picture. "You had longer hair then. How old is this ID?"

"I've been an E-7 for three years now, so it's that old."

"You looked different then."

"Younger."

Myra looked up from the ID, unabashedly studying her face.

"I know, I know," Tory said, covering her face with both hands and peeking through the fingers. "New wrinkles seem

59

to be popping up daily."

"You look better. I like the shorter cut of your hair, too."

Myra spoke the words just as seriously as she had studied her face. Her sincerity not only flattered Tory but also summoned from deep inside Tory a shyness that she thought had been long buried. It felt delightful. Gazing into Myra's earnest eyes, she recognized the feeling—the giddiness of newly awakened love. She cleared her throat and beckoned with her hand. "Come on. I gave. Now you."

Myra shook her head. "You don't really want...."

Tory tucked her head and threw her 'The Look.'

Myra gave. "Mine's only about a year old."

"Why, you had short hair then! Short hair looks great on you. It's so thick, so wavy and soft." To Tory's surprise, Myra's hand went for her tags. *Hair and tags and Craft?*

"Yes." Myra snatched her ID and secreted it back to her pocket.

"I mean your long hair is lovely, too, but...."

Myra dropped her tags. "You ready for your tour?"

Tory knew when to leave well enough alone. Truthfully, she was glad Myra stopped her. She wasn't sure how she would have crawled her way out after saying, "But this picture shows an exquisite woman with a commanding air—those high-arching brows and cheekbones. And that fetching smile. Such seduction, Myra. There's no despair in those eyes, only love and beauty. And where are the creases, Myra? What created those lines in less than a year?" Yes, Tory knew when to leave well enough alone but she didn't spare herself a mental kick in the ass.

* * *

Fairy tale land, Tory thought as she lay on her bunk with a wide grin. Never had she been in a company where the First Sergeant didn't give diddly-squat about someone's private life or where subordinates hoped to have another lesbian as their superior at the next post. And Mamasan, Tory, don't forget Mamasan. Such service in the Army. And Myra, Tory, don't forget Myra, Specialist 7th Class Myra Sturdivan. Since they were equal in rank they were expected to hang together. This had to be fairy tale land.

Joy bubbled inside her and every so often giggles burst out despite her battling to control them. What a day! Top confided his feelings and her troops divulged theirs. All she recalled was positive. Then Myra.

Myra had been an outstanding guide and a more than pleasant companion.

They had gone to the bank, shopped at the PX, strolled here and there, then taken in a movie where they ate popcorn, drank sodas, laughed and, yes, oh yes, sat close side by side.

By the time they had returned to the barracks, dinner was over but neither cared. They were stuffed with popcorn and happiness. And it seemed Myra's creases had lightened. Tory cocked her head. Myra's eyes had sparked a bit with life too. Perhaps, then, Myra had just been lonely. Maybe now that Tory was here things would get better. What goes around comes around. Myra gave her kindness and she would return it.

A lovely fairy tale land, a small camp where everything was within a mile—the theater, snack bar, bus depot, PX, everything. Everyone walked or rode the bus or a taxi. The pace was slower. Like a step back in time. She felt herself relaxing. Closing her eyes, she saw Myra as she had seen her twenty minutes ago when they stood together outside her room door.

"Come in and sit awhile," Tory invited, unlocking the door.

"You really should rest. The day was enjoyable but it'll kick you if you don't keep an eye on it. The body needs rest to adjust."

"Oh, come on. We'll get something to drink and sit on the floor and just talk." Myra was tempted. Tory could see it in her eyes. For a moment Tory thought she had noticed Myra drawing closer as if about to embrace her. But that had to have been her own imagination teasing her. Myra stepped back.

"On the hard tile? Haven't done that since Basic. If you had a rug...."

"Do you?"

"Yes, sort of."

"Good. We'll go to your room then."

"No!" Myra held up both hands.

The nervousness and anxiety Tory read on Myra's face seemed to act like a knife carving the lines on that face deeper. How she wished she could kiss that beautiful face and smooth the lines away.

"No," Myra said again. "You, uh, really need to rest." She backed up toward her own door. "See you in the morning. 'Night."

Anxiety. Tory's eyes opened. Her grin faded. Fairy tale land. Myra was hiding something. More than anxiety. Fear maybe? The dog tags outside her clothes. Fear, she confirmed. Craft popped into her head. Fairy tale land. Wasn't there always a ghost or goblin, evil witch, something, some villain in fairy tales? No, loneliness alone wouldn't create such worry lines.

* * *

So many emotions were tearing through Myra that her hand shook, missing the keyhole. On the third try, the key slid in. Mumbling thanks, she pushed the door open, rushed in, whisked the door closed behind her and propped her back against it. Holding her breath, she listened for any noises coming from the hall. Her heart pounded, sounding like a drum in her ears, pumping fear and excitement hard through her body, making it difficult to hear. The soft clicking of a door closing down the hall reached her. It was Tory's. Good. No footsteps. Good. Tory was giving her space. Very good.

Letting her head rest back against the door, she closed her eyes and released a sigh of relief. Then she bent forward and braced her hands on her knees. Breathing deeply, she waited for her heart to slow.

She half expected Tory to come knocking on her door, pressing for the day to continue. Or was she the one who wanted Tory to follow? Maybe both. No doubt, she admitted, she was guilty. This was only the second day after meeting Tory yet she felt comfortable with her, so comfortable that she nearly drew Tory into her arms. The want had been so strong it mesmerized her. The motion of her body as she had begun to move forward jolted her senses awake, kicking off the hypnotic spell.

Myra straightened and opened her eyes to the darkness of her room. Hugging herself, she thought she was smart in refusing to enter Tory's room. If she had gotten that close to losing control of herself out in the hallway, what would she have done in the privacy of Tory's room? Probably something she would have regretted later.

Smarter still was her stopping Tory from coming into her own room. She could picture it. There Tory and she would be, sitting on the rug, sipping coffee, gaily enjoying each other's company when the knock on the door would come. The knock on the door always came.

"Aren't you going to answer your door?" Tory would ask.

"Door?" she would answer, hoping Tory would realize she had only imagined a knock. "What door?" Tory would look at her as if she were something not quite identifiable, then get up to answer it herself. Then she would have to stop Tory from going to the door and Tory would want to know why. "Because it's Craft," she would say.

"So? What does he want?" Tory would ask.

"He wants me," she would have to say. "He wants to threaten me."

"Threaten you? Why?" Tory would ask.

"Because he wants me," she would say.

"He comes to your door to threaten you because he wants you?" Tory would ask in confusion.

She would have to say, "Yes. I don't understand the why of that but yes. And he wants my silence."

"Silence?" Tory would ask, now scratching her head in total perplexity. "Silence concerning what?"

Then she would have to shut her mouth because if she answered she would have to say, "Silence concerning his raping a Korean woman in the ville six months ago. I caught him raping her and he threatened to hurt me if I said anything. Then he threatened to hurt Mamasan because he knows I care about her. Then he threatened to tell everybody I'm a dyke and was buying pussy on thousand won alley, and that nobody should believe what I say because I was only trying to protect myself by telling lies on him. Then he tried to rape me, but I bashed his head with a rock and ran.

"He comes nightly now to remind me how sweet my Mamasan will be for him if I utter a word. He reminds me of the lie he'll spread about my buying pussy on Thousand Won Alley if I utter a word. He tells me how a normal girl wouldn't, couldn't possibly reject him, and that if I was a for-real dyke, he'd be glad to wear falsies for my added pleasure, and after a while he wouldn't need the falsies because I'd see how wonderful a man is.

"He comes nightly, Tory. Nightly! To remind, to tell, to threaten, to grin like the snake that ate the mouse. My word against his, Tory, and everybody likes him, believes him. He's smooth, he's a buddy, he buys drinks. My word against his, Tory, and once the word lesbian is uttered in the military, the lesbian's words are negated. Haven't you seen women in the course of your career get laughed at, humiliated, degraded, dragged through shit and discharged? I've seen them. Guys get pissed because the women won't go out with them and the next thing the women know, BOOM!, they're discharged for suspicion of lesbianism. That's a fact in the military, Tory, and you know it. A sad, disgusting, ridiculous fact but a fact just the same, and, yes, they would believe him just as soon as he mentioned his catching me buying pussy on Thousand Won Alley.

"They'd believe him because it would be his word against mine. That Korean woman he raped is too frightened to step forward...I know who she is because Mamasan knows her and told me about that woman's pain...but I can't step forward because he's blackmailing me and is backed by an Army that would just love to kick out my kind despite our good work... God save my soul, I am living in hell, being destroyed by fear that I'll be dishonorably discharged after sixteen years of faithful service...and consumed by guilt over that Korean woman."

Myra hid her face in her hand and laughed hopelessly into it, shaking her head, while tears rolled down her cheeks. "So you see, Tory," she continued in what she would have to say. "I don't want to answer the door because I'll have to explain all this and if I explain I'll be telling, and if I tell he'll go for my throat...and my throat isn't really my throat, Tory—my throat is Mamasan. And my throat is my career, my life. And I can't help but think my throat will also be you if I appear too friendly with you."

After having such a wonderful day, she had hoped her luck had changed, that she would blink and find the last six months a bad dream and nothing more. "I wish I could share all this with you, Tory," she whispered to the dark. "I wish I could share this with anybody." Then she prayed it was only Craft responsible for these nightly vicious attacks. He would leave in four months. Maybe she could hold on until then.

She rubbed her face hard with both hands, then wiped away the tears on her jeans. Snapping on the light, she marched to her latrine. With both hands she supported herself on the white sink and slowly raised her head, braving her reflection in the mirror. An attractive but, to her at the moment, ugly image looked back. Its red eyes characterized what Myra saw as weakness surrounded by scars. She lifted a frightened hand to the face in the mirror and said, "This wasn't you when you came here." Confusion entered her eyes as she continued, "Even I don't like looking at you. Why would anyone else, especially Tory?" Her chin trembled as she scowled at herself. The trembling brought on anger, the anger curled her hand into a fist and the sight of the fist repulsed her. Anger was why all of this started to begin with. With one hand still on the sink and her fist against the mirror she pushed herself back and away.

Turning around, she changed into black pajamas, clicked off the light, and curled into a fetal position on her bed, clutching her dog tags, waiting for sleep. Sleep always resisted until after Craft's knock on her door. She always either lay awake in a dark room that appeared uninhabited or sat out on the second floor fire escape until she felt it safe to return to her room.

Tonight, however, was different. Instead of one knock, she got two. The first she heard about twenty minutes after cutting off her light. The second came about forty minutes later. The second knock alarmed her, convincing her that Craft was growing even more adamant, deepening her fear, allowing her only restless sleep.

Chapter Six

"Good Morning!"

Myra jumped. She was leaving her room to go to the mess hall and hadn't expected anyone, let alone Tory, to be up at 0630 on a Saturday.

Tory sprang up from her perch on the threshold between the hall and fire escape.

"Didn't mean to scare you."

"Only startled. What're you doing out here?"

"Looking for company for breakfast. You headed there?"

"Always have breakfast. It's the best meal of the day. At least you can choose the kind of eggs you want."

With Myra leading, they scuttled down the fire escape.

"I knocked on your door last night." Tory received no response. It seemed Myra was lost in thought. "I don't mean to sound like a baby but I guess I could use some coddling until I get used to this place."

Myra stopped at the bottom of the steps and turned to her. "You don't sound like a baby. You're very far away from home. Everyone is scared at first whether they admit it or not. What time did you knock?"

"About nine."

Then it was Tory, not Craft, who had knocked the second time.

"When you didn't answer I assumed you had gone to bed or out. I guess I got a case of the lonelies and wanted to know if you'd sit out with me on the fire escape awhile."

Myra started walking again. "I'm sorry I missed you. Next time call through the door."

"I didn't want to bother you if you were sleeping."

"No bother from you."

"I'd rather not announce myself to the whole hall."

"That's true." She opened the mess hall door for Tory. "Rap four times then and I'll know it's you."

"A secret code! I love it. Do you answer for alerts?"

"During an alert the CO runs up and down the hall, banging on doors, screaming, 'ALERT!' I couldn't miss him even if I wanted to."

"My two favorite ladies," Sergeant Hart greeted. "What'll it be?"

"Good morning, Jim," Tory said cheerily. "Scrambled for me."

"And your best ham and cheese omelet for me," Myra finished.

"Coming up." He turned to the grille.

"Don't mean to pry, but I am curious. Why don't you answer your door?"

The exact question Myra had dreaded. "Health reasons." She squeezed her dog tags once, twice, then dropped them. "What's on your agenda for today?"

At least she didn't hang on to them for dear life, Tory thought. "I don't really know. I know where everything is on post. I was hoping to find some kind person at breakfast who'd be willing to show me off-post."

She cut her eyes at Myra who returned the look.

"Here you are, ladies. Scrambled and ham and cheese."

They thanked the Sergeant, moved on, picking up other items, and stopped at the coffee urn. "I suppose," Myra began, flipping the nozzle for her coffee, "some kind person would be pleased to show you off-post." She smiled and went to her usual table.

* * *

"You want to walk or catch the bus?" Myra asked outside the mess. Tory looked uncertain. "It's only a half mile to the gate but maybe we should ride. Show you how easy the buses are to use."

Tory patted her pockets. "Damn! No change. Will they take dollars?"

"No. They won't take your change either."

"What do I need then?"

"Two legs to climb aboard." Myra raised a brow, waiting for the connection. She didn't wait long.

"Damn, Myra! Are you messing with me this early in the morning?"

"Just a little. Buses on post are free and run every half hour. Off-post, though, will cost you. Here comes one now."

A dull, olive drab, school-type bus stopped in front of the Admin hut. Myra led her to an empty seat where Tory gaped at the multitude of Koreans.

"Everyone rides free." Myra blurted the words quickly, trying to cloak her nervousness and excitement over sitting thigh to thigh with Tory. "The Koreans in fatigues are called KATU-SAs. You've seen them in the barracks."

KATUSA stood for Korean Augmentation to the United States Army. Every Korean male had to serve a stint in the military. The sons of the wealthy made up a special group who did their time with the US Army that fed and clothed them better than the ROK Army. The KATUSAs not only helped bridge the language barrier but, if any fighting broke out, they would also serve as scouts since they knew the terrain better than any American soldier.

Tory turned to Myra. They were nearly nose to nose. Yesterday's experience at the movie theater seemed like an appetizer compared to this snugness. The gentleness of Myra's eyes together with the intimacy of their joined thighs quickened her heart, heating her. She wondered if Myra was aware of the sexuality she exuded.

"Yes," Tory said, but dreamily, as if she were responding to what she was seeing rather than what she was hearing. "Top told me they're sons of wealthy Koreans who pay their government to let their sons work for our Army."

"Yes," Myra said the same way Tory had. The bus was moving. Somehow her mind was able to pick that up while her entire being melded into Tory through their connected thighs. "Uh" escaped her lips but her brain could manage no more until it registered Tory's thigh pressing suggestively to her own. Then her brain went on Alert status. They were on a public bus where anybody could see them looking at each other in a more than friendly way. They were in the Army and you didn't do that in the Army, not where you could be seen, or even *possibly* seen, for that matter. And she didn't know this Tory. The others must have told Tory about her. Tory could be a plant, someone deliberately set to get close to her and determine for sure if she was one of "them." It was mind boggling the tricks the Army used to identify lesbians— intimidation, threats, interrogation, surveillance, plants— enough to make a sane mind go screaming into the endless night of insanity. Okay, get a grip, she told herself. Tory could be a plant just as Julie had been at her last post. Thank goodness she had asked Julie to only a movie instead of the sack. Get a grip. Julie never rubbed her thigh up against yours, did she? No. Okay. Tory was probably genuine. What were they talking about anyway? KATUSAs. Yes.

"Koreans," Myra blurted. "The Koreans in civies work on post everywhere. The PX, NCO Club, commissary, library, 1-2-3 Club, bus depot." Myra pulled her eyes from Tory's and glanced ahead. "We're here. The gate."

"Already?" Tory asked, disappointed more than surprised.

The bus stopped and Myra stood, relieved. "I told you we're only a half mile from the gate."

Reluctantly Tory followed, but her mind was already busily plotting. On the return trip she'd ask her to sit out a tour of the entire post, thigh to thigh.

They stepped into the short line of people exiting the camp. Myra pulled out her ID wallet. "Get your ID. The MPs will check it."

"I didn't have to show it when I came."

"That's because Henry brought you in by military jeep and the MPs know him. He picks up all the new personnel to our company."

"Oh." As Tory dug into her pocket her gaze wandered to the fence. "It's a real twelve foot high, chain link fence. I saw it when we drove in but I guess I was so busy looking at everything else and, of course, my mind was on what my new duty would be like. I guess I didn't see it like I'm seeing it now. It's intimidating in itself but with that barbed wire on top it's like a concentration camp."

"That's a matter of personal perspective, Tory. That fence marks the boundary line between Korean and American military soil. It runs the entire perimeter of Camp Bolden. To enter or exit vehicles have to go through the open, wide gate where the MP is standing."

Tory looked over. It was exactly that, like a gate in a backyard only on a much larger scale. It crossed the width of the road. A KATUSA MP faced it. MPs usually covered the gates of Stateside military compounds. That didn't bother her as much as the awesome reality of an actual locking fence. Instead of dress uniforms, the MPs wore fatigues and helmets, battle garb for a combat zone.

They entered the wooden twelve by twelve shack that was part of the gate. One KATUSA and two American MPs stood behind a counter, checking bags and IDs. Tory held up her ID as Myra did. As they left the shack Myra said, "That was the line out. The other side is the line in. Same deal."

"We have to show our IDs every time?"

"Every time."

"They'll check any bags we carry, too?"

"Thoroughly."

"What're they searching for?"

"A lot of things. IDs so no unauthorized persons like North Koreans or Koreans without passes can get on post. Bags so no unauthorized things can get through like bombs onto post or controlled items off."

"What controlled items?"

"You have your ration control card but haven't had a class yet. You will. Sugar, coffee, American liquor and cigarettes, pepper and a few others you can buy only so much of per month. It's a measure to help keep the lid on the black marketing. Only Americans can take them off-post. But I want you to take a good look at that gate."

Tory did. "What am I looking for?"

"That gate closes at midnight sharp and reopens at 0600. The last bus on post runs at midnight and starts again at 0600. After midnight, Tory, the only Americans allowed off-post are MPs on duty and those that live out here. And they stay in their hooches. After midnight, Tory," Myra paused, waiting for Tory's full attention.

Tory turned to her. "After midnight what?"

"After midnight, if you're caught off-post, you can lose your life. You've seen the guards carrying rifles along the roads when you came in..." Those guards toted fully-loaded M14s and strictly enforced the curfew. They, as well as the Korean National Police, knew that all American soldiers knew about the curfew. They would figure any soldier out after midnight blatantly disobeying the curfew was up to no good. "...They have the right to shoot."

"Mama! Has anyone been shot?"

"Not that I know of. But then I don't know of anyone who disregarded the curfew either. I for one will not risk it."

Tory was silent a moment absorbing the information, then said, "Mama! Feel free to draw my attention to any other minor details."

Myra patted her arm. "Come on. Let's go see the wonder-land of Seoul."

"Wait a minute." Tory captured Myra's patting hand, sniffing the air. "This is the same smell that was in the air the first time I stepped out onto the fire escape. Only it's stronger here."

"Smell?" Myra cocked her head, puzzled.

"It's like, oh, rotten cabbage."

"Oh! I'm so used to it I don't notice it anymore. It's different things but mostly kimchi and garlic."

Tory sniffed again. "Garlic. Garlic I can understand."

"Kimchi is salad. Only it's not fresh. They put cabbage and bok and other similar vegetables in big urns. Hot pepper and garlic and other seasonings are added. All is stirred well, then buried in the ground to ferment. Refrigeration is common only to the rich here. Here a refrigerator is not a household appliance."

"Do I dare try it?"

"Remember the class I mentioned you'll attend on ration control? You'll also learn the do's and don'ts in Korea. One of the don'ts is not to eat any kind of food or drink the water in the ville. I wouldn't advocate otherwise, but there are some things I indulge in."

"Like kimchi?"

"Not regular or what they call winter kimchi. Heck, that'll grow hair on your chest. It'll burn your throat, your stomach, and later you'll spend time, lots of time, on the commode, if you know what I mean."

Tory laughed. "What's the other kind?"

"A-gi, it means baby, or Spring kimchi. Koreans laugh and say it's for babies. But I like it. Which way you want to go?"

"You're asking me?"

"Of course. You're my leader."

Tory pinched her arm. Myra grunted with the pain, rubbing the spot. "And if that doesn't kill the wiseass in you," Tory said, "I know of a better spot."

With a smile Myra backed her rear-end out of arm's reach. "I don't think you're ready to go right yet, so we go left."

It was only eight in the morning yet the streets of Seoul were noisy with activity. They started uphill. Many shops were open and ready for business. Other peddlers were setting up their goods on the sidewalk and some on the road. Blue, compact taxis wove around them.

"Anything you want you can buy here," Myra began. "It's a wonderland if you're an avid shopper. Even if you're not, it's enjoyable to come out and just walk and watch all the people."

"It looks like a giant open flea market."

"But you'll get better quality for the same low price. See that sneaker shop?" Myra pointed across the road. "I see we're both into tennis shoes. If you stay only a year be sure and buy about ten pairs."

"Ten pairs!? I couldn't afford that many."

"At five dollars a pair?"

Tory's eyes popped. "Everything's that cheap?"

"Even gold."

"Same quality?"

"I've known guys to buy over-sized rings and sell them in the States for three times the price. Can't take gold as is out of country but you can in jewelry form. All clothes, coats, jackets, boots are tailor-made of leather, suede, silk, anything."

72

"Mama!"

Myra touched her elbow. "But, hey, don't go spending yet. Down Osan way you'll get better deals, especially on gold."

"Osan?"

"It's an Air Force base about thirty five minutes south. A lot of Americans, tourists as well as GIs from other camps, come here to shop because Seoul's market is the biggest. But it's not the best for price."

* * *

"You're sure I should drink this?" Tory asked. The cola in the glass looked harmless. They sat at a small table in a marketplace restaurant. Eight, what Tory called munchkin, tables filled the room, covered by red and white checkered, plastic tablecloths.

"Water is said to be non-potable but you won't get much from the ice."

Tory threw her The Look. It meant you're shittin' me.

With a gulp Myra answered it. "In some of the smaller villes I'd advise against it. But Seoul's sanitation is good."

The Look still bore down.

"Take them out if it'll make you feel better."

The Look retreated. She watched Tory finger the few cubes out, then drink.

"Mmm. Needed that." Tory's eyes twinkled on Myra. "Thank you." She said no more, testing to see if Myra understood she was also grateful for her time in showing her around and the special company she offered.

Myra's usual steady eyes darted from Tory to the table, back to Tory, then squinted in childlike glee as if she were tickled. "No. I should be thanking you."

Mama! Tory thought. Right on target. Would now be a good time to bring up more personal conversation? Their bowls of a-gi kimchi arrived. Myra taught Tory how to use her delicate, silver chopsticks. With much difficulty, Tory managed one or two pieces of the cabbage. Liking it, she dropped the awkward sticks and used her fingers.

Feeling guilty, Tory asked, "Am I going to get sick?"

Myra shook her head. "Too many preservatives in the stuff. No germ could live." She didn't dare mention the diarrhea that

73

eventually would follow. It was a stage the body had to suffer on its road to adjustment.

Tory stacked the empty, silver-colored bowls and slid them aside. She folded her arms on the table, leaning into Myra. "Where do you come from?"

Myra's brows furrowed. The question was direct, bold, and came from nowhere. The tone Tory used made her feel like a strange being from a UFO. "The States, of course." She received The Look. "If I tell you what state, will you tell me I've been rooting for the wrong football team?"

"I don't even like football. I wouldn't care."

"Neither do I."

"Besides, I wasn't referring to just what state."

"I know."

They locked cocked brows. The stand-off ended when they both broke into laughter. Myra gave. "Weiser, Idaho."

"Ah!" Tory squealed. "We're practically neighbors! I'm from Colorado. Fort Larson. At least I was born there. I'm an Army brat. Don't really have a place to call home."

"I know what you mean. I call the Army home, too. I haven't been to Weiser in, oh, nine years. About as long as my father's been dead. Car accident. It happened after I returned from 'Nam. My mother's remarried."

"Why so long away?"

"No family left there. My mother lives in Nevada. I have one brother. He's in prison for, well, laziness I could say. Big bucks lured him into drugs. I entered service when I was eighteen, liked it, and have been marching on since." She shrugged and showed her palms. "That's it."

Tory gazed at her a moment, then lowered her eyes to the dog tags. "No, but that'll do for now." Picking up her glass of cola, she was startled by what looked like Myra's dog tag chain going taut. She lowered the glass. Sure enough, Myra was pulling on it. Myra's eyes flitted between something behind her and the empty bowls on the table. Tory guessed the something was the entrance to the restaurant since she had her back to it. And through that entrance must have passed Craft. Calmly, Tory lifted her glass to her lips, then nearly bit out a hunk when she heard,

74

"Ladies! Good afternoon. It's a pleasure to see you out here."

Pleasure, my ass, Myra thought.

Tory looked up to see Tracer and a Korean girl she assumed was his yobo. He was tall and skinny and she half his size and grinning as if she was the happiest girl in the world. "Hi. You out for a shopping spree?"

Tracer placed a possessive arm around the Korean girl's shoulders. "Got to keep my lady friend happy, don'tcha know." He looked at Myra who was not smiling but returning an acknowledging nod. "We're here to have dinner, so if you'll excuse us?"

"Have a good day." Tory waved as Myra continued to hold the tags. Watching her, Tory thought back to yesterday when they studied each other's ID pictures. Hair had been an extremely touchy topic for Myra. Tory checked Myra's hair now and realized she hadn't yet seen it any other way but pinned up. That was expected in uniform per regulation, but not off duty. So, it was hair which stayed pinned up, tags, Craft, and now Tracer. Was the moment ripe to ask about the tags? Myra was silent, staring at the empty bowls. Whether it was or not Tory couldn't resist. "Are you aware of your habit of pulling on your dog tags?"

Myra's ears, sharp as always, especially in the small area of the restaurant, easily picked up, "...dyke...shoots an M16 like a man...." coming from Tracer.

Certain Tory had heard, Myra bit at her top lip, then raised saddened eyes to Tory. "I don't have to look to know that Tracer chose a seat that faces me."

Unwilling to let his words get the best of her, Tory glanced over. Tracer sat as Myra had claimed and his yobo turned around in order to...get a second look at the white Godless perverts, Tory thought.

"I can see the answer on your face." Myra said as they both heard Tracer say, "...like a fucking man...."

While Tory rubbed her forehead in embarrassment, Myra thought how fine her hands were—large, long fingered, olive-toned like the rest of her. Tory possessed a beauty she wanted to touch, but she felt unsure yet. If Tory knew what she was

75

thinking, would Myra again view that beauty in a small restaurant at a table for two? So damn tough in service. If she could predict that the worst possible outcome would be a simple rejection, she could handle that.

But she couldn't predict and the worst could be discharge. Myra couldn't handle that. It was a bit easier in the States. At least there were women's bars there where she had often found and met others—no risk. Here there were no bars. Here there were very few women scattered among different companies and they included more straights. So damn tough—and lonely. And Tracer's words, meant for Tory to hear, to know about Myra, were making the already difficult almost impossible.

Judging by the taut dog tag chain, Tory could tell Tracer had to be in alliance with Craft. Tory could guess what Tracer was up to, helping Craft ensure everyone, including herself, believed Myra was a contemptible lesbian unworthy of any association. He was being smart about it, mentioning no names, saying it loudly enough to hear yet softly enough to imply that his words were meant only for his own and his yobo's ears. Tory wouldn't reprimand him. That would only tell Tracer that his malice had struck the bull's eye. She reached over the table and patted Myra's hand.

"You didn't answer my question," she said, hoping to take Myra's mind off his hostility.

"...bet she pisses standing up...

Myra yanked her hand from Tory and bolted to her feet, checking her watch. "It's three-thirty and a-gi kimchi won't carry us through the next hour let alone the night. I'm going to catch dinner in the mess."

Tory gladly followed, but she wasn't going to let his words divert her train of thought. While Myra paid in won, Korean currency, Tory asked again, "Are you aware of your habit?"

Smiling wanly, Myra led the way back to post, thinking that Tory was being kind by disowning his contempt. She said, "I can't help but think that your parents must be very proud of you."

"Oh?" Comments like that always tickled Tory.

"You obviously followed in your father's footsteps and are

76

proving yourself successful. You're not only attractive but bright."

Mama! Tory thought. Let's go for the orgasm!

"Not only bright but congenial," Myra continued. "Everybody in the office is already won over by you. Even Craft and Tracer."

"Does that upset you?"

"Heavens, no! It makes me proud to have the privilege of showing you around. It makes me feel special."

"You are," Tory said, but in a voice too soft to be heard.

"I guess what I'm trying to say..." They entered the gate's shack, showed IDs and exited onto post. " Let's walk, okay?"

Preoccupied with the present conversation, Tory readily agreed, forgetting the planned thigh to thigh tour of the post from the bus.

"I guess what I'm saying is that it's obvious you like to be in the know about everything."

"And that's wrong?"

"Just the opposite. But sometimes the timing for some knowledge is wrong. And sometimes learning what you wanted to know has a negative effect. You know what I'm saying?"

"But more often learning has a positive effect, so positive that it makes you happy."

"I suppose I can't argue that."

"But, you're saying you won't answer my question so back off."

"Close." Myra smiled. "The answer is quite."

Chapter Seven

"I don't get it." Craft stuck a chaw of tobacco into his mouth, bulging his left cheek. His focus was set in the distance as he leaned back against the barracks.

Tracer took a long drag on his cigarette, then chuckled gutturally. His eyes were set on the same thing, Barrett and Sturdivan leaving the mess hall, going to the bank on this end of May sunny afternoon. "What?"

"What the fuck's the deal? Barrett knows what Mikey is. I gave enough hints. Unless she's a stupid bitch."

Tracer toked again and chuckled more. "Or she's the same as Mikey."

Craft's brows lifted in surprise. He spat a brown glob onto the grass. "No way. She's too feminine, man! And she treats me good. Hell, she'll let me off practically whenever I want. She's fair, you know? And she's been in charge only a month but she runs that office better than any NCO I've known and I've been in the Army five years, I should know." Tracer listened with a sly calm. "We get things done quicker and better with her. She's better organized or something."

"Like Mikey in supply. Johnson and Guiterrez always get time off."

Craft spat again, lost in thought.

Tracer flicked ash off his cigarette. He checked Craft's response as he said, "Mikey's got quite a few curves, too. That's why you want her."

"Fuck, Tracer! You know I just spread that dyke business so everybody would stay away from her. She's mine. I figured if I told Barrett she'd stay away, too. Sturdivan gets enough lonelies, she'd come running to me for comfort. But nooo!

Barrett had to come."

"I hear Top sicced her on Mikey from the get-go."

"What the fuck for?"

"Concern over Mikey's mental state. You know, ole buddy, since you started that nightly ritual with her she started acting funny."

Craft spewed another brown glob onto the grass. "Damn straight! She deserves it. Don't want nothing to do with me. Fuck her! Besides, I gotta keep her in line because of that Korean hole. Like my ole man used to say, 'Boy, there's only two ways to handle a woman, with the tongue or the hand. If one don't work use the other. Always watch her.'"

"Yeah, man. He was right, too. If I wasn't stuck in this goddamn hole of a country my ole lady wouldn't be divorcing me. I'd be Stateside keeping an eye on her and handling things."

"That's how the ole lady got away from my ole man. She ran off when he was too drunk to watch her. But I ain't gonna make the same mistake he did. I'm gonna watch Sturdivan."

"Yeah, man, but don't worry about that Korean. She wasn't nothing but a whore. No court'll listen to her word. Most you'd get would be a slap on the hand and advised to be more careful in picking holes. But it's good you keep Mikey in line like that. Keep her scared, she'll do what you want."

"Hey, man, I owe you one for that idea, too."

"Hey, man, nobody's making you do what I say." Under his breath Tracer mumbled, "Can't stand a fucking dyke."

"What?"

"Look, man. Look at them. Don't they look real happy together? You know, man, I never peeked in Mikey's room to see if she sucks the tits on that blow-up doll you dropped at her door. I don't know if she's a dyke. But if Mikey ain't, what about Barrett? If Barrett is, who's to say Barrett won't change her?"

"Naw! I'll get her yet. She'll break down."

"Yeah, man. Is that before or after she becomes one?"

"You really think Barrett is?"

"Hey, man, I don't know. But if she is, she's gonna be messing with your goods real soon, don'tcha know."

"No fucking way! I'll kill her. I'll—"

"No, man. You're thinking wrong. Barrett's hard-core. You fuck with her, you'll be eating shit. She's stripes, man, not a specialist."

"I don't give a fuck." Craft spat the entire glob of tobacco.

"Look at yourself, man. You're popping. Your blood pressure's up. Come on, man." He laid a supportive hand on Craft's shoulder and turned him in the direction of the gate. "Let's get some pussy and figure it out."

* * *

Three days after Craft and Tracer went to the ville to "figure it out," Myra crouched before her trunk. Its lid rested open, making it look like a homemade trap for small animals, one that stole freedom but didn't physically injure unless forgotten.

Since Basic Training her trunk had served her well. In the beginning it acted as a safe port, a place where she stashed contraband. As long as it was locked no inspection could touch it. She had hidden chocolate bars, jelly beans, potato chips, sodas, cheater pads for polishing boots, cheater cream for polishing brass, dirty laundry and other things. Later it harbored civilian clothes and fragile items that she wanted to preserve—pictures of her family and friends, gifts from past lovers, memorable certificates for outstanding completion of military schools, souvenirs from different posts.

Now she could only stare at the contents of the trunk and shake her head. The things inside came from Craft. He had told her so early on when he started his nightly knocking on her door. Other than his word, there was no evidence they came from him. The things were always wrapped in brown paper and left at her door with "Sturdivan-Mikey" stenciled on them. She had taken every one of the packages in mainly to get MIKEY out of the public hallway.

She understood why Craft wanted her silence. But she didn't understand why he sent her the things inside her trunk that confused and disgusted her. That Craft could be so enchanted by her that he'd terrorize and berate her in the name of love awed her. Love and abuse should not walk

80

hand-in-hand. Yet here in this trunk were reminders that love and abuse existed as one for some. Why else would Craft have sent her vibrators, thickly padded bras that he promised to wear for her pleasure, a blow-up female doll, a double-headed dildo, pictures of nude females he'd "allow" her to peruse while he "sucked" her off, and a satin pillow with "her and her" sewn on it with a penis, hard and straight, dividing the two? All items to make her feel shame and goad her into proving she was straight. Why couldn't he just accept that she was different? Why did he just take her difference and her disinterest in him as a challenge?

Myra knew she should trash the stuff but fascination prevented her. She did not understand her own fascination. The effort she exerted trying to understand the whys of it all left her weak and baffled.

She laid two firm hands on the open lid. This evening, this third day of June, held the clincher. At dinner she had decided to show Tory her room. Tory bubbled, excited over finally getting to see what Myra's mystery was. The only secret she wanted to keep was her attraction to Tory, yet continuing to refuse her created suspicion. At dinner she convinced herself that all would be okay if she were alone with Tory. She would maintain distance, keeping the friendship just that until Craft left so Tory would not be added to his hit list.

But fifteen minutes ago she had gone to the mess to get ice, then the dayroom for sodas in case Tory wanted something cold instead of hot coffee. She had had her head down shuffling the cans deep into her plastic bag full of ice when she rounded the corner out of the dayroom, heading for the stairs, and bumped into

"Miiiikey," Craft laughed, holding her by the elbows. "Are we in a hurry to get somewhere or *see* somebody?"

Myra shook herself free. "That's none of your business." She tried to go around him but he stepped in front of her, grinning. She had to stop and make it look like everything was all right because others were passing by.

Craft brought his head down level to Myra's, anchored his eyes on hers and whispered menacingly, "Mikey, I told you. Ain't nobody but me going to have you or go out with you. The

81

sooner you accept that the sooner you'll be happy. And I'm only concerned about your happiness. I noticed lately you and Barrett's been getting chummy."

Myra's heart was pounding in her ears but she managed, "Get out of my way, Craft."

He smiled, exposing a mouthful of sharp teeth. "You gotta admit, Mikey, I've been very patient with you. But this seeing Barrett is trying my patience. I'm going to say this only once so listen carefully. Don't see her again. If you do you'll regret it. You look like fucking dykes together."

Scowling, Myra raised her bag of ice and cans, ready to swing. "Get out of my way."

He laughed and stepped aside.

His warning was the clincher. She would "regret it" if she didn't see Tory. With a knotted stomach, she kept one firm hand on the lid of the trunk and grabbed her dangling dog tags with the other. Closing her eyes, she recited to herself as she often did, "I am okay. Hang on. This will pass. I am Myra Sturdivan, lesbian, child of God. No one will intimidate me into being what I am not. I am okay."

Opening her eyes, she scowled at the contents of the trunk, then slammed the lid shut.

* * *

Tory's first month at Camp Bolden had crawled along, though she adjusted quickly and smoothly. The time should have sped by. The reason it hadn't was Myra. Myra had eased her into Korea and Admin Company, making her feel comfortable. But she maintained a hard shell, one that Tory continuously studied, hoping to find a crack. No crack was spotted. She didn't want to risk being rejected or appearing too aggressive or finding out that her judgment of Myra was wrong, so she didn't knock again on Myra's door. Instead, she had waited for an invitation.

Now, finally, her patience, though more often her impatience, had paid off. Now Tory stood, swaying from side to side on two weak knees, flustered over whether to knock or rap the four count as Myra had instructed a month ago. While she struggled with that dilemma she also admonished herself. "Now, Tory, don't jump her bones as soon as the door closes behind you. You may want to, but don't. Even if you find out for certain where she's coming from, don't. Take your time, be polite, keep your hands in your pockets. Don't make an ass of yourself. If you get nothing firm on where she's coming from, look around and find some clues. Don't just—" A bang from inside the room startled her. Her hand jerked up and pounded four quick times on the door.

The four bangs on the door sounded like gunshots. Myra jumped to her feet. She knew she should answer it but she was frozen in her spot, listening to her heart hammer in her ears and feeling her face burn. Was she doing the right thing, allowing Tory into her room? Sure as shit, Craft or his right-hand man Tracer was watching from down the hall, seeing Tory knock, waiting to see whether or not she entered. What would either one do? What could either do? Hadn't she already experienced the worst? Wasn't near total isolation from the others enough? Weren't the scars on her face evidence of sufficient punishment?

Propping a concerned ear to the door, Tory listened but heard nothing. Had Myra fallen? No. Sounded more like a locker fell. On Myra? She struck another four times, pledging to bust the door down if she got no response.

The second wave of whacks smacked Myra into action. She rubbed her palms on her pant legs and checked herself in the mirror. She had showered—check. Neat creases in her jeans—check. Silken, hopefully alluring, black blouse—check. Too alluring? Too late—check. Clean room—check. No shoes. She panicked. Put on shoes or answer the door? She padded to the door in her black socks.

As she opened the door her eyes popped. Tory was flying at her with the mad speed of a Kamikaze pilot.

Tory's eyes popped at the same time but it was too late for an apology. She went blasting into an incredulous Myra whose mouth fell open, releasing a whimper, as she hotfooted a backwards retreat, holding on to a Tory crying, "MAMA!" Searching frantically for grip, Myra's socked feet slipped and slid on her carpet until her heel struck her yo, her bed, tripping her back-first onto it. She knew she was a goner before it happened. Still, she sank all ten fingers into Tory's arms,

83

vainly reasoning that somehow Tory would stop the inevitable—they went down together.

Tory did manage to shove out an arm, stopping her weight from hitting Myra hard. As soon as they realized they had landed and weren't dead they released held breaths. Tory dropped with relief onto her elbows.

They were pelvis to pelvis, breast to breast, faces only inches apart. The danger being past, their senses alerted to each other. They absorbed every bit of their joined, perspiring bodies, breathing in each other's scents, feeling each heart thrash to the beat of the other.

Wide-eyed, Tory rasped, "Are you all right?"

"Uh," Myra uttered. Tory's warming crotch was touching hers and Tory was showing no sign of even thinking of moving it. "Yes," she muttered. The closeness of Tory's lips dazed her. They seemed to wink with the promise of satisfaction guaranteed. "I'm fine." With much effort she brought her eyes up to Tory's. She saw the same want that she herself was struggling to contain. Her mind cried, Oh, God, am I ever in trouble, while her voice asked, "You?"

"Okay." Tory waited, hoping for the sign that said, come on. It had been too long a month, too long near someone she wanted to touch but didn't dare—too long. Her charcoal eyes darkened with hunger. It wasn't deliberate. It was a natural reflex, though if Tory could have, she would have held it in check. Her hips, as if with a mind of their own, gently nudged into Myra as if to say, Hey, guess what.

Myra's didn't have to guess. It knew exactly what and responded appropriately. Her mouth fell open from a rush, taking in a sharp breath. "Uh...is that musk you're wearing?"

Tory moved closer into her. "Yes. Like it?"

"It smells wonderful."

"So do you." She took in all of Myra's close features, from the beautiful doe eyes that held nervousness, but also want, to the creases and full, inviting lips. Tracing down her lovely neck to her nearly-exposed creamy breasts, she whispered, "I like your, uh, blouse."

"Thank you." Myra glanced down at Tory's lavender T-shirt. The two buttons on top were undone. Tory's full softness touched her own. "I, uh," she cocked an uncertain brow, "like yours, too."

"Your blouse is open by three or four buttons."

"It wasn't meant for this kind of activity."

Tory closed in to an inch. "I think it was.

My, but isn't she handsome, Myra thought. Then her eyes jerked to the side. Gently, she took Tory by the waist and steered her to the side and off her. Thumbing Tory's bottom lip, she said, "The door." Myra closed and locked the door. Holding the bolt, she stood still, facing the door, wondering how this had happened so suddenly. She heard Tory behind her, approaching. Her steps sounded light, calculated— tentative? If she turned around now, would she see the same look of desire or a second thought apology? Tory was close. Every excited, jumping pore in her body said so. She glanced down at her tags, then cautiously turned to face her.

Tory was intent. Holding Myra's eyes captive, she slid the back of her fingers from the button on Myra's jeans down her flat belly to the soft swelling below. There she paused and placed over that hand the back of her other. She stepped into Myra and allowed her only a hint of her own desire. She got what she hoped for. Myra's mouth fell open again from what Tory knew was a hot, fluid rush—just like her own.

"What," Tory's voice was thick with desire, "was that we fell on?"

Myra stayed perfectly still, unwilling to break this moment, and pivoted her eyes toward what Tory had asked about.

Refusing to let Myra escape, Tory turned her head as if for a kiss and recaptured Myra's eyes. "What?" she asked again, sliding in a thigh.

Myra's socked feet slipped willingly apart. Her desire reached out for Tory's, offering, but Tory was teasing, letting her have only so much. Myra wanted more. She anchored her eyes boldly on Tory and asked, "My yo?" to camouflage the slipping of her hands up Tory's thighs and under her shirt, resting half in and half out above the zipper of her jeans.

Tory didn't have her stripes for nothing. The camouflage failed. She felt every move of the silken warmth of Myra's hands. As if on command she raised her hands to the same position as Myra's, flexed her knees and pressed herself up and in, giving her what she wanted but still not all. "Yes," she breathed. "Your yo."

"It's..." Myra began, pulling the zipper of her own jeans down, the touch of Tory's hands there sending shivers through her.

Tory opened wide what Myra gave and watched arousal color her cheeks. Was it her imagination or were the creases fading?

"...a modified version..." Myra continued, unzipping Tory's jeans, opening them as Tory had done hers, "...of a..." She stopped for breath. Tory's hands, strong and sensual, were pulling her blouse out, slipping free the last few buttons. "...Korean bed. It's three pieces of six-inch thick foam...covered with cloth and...sewn together."

Tory could listen to her voice all night. It was so precise, so calm, so gentle. It seemed as if it alone were making love to her. "Go on."

Myra wasn't sure she could. Her breath was shuddering. "It can be folded." Another rush swept through her. She closed her eyes and leaned her head back as Tory lowered herself, kissing her vulva. Her hot breath penetrated her nylon panties, making her flesh quiver. She forced herself to continue. "It can be folded to use as a sofa or laid flat as a bed." She said it fast, her breath gone.

Tory kissed her way up to between her breasts where the dog tags lay. Opening the black silk blouse, she took a breast into her mouth, sucking, biting the hard nipple. She encircled Myra in her arms and brought her in tight, gobbling the other breast. Heated and past ready, she captured for a final time Myra's eyes—they were fluid and pleading—and rasped, "It must be very good for the back."

Myra took Tory's head with its rich hair and now black eyes into her hands. Shuddering, about to come, she could only mouth a "Yes." Tory couldn't hold back any more. It had been too long. She slipped one hand behind Myra's head, holding her firm, the other into her pants and her wetness. Watching Myra suck in air, she plunged three fingers, four, filling and taking. Burning, Tory tilted her head and breathed, "Come to me."

Myra crushed a hungry mouth on Tory's and they cried out their orgasms into each other's breath.

* * *

Craft skulked behind the wall of the inside stairs, spying. That bag of ice and sodas had told him Myra was staying in, not going out. He'd never seen her get ice before. She had to be entertaining somebody and if she did after he had told her not to.... He watched Barrett leave her own room and go to Myra's door, pause, then knock. When Myra didn't answer he grinned to himself, believing his earlier threat had done the trick. Hearing Barrett knock again, he said to himself, "Knock forever, dyke. She knows better than to let you in." When he saw Barrett back up his brows furrowed in puzzlement. He was even more puzzled when he heard the opening click of Myra's door just as Barrett hurled herself at it. His puzzlement turned to anger when he realized the click of Myra's door meant she had opened it for Barrett. She opened it, he said to himself, stunned. And after I told her not to. He heard another click and looked. No Barrett was in sight. Myra had not only opened her door to Barrett but let her stay. She had defied him. Next thing she'd probably do is open her mouth about that hole in the ville. No fucking way was she going to do that. "If one don't do it, use the other," he heard his ole man say. And Tracer had agreed, had said it was the only thing left to do. Craft walked away with a hard penis and two clenched fists, saying, "All right. The tongue didn't work. Now it's time for the hand."

* * *

Myra began to get up off the yo but Tory pulled her back down. "No, no, baby doll. You're staying right here."

Myra laughed. She hadn't felt this good in—she couldn't remember how long, but it was never. Her feelings for Tory were stronger than any she had felt for any other woman. "I'm going to dress and make that coffee you originally came into my lair for." She raised both brows playfully, suggesting she had actually planned Tory's flying into the room, their falling entwined onto the yo, and the subsequent lovemaking.

Tory touched Myra's hair that was a total, beautiful mess

but still pinned up. "Coffee I'd like. How about leaving the clothes, though?"

Myra threw her eyes up and back toward the window. "I don't know how long we've been at it, but it's dark outside and there's work tomorrow."

"I hate it when you're right." She slapped Myra's arm. "Go on." After watching her dress, Tory put on her own clothes, albeit reluctantly.

Myra made the coffee in a drip pot she kept on her old, wooden desk. Waiting for it, she straightened her hair, then stood, arms folded, with her back to the door. A satisfied grin stretched from ear to ear.

Tory glanced up from tying her tennis shoes, then did a double take. Myra was radiant, glowing from—here she mentally patted herself on the back—what could only be their first lovemaking. "What?"

Myra shrugged. "This has been an incredibly wonderful evening."

"My sentiments exactly." She started toward her.

Myra threw up a halting hand. "Please, stay right there. I said that because it's true and because I don't want you to get the wrong idea. After we have coffee I'd like you to leave."

"Oh, hey, I told you why I came flying in here. I thought you were—"

"No." Myra shook her head. "That's not why I want you to leave. It's lovely that you're so protective."

"Then I don't understand. We just made love."

"I'm more than aware of what we just did and that's exactly why." She saw Tory's brows crease in confusion. "Remember our first meeting on the fire escape? When I said there were always eyes? I know you thought I was bonkers, but it's true. One reason I want you to leave is so you'll be seen leaving and not seen spending the night."

"Myra, babe, don't you think that's being a bit paranoid?"

"Trust me, Tory. You will be seen. The second reason is, well, all of this happened so quickly. I need time to savor this alone."

Smiling, Tory said, "I think the coffee's ready." Seating herself at the desk's chair, she spooned cream and sugar into

Myra's one cup. Myra took a seat on the edge of her desk. Caressing Myra's knee, Tory offered her the first sip. After Myra accepted it, she looked at the yo for the first time. With wider eyes she took in the entire room, breathing out a "Mama!"

If Tory had been standing at the door, she'd have seen the yo in the far right corner on the floor. A bright white quilt with a red rose print covered it. There was not one flat, military-type pillow but four very civilian, fluffy ones. The satin pillowcases and sheets were soft yellow. Heavy, burgundy drapes shrouded the window of the far wall. Centered in the window was a set of tubular, silver wind chimes. In the far left corner stood the desk. A long, wide, lacy doily dressed it. The coffee pot was on the right, pictures of family and friends on the left.

On the wall above the desk hung a poster bearing the image of an amazon, dark-haired and grave, clad in jungle fatigues, combat boots and a helmet with a dangling chin strap. Camouflage paint covered her face. Boots braced shoulder-width apart, she toted an M16 rifle on the ready and a bandoleer filled with M16 rounds. Her hips supported an olive drab field belt with a canteen on the right and gas mask on the left. A tattooed double women's symbol peeked below her rolled-up shirt sleeve. The poster's caption read, "The Army needs a few good women."

Myra followed Tory's eyes and was pleased with her open-mouthed, silent comments. As Tory gawked at her poster she said, "I fell in love with her the moment I laid eyes on her."

Tory nodded, seeing Myra in it. Captivating sexuality and strength illuminated the woman. "I can see why."

Pulling her eyes away, Tory continued. Below the window stood a foot high, Korean table holding several plants and an alarm clock. The plants were lush with care, creeping up both sides of the window and along both side walls near the ceiling. A four by six looped rug adorned the right wall above the yo. On a lavender backdrop it portrayed a pristine white unicorn with a collar of flowers and a sparking golden horn, flying amid the stars toward the moon. A ten by twelve orange rug bearing a panther in a stretching, alerted stance, encircled by jungle vines covered the floor. Later Myra would explain it wasn't a rug but an imitation mink blanket.

At the foot of the yo but tight against the right wall were a trunk and gray metal locker. It looked as though the trunk was trying to hide. Along the left wall by the desk was another locker. Two lockers didn't surprise Tory. She herself had two. It was the wall! From floor to ceiling mirrors covered the entire left wall, giving the room a spacious, majestic feel.

On the front wall, to the left of the door, hung a circular dart board above a solid, two-foot tall brass urn holding six-foot red, white and purple feathers. To the right of the door was a white poster board with a large red arrow pointing to the latrine. Above the arrow in black, block letters was printed the word PRIVATE. Under the word in smaller letters was, *Unless you're family.*

Awed, Tory slowly came to her feet and walked to the center of the room where she did a complete circle, gaping. With a hand to her mouth, speechless, she stopped.

Myra squinted in childlike pleasure. "You like it?"

Tearing her eyes away, Tory focused on her. "Like it!? This doesn't even resemble a barracks room. It's so warm, comfortable. It hugs you. No wonder you keep everybody out. How do you get around inspections?"

"Higher-ups like us are free of any and all inspections."

"I'm glad. I've been sick of those silly things since Basic." Tory took the cup of coffee Myra offered.

With a smug smile Myra looked around, then shrugged. "I can't take all the credit. Mamasan helped me some. But this is my home for at least another sixteen months. Might as well make it livable. I'm lucky. The sun shines in beautifully. My plants love it and I've got to have growing vegetation of some sort. I grew up in a country environment."

Tory returned the cup to her. Myra refilled it. "And the wall rug?"

"I made that. When I saw the pattern in the PX, I greedily snapped it up. It was the last and I didn't care who else might've been looking for the same thing." She handed the fresh cup to Tory.

"It was the last," Tory sipped, "probably because there are

more women here searching for the same thing."

"Lovely. I never thought of it that way. I assumed the person responsible for supplying the PX goofed by ordering that." She paused in thought, then said as if thinking out loud, "It's sad though."

Hearing the change in Myra's voice more than the words, Tory turned from the wall rug to her. "Why's that?"

"Well, there're different reasons for the women being here. It's not just that they randomly came down on orders. When I was stationed at the Southern tip in Pusan there was a woman there that I had the hardest time getting to know. It turned out she'd been sent to Korea as punishment. One of the officers at her last Stateside duty station began to suspect her. He dogged her but couldn't get her to admit anything. She said he finally just blew up at her one day and accused her of being a dyke because of the way she looked. He couldn't stand her face anymore so the next thing she knew she was on orders for Korea. And she wasn't the only one I heard that similar story from."

"She was scared. That's why you had a hard time getting to know her."

"Yes. But you know she said she was glad she was sent here. She said in the States she had to watch everything she did, including the way she walked, talked and even breathed."

"She lived in the barracks I bet. Everyone's so close everyone knows everything about everyone's business. What they don't know they make up."

"Exactly. Here she still lived in the barracks but said she could breathe easier."

Tory cocked her head in thought. "Hmph. That's probably what Top meant. We had a talk my first day here. He made sure I understood Korea was considered a combat zone and screaming queer to get out would only bring harassment, not out."

"Only thing that matters is a body capable of toting a weapon. Heck, you know that from 'Nam. There you could've walked around in a suit and tie and nobody would've cared until you got back Stateside. Then all of a sudden it would matter again. We can die for our country but we can't live in peace for it."

Musing over that, Tory went to the desk where Myra still sat and refilled the cup.

"Since that woman told me how she was able to breathe here," Myra continued, "I often wondered about myself. Don't get me wrong. I genuinely love being here. I love the country, its people, their simplicity and honor. I like the way everything is smaller here and the slower pace. But I wonder if part or even the major reason I kept extending and requesting to return is because I knew I can breathe a bit easier here, too."

Sipping her coffee, Tory raised her brows. "Like here you're allowed to actually exist as you are. Sort of like you're accepted."

"No, not accepted. Tolerated, I think, but even that's stretching it now—lately. The others suspect I'm a lesbian, so they avoid me. Some, like Johnson and Guiterrez, like me, but to avoid being ostracized themselves they stay away too. In front of others, that is."

"Hmph," Tory said, thinking. "Like prostitution here. You told me prostitution isn't legal but the Korean government turns its head."

"Something like that. The Army often turns its head on homosexuality, when that suits its needs. They'll harass if they suspect, but unless we blatantly admit to being dykes, cause some sort of trouble or get caught doing something in public we won't be brought into the Captain's office. I know I won't be dragged in and discharged just on suspicion, no matter how many avoid me like the plague, so I feel like I can breathe easier here. It has nothing to do with my being a dedicated soldier, so I'll never admit anything, and I'm surely not going to be caught in any act."

"I'm sure that's why that woman you knew in Pusan said she could breathe easier here too."

Myra squinted. "I guess for a turn of the head we're willing to exist in a combat zone, even grow to like it. Anything. Just as long as we can live."

"Yeah," Tory agreed. "But I've talked with Top and I can assure you he's more liberal."

Myra cocked her head. "Are you kidding? Top's an unusual man. That's why everyone likes him so much. But what do you think would happen if we held hands in front of the Admin hut?"

Tory grimaced "We wouldn't make it to retirement?"

"We wouldn't make it past the Captain's office. He's said more than once he can't stand queers. Top may be liberal and he may run the company, but the Captain has the final word. He wouldn't be able to stop the Captain from having us kicked out. Besides, if you come out to Top it's as good as breaking the contract."

"Oh, yes." Tory smiled. "The one I signed, saying, oh no, not me, I wouldn't do that!"

"Don't take what I'm saying lightly, Tory."

"Myra," Tory lifted Myra's chin and pecked her lips, "laugh. I'm not taking you lightly. But if you don't laugh somewhere, sometime you won't survive. And if you don't survive, who's going to be around for no other reason than to spite the fuck out of them?" Myra did laugh and Tory said, "Now, tell me about Mamasan."

'Mamasan? What do you mean?"

"Where do I stand?" With Myra's brows creasing yet more, Tory explained, "Henry told me you used to hang with her a lot but you haven't lately. Was it a breakup? What happened?"

"Oh! No. We weren't lovers. I, uh...." Myra wasn't sure how to proceed without dishonoring her word. Craft had raped Eun Lee who had cried on Mamasan's lap over it. Then Myra herself had cried on Mamasan's lap over it but on a separate occasion. Myra wanted to report it but knew she'd only endanger herself since she didn't know who the victim was. Mamasan understood Myra's fear of being harassed and humiliated, then discharged by a homophobic Army. She also understood Eun Lee's fear of her parents. Though she had sworn silence for Eun Lee, she wanted the American rapist to suffer as he made Eun Lee and her American friend suffer. She got together with Myra, then they got with Eun Lee. Myra was willing to face being interrogated about why she was in Thousand Won Alley if Eun Lee was willing to face her parents, but no amount of urging would make her come forward. The result—Mamasan and Myra swore silence for Eun Lee while Mamasan was supposed to continue trying to persuade her. No one but the three of them knew about the rape.

As an added heartbreak, Myra stopped going to Mamasan's hooche to keep Craft's mind off Mamasan and hopefully prevent him from even thinking of hurting her, too.

"I, uh," Myra said again.

"I, uh. You're stuttering an awful lot there, Stuuurdi."

But she hadn't told Mamasan about Craft's threat on her. She didn't know if she was doing the right thing or not by keeping it a secret from Mamasan. She did know she didn't want Mamasan living in fear as she herself did. "I'm scared, Mamasan" was what Myra had told her when she asked why Myra wasn't coming to her hooche anymore. "He threatened me, Mamasan." Mamasan didn't like it but accepted it and the next day she put the switch blade with its case in Myra's hand. "You carry this always. If he even looks like he's going to try something you slice it off. You slice it off for Mamasan and Eun Lee if not yourself."

"Myra, if you weren't lovers I believe you. If you bought sex from her that's okay, too. But I need to know where I stand."

Myra forced her thoughts back to the present. "No, Tory. there's nothing sexual between us. Yes, I love her but not in a sexual way. Sometimes I think of her as the sister I never had, sometimes a friend, sometimes even a mother, especially when she comes down on my case for something. Most times she's a combination of all three. We clicked. She knows where I'm coming from and she accepts me. Sometimes I think she likes me because of what I am."

"Is she a lesbian, too?"

Myra grinned sheepishly. "She won't tell. Not too long ago she did say, though, that she had found happiness thanks to me." Myra shrugged. "Maybe she'll tell me one day. I think, too, she appreciates me because my being here makes her work day more comfortable, like she's not working for a bunch of strangers."

"So why did you stop seeing her?"

"I didn't. Not really. I'll sometimes share a ramyon lunch with her at the end of the hall where all the Papasans and she gather for it. And usually she comes to my room when I get off. She knows I always make coffee. She'll bring her mug and sit a while."

"But you don't see her at her hooche any more."

No, Myra wasn't going to tell her why. "You can thank Mamasan for that cup of coffee you got your first night here."

"She said it came from you."

"Sort of. She took the cup I was about to drink from out of my hand and told me in not so nice a way I wasn't being a good hostess. She said she could see I was attracted to you by the issue I gave you and that if I didn't know how to treat you, then she would do it for me."

Tory easily read the sincerity in Myra's eyes, then hooted. "Yes. I see why you'd see her as a mother then." Reclaiming the desk's seat, she placed the cup down and turned to the pictures. She picked up one showing a man and woman. "Your parents?"

Myra answered, "Mm-hmph."

"You look exactly like your mother."

"You think so? I always thought my mother was so beautiful."

Tory raised her eyes to Myra. "Yes. Exactly like her."

Color rose in Myra's already glowing cheeks. Her right hand came up and gingerly touched one of the creases.

Tory took that hand in her own and kissed it. "Yes, you are beautiful." Seeing Myra redden yet more, she lightened. "Now me! I got everything from my father. His complexion, his eyes, his hair, his voice, and even his fondness for women."

Myra laughed. "And I'm sure you've met with successes too numerous to count."

Pleased, Tory stretched it. "I do not kiss and tell. But I will disclose to you, only to you because I know you will keep silence, my most intimate, innermost fantasy." Cocking a suggestive, albeit comic, brow, she whispered, "You see this complexion? Yes, you do. It's Greek. One day I hope to trace my family roots back, all the way back to, yes, the Isle of Lesbos. There I hope to find that my great, great, great, great, and so on grandmother lived a life of utter ecstasy, surrounded by a harem of beautiful women and that she had a child only to

95

ensure that one day I would be born to carry on the family tradition."

Myra hooted. "Good God, what a brazen dream!"

Tory stuck her tongue out at her. "It's mine after all." She replaced the picture and picked up one showing four smiling women holding each other about the waist. Her attention was drawn to the woman on the right. She was the tallest and looked familiar. Pointing at her, she asked, "Who is she?"

"Grinder. At least everybody called her that."

Tory put a thoughtful finger to her chin. "I swear she looks familiar but the name doesn't spark."

"I don't know her real name. From what I understand she was named Grinder for her skill in smashing a volleyball, but I never saw any of them play. They were part of a bunch that hung together at Fort Hill."

"Were you stationed in Oklahoma before coming here?"

Myra nodded. "I hung with them a bit but didn't really get to know them. The rumor was that Grinder had run away from home at a young age. She was hiding out and didn't want to be found by using her real name."

Tory's breath caught. An idea struck her that was too good to be true. Bringing the picture closer, she scrutinized Grinder's face. Those blue eyes twinkled just like– "How old is she?"

"Oh, early twenties, I guess. You know her?'

"She wasn't in service?"

Myra shook her head. "She's civilian. Held a job in, uh, computer repair, I think."

Tory continued to stare at Grinder with determination. She ran her fingers through her hair, trying to force some recall. Grinder was tall just like.... "Do you have her address?"

"Sure. Well, actually I have Carol's. She's the blonde next to her. They live together."

Clenching a victorious fist, Tory grinned, then thrust the picture at her. "Take a good look. Does Grinder remind you of anyone?"

Myra reared back. "I always thought Top looked like her."

"BINGO!" Cocky with certain success, she asked, "You think it's just coincidence that Grinder sounds very much like

Top's name, Grindulman?"

"You're not saying...."

Tory threw a you-know-exactly-what-I'm-saying look.

"His daughter?"

After Tory explained what she and Top discussed in his office on her first day, Myra got off the desk and sat cross-legged on her yo. She stayed in silent thought until Tory couldn't bear it anymore.

"Give me the address, Myra."

"Honestly, Tory, she does not want to be found."

"I swear to God and all that's holy I'll be discreet. If she is his daughter I will not give him her address unless she puts it in writing. Of course, I won't mention it to him until I'm certain."

"I understand she's afraid of her father."

"She's afraid of her last scene with her father, not necessarily him. The man's in mourning, Myra. It's been four years and he grieves like it happened yesterday. You should've seen his face."

"That's why he's so liberal." Myra hesitantly retrieved her address book from her locker. "She may not be his daughter."

"By writing we can find out. All we would've lost is a stamp. If so, we may just make two people incredibly happy. Do you know for sure that Grinder wouldn't really love to see her daddy again? A daddy who's willing to accept her as she is?"

Myra rubbed her address book between two praying hands.

"Don't you think it'd be just plain kind to be able to let him know that his child is safe and not dead?"

Myra inked the address onto a slip of paper, then offered it to her. Tory took hold and Myra held on. "Promise you'll be cautious with this."

Tory raised her right hand. "I swear on all the Bibles you can stack that I will. I will not betray a sister. Do you think I, a lesbian, could survive eighteen years in the Army without being so?"

Myra released the paper.

"Well," Tory started, handing the cup to her, "you need to

be alone and I need to start a letter. May I assume I'll be invited back?"

"You're welcome anytime and you know it."

"Just can't spend the night."

"One day, I'm sure, I'll tell you all about it."

Tory spread her arms. "Do I get a kiss good night?"

Throwing up a halting hand, Myra cautiously stepped around her to the door. "Not a chance. You'd be staying for certain if you got that." She opened the door. "Tomorrow? Same time?"

With the back of her hand Tory stroked Myra's cheek at arm's length, then took a last look around. Yes, indeed, this was fairy tale land, this room the palace, Myra the princess.

* * *

On the fire escape Myra sucked in a lungful of warm June air and raised her eyes to the sky. The moon was full, the stars bright. The heavens seemed active with excited, reassuring voices whispering about futures and good times to come. She listened with a smile and eyes half closed as she breathed, "Oh, what a night." She felt drugged, as if everything were in slow motion, sedate and peaceful.

The distant mumbling at the other end of the hall intruded on her enjoyment of reliving what had just taken place, her first lovemaking with Tory. "Tory," she heard herself say with a tongue that could still taste her sweetness. This moment was too precious to share with the voices from down the hall. She floated down the escape on white sneakered feet, grinning above her bright orange T-shirt.

At the bottom she went behind the building, heading for her new hidey hole. Twenty yards into the woods she came to a ten foot irregular patch of cleared ground encircled by protective trees. In the middle was a rock, smooth and clean. She went to it but didn't sit on it. That would've taken more energy than her drug-like condition was willing to give. Instead, she sat on the ground, leaned back against her rock and gazed up at the stars. They seemed to shine just for her.

Right now there was nothing else in the world but the miracle of love and its healing powers. The touch of flesh, love's reward to two souls uniting, becoming one. In the stars she saw Tory's eyes, deep and rich, sending their message of desire, passion, love too fervent to be caged. The clouds were her lips, enticing, persuading, giving, the gentle breeze her whispers of love, the shadow of encircling trees her arms, arms that cast the nightmares out and replaced them with promising dreams. A fairy-tale come true.

She thought she should share this with Tory. Maybe she was paranoid. Maybe she should have let Tory sleep in her arms. How wonderful that would have been. Maybe.... No. The night wasn't over yet. She could still share it. She slowly lifted herself, backing onto the rock where she sat motionless, waiting for her muscles to awaken. That's what she'd do. She'd....

A big, hard hand slapped over her mouth. It stank of tobacco and pulled her tight into a harder chest. She hadn't heard anything, not a twig crack, a branch swish, nothing. The hand was smashing her lips into her teeth. Another hand crossed over her chest and grabbed her breast, squashing and pushing. She twisted to free herself but he was strong, clamping her against his entire body. His penis hardened against her. The pain in her breast was excruciating. Tears burst from her eyes. She tried to bite but couldn't move her mouth. She pinched his arms but he didn't seem to feel it. She reached up for his hair and heard, "Ooooh, Mikey! You do have something there!"

That revolting voice. Cold goose bumps exploded over her skin. She could see his repulsive smirk. She screamed into his hand, twisted, jerked, strained every muscle. Sweat and panic burst from every pore. Her tears blurred her vision, stinging her eyes. All she could see was his dark humping form in the alley.

He rubbed his whiskered cheek against hers, scratching her, and clamped her tighter. "Mikey, cut the shit. I got to do this. It's for your own good. I don't know what Barrett's done to you but whatever it is it's too much. You defied me. You let her into your room. And after I warned you not to. Next thing you'll be letting her into your pants."

Her struggles seemed useless. His arms felt like steel

bands. A whimper of helplessness choked her.

"I warned you, Mikey, and you still saw her. Now for your own good I got to do this. But when I'm through you'll thank me. And the best is that I put in for a year's extension...."

"Extension" zapped through her head like a searing streak of lightning. Bright white light flooded her. The next thing she knew she was on one knee, stopping her fall to the ground, her sneakered feet slipping and pushing against fallen leaves, exposing sharp rocks.

Craft shook his head, clearing the ache in his eye. Myra had hooked it and if he hadn't let go she would have torn it from its socket. He caught her arm and threw her backwards onto the ground.

Myra cried out. The rocks cut into her back. He was coming at her. She lifted both feet and caught his chest. She heaved him back. The rocks cut deeper into her buttocks as well as back. Scrambling on all fours, blood spotting the back of her shirt, she headed for the trees, the barracks, but was caught in his rigid grip and whirled around.

"You bitch!" he spat in her face. "This is for my eye." He backhanded her hard across the face. "And this is for seeing Barrett." He whacked her again on the same side.

Myra's head snapped to the side. Spots flashed. Her knees shook, then buckled.

He grabbed her again. "And this is for thinking you're too good for me." He hit her again and again and again, whipping the same side of her face. His knuckles beat her eye, her cheek, her lips. Then he slung her to the ground.

She landed hard on her stomach. Blinding pain tore through her breasts, her face, her arms. Glass from broken liquor bottles, remnants of past parties, dug into her belly, legs, arms. Just as she became aware of what she had landed on she was flung onto her back, felt her shirt and jeans being ripped open, his body straddling her legs.

"NOOOO!" she screamed and sank fingernails deep into his cheeks, clawing down. He howled. She grabbed a piece of branch and swung it with both hands, hitting his forehead. Her breath was hard. Her heart raced. Her only thought was that this was absolute madness as she scrambled over the

100

cutting glass and was kicked by a hard boot flat into it.

"This is for your own fucking GOOD!" He unbuckled his belt and spied her right hand closing over a stone. Remembering what she had done to him last time with a rock, he stomped her hand. He heard her scream as he scraped his boot across her knuckles, tearing flesh. Seeing her other hand searching, he stomped that one, too, scraping more flesh.

Pain, pain, hot, searing, tortuous pain. Whimpering, she pulled her hands in and under her. Pain burned her entire body yet the sound of his zipper coming down speared through it. She prayed. She forced her mind to think. Had to be a way out. Nothing came until she felt the touch of the case carrying her switch blade. Her hand had automatically clamped onto it. Mamasan's gift felt like a kiss from Tory. Then she felt him straddle her again.

He growled, "And this is going to look like child's play compared to what I'll do to your sweet Mamasan if you tell our little secret."

He pushed her onto her back and she pulled the switch from its case, hid it in her two bloody hands and hid her hands between her curled legs.

He hunched over her legs. He was sweating and panting. He grabbed her fallen hair in a fist, spitting, "Spread your fucking legs!" She didn't do it. He raised his hand high, snarled, "I ain't playing no fucking games," and came down on the same side of her face. He hit her eye with a hard, direct fist.

His face had to be only inches from her—she smelled the tobacco on his breath—but she couldn't see it well. It was fuzzy and wavered on top of her. Something was wrong with her eye. Her head was reeling. Her bladder released. Her legs went limp. As if in a nightmare she watched through one blurry eye as his face changed to shock and horror and finally a grimace of pain. His body rose upright over her own and her hand went up with it. Her senses threatened to black out, then suddenly came alive. Her hand held her switch and her switch was deep inside his inner leg.

Using the last bit of her strength, she pushed the blade deeper and rolled him off. His hand closed over her own holding the switch. Repulsed by the touch, she yanked the blade out. Blood gushed from the wound. He grabbed onto the hole in his leg, growling and groaning.

Trembling, exhausted, sweat and blood and dirt mixing, she crawled to her knees. Her blade dripped with blood. It looked dirty. She cleaned it on the back of his hands, slicing the knuckles he had used on her face. Her knees shook so badly she could barely control them but she managed to stagger to her feet.

Chapter Eight

"Baaarrett! Baaarrett! Bali bali! Baarrett!"

The private on chow duty could only hold back the Korean woman fighting to get past him. "Hold on, Mamasan. You can't come in here."

The long table where Tory, Johnson, Guiterrez, Walker and Henry sat was separated from the private and distraught Mamasan by three feet and a thin, wooden lattice barrier. Sitting at the head, Tory had her back to it. Craft and Tracer hadn't showed up for breakfast. It was 0700 and Myra, who was always at her own by 0700, hadn't come yet either. Tory heard the commotion just as Johnson stood to get a better view.

"What's up?" Tory asked, folding the military paper she was reading.

"I don't know, Sarge, but Mamasan wants in bad. Sounds like she's putting a curse on him."

Tory went to Mamasan who was wringing her hands on her work skirt, crying, "Baarrett, bali bali, Stuuurdi!" Then she started gibbering in Korean, hands flying to her face, slapping it, then pounding on her face, then fingers poking and slicing on her arms and legs. Tory caught Mamasan's wrists and dipped her knees, leveling her eyes on Mamasan's.

"Easy, Mamasan. Slow down. I don't understand. Take a deep breath." Tory inhaled, showing, and Mamasan did the same but it didn't help.

"Stuuurdi. Bad. Hurt. Bali bali." She took Tory's wrists, pulling.

Tory broke a hand free and raised it above the barrier. "Johnson, my hat!"

Johnson bulls-eyed the cap into her hand and Tory took off running. "Think we should follow?" she asked the group.

Henry rubbed the back of his neck, grimacing. "No Tracer. No Craft. And now Sturdivan. I have a rotten gut feeling. I got to watch the office when Barrett's gone. You go, Johnson, but as backup. Keep your distance."

Johnson bolted out the door.

* * *

The smeared blood on Myra's door tumbled Tory's stomach. Mamasan unlocked it. As it opened she put a protective, halting arm across Tory, saying, "Bad, bad," warning her to brace herself. The door open, Tory saw Myra splayed out naked, face down, on the yo. Mamasan throatily hissed, cursing Craft in Korean, pulling on her, pointing to the floor. Tory followed her point to the switch blade lying open and what looked like dried blood on the blade close to the handle. Her breath caught, her own blood went cold and her face ashen, as she spotted the torn and bloody orange T-shirt and jeans. She grabbed onto Mamasan's hand. There were large, ugly bumps, bruises, abrasions and cuts over Myra's back, legs, buttocks, everywhere. The knuckles of both hands were torn and her always neat hair a shambles with one pin left, hanging. And she wasn't moving.

Feeling Tory shudder, Mamasan enfolded Tory's hand with her other, kneading it, squeezing the strength out of it for herself as well as giving her own to Tory.

Okay, Tory said to herself, don't panic. Yes, you made love to this woman last night, expected to make love again tonight, but don't panic. What's the first thing you need to do? Check for breathing. Right. Myra wasn't moving. She was afraid to go closer.

Mamasan spoke rapidly to Tory in a combination of English and Korean. "I know who did it. I know.I was afraid for her. She dear to me. Stuurdi protected me from losing my job by not reporting that I shower in her room.Then she protected Eun Lee with her silence. I protected Stuurdi." I gave her that knife." She pointed to the blade lying on the floor, then to herself, then Myra. She shook Tory's hand in her two, demanding that she listen. "She accepted me as her equal, her friend, opened her home and her shower to me, shared her coffee with me. My days working here are bright because she's here. She made me feel like someone important, not just worker. But more." She squeezed Tory's hand and nodded and pointed down to Myra, "Help her. Get me liniments to clean the cuts and I will take care of her."

Unfortunately, all that Tory understood was "I know who did it. I know. I gave her that knife." Just the same, grateful for Mamasan's support, Tory closed the door behind them and together they made their way shakily to the yo.

As they look down on Myra Mamasan said again, but in clear English, "Help her!"

Tory freed her hand and patted Mamasan's reassuringly. While Mamasan wrung her hands on her work skirt Tory wiped her own on her fatigue pants.

Scared, Tory looked over to Myra's face which was turned to the wall. It looked okay. She put an ear to her back and felt the sweet rise and fall of breath. Placing a hand under Myra's, she called into her ear, "Myra, baby doll," and got a groan. "Come on up, baby. Slowly. Nice and easy." She felt Myra's weak grip squeeze her hand. "That's it. Easy. You know who I am, baby?" It took a moment but she finally heard, "Tooory."

"That's right, baby. Think. Do you feel anything broken?"

"No broken," she whimpered. "Hurt."

"Yeah, baby, I know. Lie real still. It'll be all right. Just lie still. I'll be gone just a minute. I'm going to call the medics...."

"Noooooo!" Myra wailed, clamping tight onto Tory's hand despite the shooting pain.

"Baby doll, you need—"

"Nooo." Struggling, she rolled onto her back, hanging on to Tory's hand, pulling it under her neck.

Myra cried out the agony of her turning, but the horror of Myra's face nearly stopped Tory's heart. Her bladder threatened to release. She faintly heard Mamasan hiss. The side of Myra's face that had been hidden was hideously swollen, cut, discolored, her lips puffed and split, making speech difficult, her eye swollen shut. Tory bit back a cry of anguish. "Myra, I have to get you medical help."

Myra clung to her hand and reached with her other to the back of Tory's head. Weakly she took a fistful of hair, opened her good eye and pulled Tory into it. "No. Nothing broken. Have two months leave. Fill out form for two weeks. I'll heal."

"But, baby, your eye."

"No. I refuse. No medical. No investigation. No court. No trouble."

"Why?" She watched Myra throw a scared eye to Mamasan. "What're you hiding?"

"Nothing," Myra growled. Tugging Tory's hair for emphasis, she said again, "Nothing."

Tory looked into that scared eye and knew there was something , but arguing right now would do more harm than good. Myra was refusing medical and Tory couldn't force it on her. Without moving from her position, Tory pulled a pad and pen from her shirt pocket and wrote on it, using a piece of the yo as a table—Johnson, give Mamasan alcohol or peroxide, bandages, aspirin, and ice from the mess. Open and manage supply. Tell Top I'll be down as soon as possible and nothing else.

"Mamasan," she called, turning her head, ripping the sheet out and giving it to her. "Take that to Johnson. Bali bali." Mamasan snatched the note, hissing and leaving. "And close the door." She bowed, closing it.

Myra released her hair and gingerly touched Tory's lips, their beauty, their promise of love better than any pain killer. Tory kissed her fingers, then ever so lightly kissed her swollen lips. "You're going to be all right, babe."

Myra fingered Tory's cheek. "Now. Yes. Kiss me again. Hold me." Fresh tears spilled.

* * *

Staring down at the note in both her hands, hurrying, Mamasan smacked into Johnson who was standing by the inside stairs. Johnson took hold of her shoulders and halted her. "Okay, Mamasan. What?"

Mamasan liked Johnson, had nicknamed her the 'gentle giant' but right now she shoved the note at her and pulled her

106

down the stairs.

Scurrying, Johnson read, her ice-blue eyes widening, her heart feeling nearly as sick as Tory's. She asked Mamasan what was wrong but got only the same explanation and hissing that Tory had, leaving her confused. Her order to tell Top nothing was a giveaway. Whatever was wrong with Sturdivan was no accident and Craft, she was sure, was involved. If he hurt her...well, she didn't want to say what she'd like to do to him. She squared her hat on her sandy hair and quickened the pace.

Mamasan waited by supply's door, holding a pillowcase filled with peroxide, cotton balls, bandages, band-aids, aspirin, antiseptics and Tylenol. Johnson had gone for ice with a plastic bag. She was returning, not ten feet from Mamasan, when Top came from behind with his bat, grabbed the scruff of her shirt and just about carried her to the door, demanding, "There's a whole lotta silence and a whole lotta eyes glued to the floor this morning. You seem a bit rushed. Want to tell me what's going on?"

Surrendering only to his rank and her respect for him, Johnson was on tiptoes, suspended from Top's fist. "I swear to God, Top, I don't know. Mamasan came into the mess this morning.... And that's it, I swear. Here." She raised the note, offering it to him.

Growling, Top snatched the note but didn't release her. "Well, what's wrong with her? She fall down? What?"

"Top, I swear. I stood by the stairs. I didn't see her. Only Mamasan and Sarge saw her. Sarge is still in her room and Mamasan doesn't speak enough English to tell."

Top rolled the cigar in his mouth, thinking and eyeing the Mamasan shouting, "Bali bali" and hissing. He could go up and see for himself but a long time ago he had learned to value female judgment—the hard way. His wife had warned him that if he rejected his daughter's wishes his daughter would reject him and he would live in misery regretting his harsh actions. She'd been right, too. His daughter rejected him and a couple of months later his wife, blaming him for the loss of her daughter, rejected him, too. If Victoria was up there, Myra was in good hands. Still, "Get up there and find out if I need to get a medic. Tell Barrett she can take as long as she needs but I need to know that much." He shoved her off.

* * *

Tory held her and kissed her and would keep on until Myra told her to stop, and she wasn't sure even then that she would. "Baby, where'd you go last night?" Myra whimpered. "Ssshh. You're safe now. You can tell me."

"Hidey-hole." Myra hurt, but, because of a mouth that didn't want to move, having to use a few words hurt even more.

"Yes. Your secret place. Where is it?"

"Back of building. Into woods. Space, smooth rock."

"Okay. About mid-building? Is there a marker?"

"'Bout half. Fallen tree."

"You went there to be alone. Then what happened?"

"Stars. Like your eyes."

Tory raised her head and smiled. "My eyes are like stars?"

Touching near Tory's eye, Myra smiled as much as her injuries allowed and blinked her good eye in a nod. "Clouds. Your lips." She brought her fingers down to Tory's lips and received a kiss. "Was coming to tell you."

"And that's when it happened?"

Her chin trembled as she nodded.

"Heard nothing. Came from behind."

"It's okay. Take your time. He grabbed you from behind?"

The trembling and tears continued with the questioning and answering until Tory had the entire story of the night before and the packages left at her door and the nightly hauntings.

"You keep saying, 'he,' baby. 'He' is Craft, isn't he?"

She watched to see if Myra went for her dog tags, the only thing she was wearing, but she didn't. Myra was holding onto her. "Craft's been terrifying you for months, hasn't he? Watching and following you all the time?"

Myra nodded, pulling Tory into her.

"I'm going to have the MPs pick him up."

"Nooo!" she wailed, shaking her head. "Charges, investigation, then court, then he'll.... No more Mikey," she pleaded.

"Then he'll what?" Myra shut her mouth and shook her head with resolve. She wasn't referring to Craft but the Captain when she cut herself off. Her fear didn't revolve around only what Craft might do to Mamasan or Tory but also what the Captain would do to her herself.

"No MPs."

"Baby, he beat you, held you against your will, would've raped you."

"No MPs."

"Baby, I can't let this go by."

Myra clamped hard onto her. "Yes! leave alone. Promise."

The door opened. Mamasan rushed in carrying the two filled bags and placed them on the floor by Tory.

"Close the door, Mamasan," Tory said, digging into one.

"Baarrett, Joohnson." Mamasan made a talking duck with her hand.

"Johnson, I told you to open supply."

"Yes, Sarge, but when I explain you'll understand."

"Damn." Tory went out of the room. Johnson stepped back from Tory's anger while explaining her encounter with Top. "Okay." Tory touched Johnson's arm. "I wasn't angry with you anyway."

"Does she need medical, Sarge?"

Catching Johnson checking the blood on the door, Tory shouted, "Mamasan! Clean this up now!" then ran a frustrated hand through her hair, catching also the look in Pam Johnson's eyes. The anxiety in them spoke of more than just concern for a superior. She had often wondered about Pam, but now she was certain. "You're in love with her, aren't you?"

Stunned, Pam turned red. "I, uh, uh—"

"Care for her," Tory helped, smiling broadly. "It's okay and I assure you our secret is safe."

Pam visibly calmed.

"Yes, she needs medical." She grabbed Pam's elbow to stop her run. "But she's refusing it."

"If she needs it we'll get it."

"We can't force it on her and if we tried we'd be taking a chance with it doing more harm than good."

"What happened?"

"Just tell Top no medical is needed."

"Craft did something to her, didn't he?"

"We're not sure of—"

"I am. I've been sitting at that breakfast table longer than you. I hear him talk. I hear the others. Tracer's in it somewhere, too."

"We'll talk later. I need to get back in there. Tell Top and take care of supply. As of right now Myra's on vacation. Got that? Go."

Reluctantly, Pam turned.

"Oh, hey!" Tory called, "Keep your eyes and ears open." Pam threw her the thumb's up sign.

* * *

Ripping around the corner in the Admin hut, ready to destroy anything blocking her path, Tory stormed into Top's office, grabbed his bat, said, "Come with me, Alan," and left.

Top jabbed his cigar into his mouth, mumbled, "Goddamn glad the Captain's at a meeting," and rushed out. "Sergeant," he called to her back ten feet ahead, "I hope this forced march is just your way of telling me you're concerned about my health."

Without answering she steered right around the back of the barracks building. Top chomped down hard on his cigar. Victoria always laughed at his jokes. This did not feel good. As he rounded the building he spotted her before a fallen tree, pacing, waving the bat like she knew how to use it. No, this did not even look good.

When he caught up she tore into the woods and found the place Myra had described. He looked around and she pulled a small camera out of one of her pant's pockets. She was preoccupied with searching the ground and taking pictures so he sat on the rock, resting elbows on knees, and waited.

Crouching by one particular spot, Tory said through clenched teeth, "Take a good look at this area, Alan."

His sudden sour stomach told him not to, but he did. Fallen leaves covered the ground, but it wasn't flat—hills, holes, rock and glass.

"Does it tell you anything, Alan?"

Top rubbed a helpless hand over his mouth. "Looks like a couple of big animals been rolling around or fighting."

Tory whipped angry eyes on him. "Wrong, Alan. One big animal and one small victim fought here."

"That's, uh, dried blood there by you. How bad is she?"

"Thankfully, this is not Myra's."

"Craft's then."

She nodded. "Over there between those trees where the glass is. That's Myra's. We have a real problem here, Alan. Intervention months ago when she came to you for help might've prevented this from happening."

"You mind telling me what happened first?"

Tory spoke, then watched him rub his face with both hands. He stood up, retrieved his bat, turned his back and leaned on it with his head down.

"Okay," he said, keeping his back to her. "Simplest first. We'll call it vacation but don't put no damn form in. She'll just disappear awhile."

"I spent a good hour and a half cleaning and bandaging her abrasions and cuts and those were the lesser of her injuries. She asked for only two weeks but it looks like a good four to me."

He waved it off. "That don't matter. She don't want no charges?"

"None." She watched him rub his mouth again. "She told me he's been terrorizing her for months, knocks on her door nightly to let her know he's always watching her. She said she had to stop visiting Mamasan in the ville because of him."

"What does Mamasan have to do with it?"

"I don't know. But there's more. She said he leaves obscene gifts wrapped in brown paper at her door. And I talked with Pam. She spotted Craft a few times dropping those packages off. And...well, I feel like a sneaky bitch but I coaxed Myra back to sleep before I left and checked her foot locker. It's full of shit he sent. You can use your imagination."

"Did he leave his name on the packages? How does she know it was him?"

"She said early on, before she realized he was going to harass her nightly, she'd answer her door. Craft was always on the other side. He would tell her flat out that he left it and what he wanted her to do with it and then would laugh at her".

"Goddammit!" he cried. "Myra didn't come back to me. I thought my talk with the boy did it."

"A talk from the First Sergeant would probably have done it if you'd been dealing with a normal boy. Seems this boy isn't. And Myra apparently saw that. She took up carrying a switch blade. She took up searching out places where she could hide for awhile and get some peace. Others started thinking she was crazy and that Craft was right about her. She was ostracized. Frankly, Alan, I'm surprised she's not crazy."

"Why no damn charges?"

Scowling, Tory stared down at the blood. "Why? The boy's got everyone believing she's a lesbian. She's afraid an investigation would only end in fingers pointing at her. She's afraid she'd end up discharged and he'd maybe pull three months in the stockade, then continue his military career. No big thing really—for him."

"No, ma'am." Top shook his head vigorously. "No. That don't matter. Ain't nobody got the right to assault anybody just because she's a lesbian."

"He attacked her because she won't go out with him."

"That don't matter neither. Nobody got the right to assault anybody unless it's in defense and then it ain't no assault. I'm going to go talk to her."

Tory stood and placed fists on hip. "No, Alan. Four, five months of being watched and terrorized and running. The woman's exhausted. What happened last night stripped the last bit of strength from her. Let her heal. Maybe then she'll think differently. Besides, she's hiding something. She has a deep scared look, like something's happened before, but she's afraid to tell because telling might make it happen again."

"You think she's protecting somebody?"

"I know she's not telling."

"You willing to go against her wishes? Take charges out on him?"

"I believe if I did that it'd put her in the hospital for sure. Right now besides Mamasan I think the only ones she trusts

112

are you and me, and if we go against her wishes.... No, it'd do no good anyway if she refuses to testify. But I'm sure as hell not willing to let it slide either."

"Okay." He shook his bat. "I'll start by beating him bloody."

Tory put a halting grip on his bat and held it. "No, Alan. This is *my* baby. You put Myra into my hands, remember? And I was making headway. He's mine. *He* is *mine*."

Top chomped down hard on his cigar but didn't argue. He had no doubts Victoria could handle it. But something about this whole thing reminded him of Valez. Something went screwy with her. He had smelled it but the Captain refused to discuss it.

"I'll keep you informed, of course. In advance. You can rest assured I'll do nothing to get either one of us in trouble." She raised the camera in her hand. "I've taken pictures of her, the torn jeans and shirt, the bloody switch blade, this area. I carefully put the jeans, shirt, and switch in a plastic bag. Myra may not want to press charges now, but when she is ready I'll have been prepared. So, okay, we heed her wishes. She's on vacation...."

* * *

Tracer wrapped torn strips of sheet around Craft's leg. "Yep, another inch, man, and you'd've been singing soprano for the rest of your life."

"Will you shut the fuck up and just wrap."

"Hey, man, I'm hungry. Ain't missed breakfast in a long time."

"This was your fucking idea." He closed his eyes against the burning pain, then opened them, glad the fucking KATUSAs were out of his room, gone to chow. "Half-headed bastards" never missed a meal. "You said it was the only thing left to do. Get to her before Barrett did."

"It was a thought, man...."

"You said I'd be doing her a favor. She'd thank me."

"I said probably. Besides, that's your ole man talking. You're just like him."

"He was right, too. The ole lady ran out. She deserved what she got."

"Oh, man. He was a drunk. Drunk up all her money she earned in the laundry mill in Pittsburgh. You're mad at her for leaving you alone with him. You joined the Army as soon as you could so you could eat again."

"Oh, right, man. But you ain't mad at yours for divorcing you? You ain't good with women. That's why you hooked onto your ole lady when she was mourning her dead husband. She needed a shoulder to cry on and you sucked her in."

"Shut up, man. I'm warning you, man."

"And this thing with Mikey. You wanted her, too, even before your ole lady started the divorce, so you sicced me on her to see if maybe there might be a chance for you."

"Hey, man, raping her was something to enjoy in your head."

Craft raised a shaking, halting hand. "Hey, man, I don't want to fight, okay? Let's just stop right here, okay?"

"Okay. Anyway, how was she?"

He pelted Tracer's forehead with the heel of his hand, then pinned the wrapping. "You think I'd have a fucking hole in my leg if I got any?"

Standing, Tracer burst out laughing. "Oh, man, this is too much! All this trouble, your face scratched to hell, a hole in your leg, sliced knuckles, a red eye, a knot on your head, and you ain't even fucked her?" Stretching out on his bunk, he laughed so hard he wiped tears from his eyes. "Oh, man, this is too much."

Craft threw a boot at him. It struck his hands as he was wiping away more tears. Startled, then realizing what happened, Tracer snarled. His green eyes turned red. He snatched the boot and whipped it back at him, striking his wounded leg, making him howl in pain.

"Hey, man, don't you ever throw no shit at me. I let you hit my head. I figured you were hurting and needed to, but this shit I don't take. What that little girl did to you ain't nothing compared to what I'll do if you do this again."

"Tracer, you fuck, I ain't never gonna listen to you again. I'm gonna get charged, man. The fucking MPs are gonna be knocking on my door. She's going to tell, man. She's going to tell everything."

"Quit your crying, you damn pussy. If that was gonna happen it would've happened before now. And remember what happened to Valez, too. But I think you'd better start thinking up a reason for your face and leg quick."

Craft stared, hard in thought. Neither one knew exactly what had happened to Valez but he did know something happened to her but nothing happened to the guys. The thought comforted but still....

"Goddamn! What the fuck am I going to say?"

"I don't know, ole buddy, but we better think up something quick. We're due at work in ten minutes." He raised his fists to his mouth and laughed behind them.

* * *

Rolling his cigar around in his mouth, Top squared his cap on his head and looked down the road. There was no twinkle in his eye. Tory, beside him as they stood in front of the Admin door, watched him wringing his bat. "She's going to need some help for awhile. You going to do it or you got somebody in mind?"

"What do you mean, Alan?"

"I mean she's got to eat. She's got to be bathed and changed and all. Another problem is I doubt Pamela can run supply on her own that long."

Tory folded her arms and looked down the road with him. "As far as supply's concerned, Pam can handle things better than you realize. If she has any questions I can't answer I can run messages to and from Myra."

Top nodded, satisfied. "What about Myra's personal?"

"I'll handle it. Mamasan will help too, I'm sure. They're good friends. It's the best way to keep things quiet. For now. Besides, for the next day or two I doubt she's going to be doing much more than sleeping. I'll get some foods from the commissary. I know hot plates aren't allowed in rooms, but I'll need something to heat—"

"Victoria, ain't nobody going to go into your room and any such mention has been forgotten." He mumbled out of the corner of his mouth, "They sell them at the PX."

"Duly noted, Alan." She stared at the bat in his hand. "I'm

going to get a few things. Be back in half an hour."

* * *

From the hall Top looked over the large Admin office where, to the left, Craft had his back to him, digging into the file. Victoria's office was a separate room to the right. Outside her office was Henry's desk. Henry was sitting at it, his head in his hands, pretending to read while sneaking peeks at him. Walker's desk was in front of Craft's. She was typing and when she spotted Top her fingers started flying over the keys. Tracer didn't have a desk. Flipping through a magazine, he sat by the pot-bellied stove resting in the middle of the floor. In the winter everybody took turns filling it with kerosene and firing it up. The barracks had central heat but not these Quonset huts.

When Craft turned he caught sight of Top. Top's usual big presence looked even bigger. He watched Top stick his cigar in his mouth and smile at him. Craft began fidgeting with everything and anything on his desk.

"Looks to me, boy," Top began, "like someone didn't want to cooperate with you." Craft might've been good at terrorizing Myra, but Top had years of training in sarcasm and terror tactics.

Craft's pallid complexion this morning turned whiter. He reached up and touched his cheek. The angry welts were puffed and red. "Oh, yeah," he half-smiled. "You know how yobos can be. She didn't like what I paid her."

"Mm-hmph," Top grunted. "Yeah, boy, never can tell when one's just going to piss on your parade. Stand up. Let me get a better look."

Craft's eyes darted about, searching for a way out. Hesitantly, he stood, wavering from the pain in his leg. Top scrutinized his face and eyes. Craft reared back and stumbled against his file cabinet.

"Your leg hurt, too, boy?"

Craft's thin lips twitched up, then fell. "Yeah, you know when she scratched me I fell back and twisted my ankle."

"Mm-hmph," Top grunted again and looked down at the leg that was thicker than the other. With a malicious twinkle in his eye, he stared straight into Craft's and squeezed the padded area. His twinkle didn't waver as Craft's eyes bulged and his teeth gnashed together, biting back a scream. "Yeah," Top said, "I can see that ankle's smarting real bad. Walker, go to supply and get me some alcohol."

Walker slammed her chair back and raced out of the office.

"I can see now that those scratches need some attention."

"Hey, Top, they're all right. I cleaned them real good."

"Well, hell, boy," he said, taking the alcohol from Walker. "Can't never be too safe in this country. Sit down and tip your head back."

Unwilling, fear in his eyes, Craft did and Top poured the alcohol over both cheeks. Craft screamed as his cheeks burned. His eyes teared and his hands clamped onto the desk with a death grip.

"See," Top said. "There was still some germs." He calmly handed the bottle back to Walker and left the office.

* * *

The wooden board on the wall held rows of keys. Keys to anywhere in Admin Company. Tory sat at her desk staring at it. A few minutes ago she had dropped off food items and the hot plate in her room, then checked on Myra. She was still sleeping so Tory found a KATUSA by the name of Pak who could speak English fairly well, then Mamasan.

"Pak," Tory said in the hall outside Myra's door, "ask Mamasan to repeat everything she said a little while ago in Sturdivan's room."

Pak bowed to Tory, then turned to Mamasan. When he finished Mamasan looked sheepishly at Tory, shaking her head in refusal. She said something in Korean and Pak turned to Tory. "Mamasan say she hopes you will not be angry with her. She say she will repeat only if Sturdi say is okay...."

No amount of coaxing budged Mamasan. She had heard Myra tell Tory she wanted no problems, so Mamasan would not talk. She also remembered the story Myra had told her about Valez. Mamasan did not want what happened to Valez to happen to her friend.

Tory blew out a heavy breath. Leaning in the corner behind

117

her was her very own, brand new wooden bat. Handling Top's had given her a calm, reassuring feeling.

"Leave no room for error," she said aloud and went to the key board. There was an extra key to her own and Myra's rooms and two master keys. She took them all and pocketed them. Then she opened the manila folder carrying the names of everyone in the company and their room numbers.

Thumbing down the list she found Craft's name. Room number 322 was typed beside it. "Damn!" Thumbing again she found Tracer's, 322. "Goddamn!" She blew out an exasperated breath, then closed her eyes against the pain for rest—she had been in this company only one short month. And in that time she had adjusted to a foreign culture, learned a new job, befriended, per directive, a soldier who acted at times odd, fell in love with that soldier, and the very next morning after finally getting to make love to that soldier.... Tory opened her eyes, her teeth gnashing. Damn it, Myra! You could've told me sooner what Craft was really doing. Even after we made love you didn't tell me. You didn't tell me it was Craft watching you. You said only, "You will be seen," when you wanted me to leave your room. You didn't go back to Top and tell him either. If I had been in Top's shoes I would've guessed that everything was all right after I had talked to the boy, too. This could've been prevented. I could have done something sooner but you didn't tell. Dammit! You didn't tell. Tory looked at the sheet of names and rooms again. "Well," she said aloud, "now I know." During the next five minutes she resolved who would go where, then opened her door onto the large Admin office.

"Tracer! On your feet and in here now!"

Tracer jumped and Tory closed the door. As she made her way to her desk chair she plucked two keys from the board.

"What can I do for you, Sarge?"

The sweet tone of his voice irritated her. His face wore a smile. It looked innocent enough until she checked his eyes. His eyes wore the look of knowledge, making his smile vile. Also, she remembered all too well his vicious words in the restaurant in Seoul.

"You can stand at attention and listen. I will say this only one time. Think you can handle that?"

He clicked to attention and stared straight ahead. "Yes, Sergeant."

"I will hand you two keys. One is to room 102 and the other to 125. You will contact by phone Miller and Jenson. You know where they work?"

"Yes, Sergeant. Motor pool and finance."

"You will tell them to return to the barracks ASAP for room movement. High priority. If their superiors have a problem with that, they are to contact me. Miller and Jenson are to move their belongings to room 322. You will move to 125. Craft, I understand, is having difficulty walking so you will also move his belongings to 102. Being that your room is on the first floor, you will have no, I repeat, no reason to be at any time on the second or third floors of the barracks. Do I make myself clear?"

"Yes, Sergeant. May I ask why?"

"No, Private, you may ask nothing."

"Yes, Sergeant."

"Private, you have no more than thirty minutes to complete this entire task. And I mean thirty. Every minute you are late reporting to me will earn you one day of extra duty. Do you understand?"

"Yes, Sergeant."

Tracer didn't look concerned and Tory knew why. She placed her fists on her desk and leaned into him.

"And, Private, let me make myself clear. I'm quite aware you have only two weeks left in this company to work and another to out-process to return Stateside. If you earn more extra duty than you have time left in country I will, I repeat, I will contact your commander at your next post and explain that you will be late arriving."

Fear replaced the cocky glint in his eyes. He didn't have much to move since he had already sent the bulk of his belongings to his next post. But Craft had a mess of shit to move, including a TV and stereo. And he wanted the States, wanted out of this "shittin' asshole of a country," wanted....

"Private! Do you understand?"

He glared at her. This bitch was for real. "May I set my watch by yours, Sergeant?"

Tory allowed him that much. "Now MOVE!" He raced out of her office and came to a screeching halt at Walker's phone. As Tory closed her door she heard him say, "Craft, you bastard, gimme your locker key."

* * *

Tory allowed herself five minutes of quiet before calling Craft in next. She wasn't unsure. She knew exactly what she was going to do. She was afraid. Being the NCOIC, she needed to remain professional. But that was easier to understand than accomplish in this situation. This one she was emotionally involved in. And this was the first of this nature she had to deal with. She couldn't just simply charge him. She could call the MPs but they'd need a statement from Myra and right now Myra was refusing. Without Myra's statement the MPs would have no reason to arrest. Tory did, however, have reason to do the next best thing, barracks arrest for the safety and security of other personnel as well as the victim. She'd also prepare a report stating the victim was under duress, unable of proper judgment, and in fear of the consequences of her testimony.

She brought her new bat out of its corner and held it in both hands, rubbing and absorbing its cold hardness. Now she understood why Alan kept one. It wasn't to show force or to intimidate, though that it did. It was to draw power of self-control from it—gain the necessary objectivity to detach emotion from the task at hand, gain the strength its inflexibility offered. She drew it to her chest and closed her eyes, preferring to beat Craft with it rather than pull objectivity from it. She squeezed her eyes tight, wringing it in her hands.

A few minutes later Sergeant First Class Barrett opened her door. She stood still with the bat in her left hand. Walker and Henry spied the bat, then exchanged terrified glances. Only Top walked with a bat but not all the time. When he did he had a distant, cold look in his eyes and they knew from experience there was one helluva battle about to be waged and he would leave casualties. Their Sarge had that same look in her eyes. They put their own eyes on their work and their legs shook under their desks. They did not even want to witness what was about to come down, let alone be involved.

"Specialist Craft!" They heard her call his name with a voice that not only said I'm controlling myself so walk very carefully but also you are not just in deep shit, you are shit. "Come into my office and I mean five minutes ago."

"But, Sarge, I can't walk...."

She brought her bat up and squeezed. "Do you want me to help you?"

Without moving their bowed heads, Walker and Henry watched him leap on his good leg into her office. She closed the door firmly but quietly.

Barrett stood behind her desk. Both her hands clutched her bat in a lowered position. She glared at him. His eyes were unusually wide.

"You mind if I sit down, Sarge? My leg hurts."

Barrett smiled and calmly said, "Yes."

He eased himself into the extra chair as if she had given permission. When he was settled and had smiled a thank you, she smiled back, asking, "Are you having a problem with your hearing as well?" When his face took on a confused look she growled, "Yes, I do mind. Get out of my chair before I knock you out of it."

With the sight of the bat rising, Craft jumped up.

"Stay on your feet, Specialist, and explain to me what happened."

"What happened, Sarge?"

"Be advised your playing dumb is only pissing me off."

"Okay!" He gave her the same story he had given Top.

"Specialist, do I look that stupid?"

Craft gulped.

She walked around her desk to his left rear and spoke softly into his ear. "Did you think up that lame excuse all by yourself or did you have help?" Again he gulped and sweat broke out on his forehead. "Did you really think that nothing would result? Did you perhaps think she would *thank* you?" He turned ashen.

Barrett walked calmly back to behind her desk and smiled at his sick pallor. "What kind of trash have you been reading that you would actually think she would *thank* you? Better still, what kind of trash have you been *listening* to?" He still wouldn't answer. "Tell me, Craft. Do you believe in fairy tales? Did you really think you were the good prince bearing the magic rod that would win the princess' love?"

His chin trembled. "I don't know what you're talking about?"

"Then why are you sweating?"

"My goddamn leg hurts and you're making me stand on it."

"I'm sure it does. But I assure you you're sweating over thoughts like abduction, threats, harassment, stalking, maiming, attempted rape. Little charges."

"No fucking way, Sarge." His chin quivered forcefully. "She wanted it. She had me meet her. Told me she wanted it. Said it would do her good. I told her I wasn't interested. That's when she scratched my face. She came at me like a wild animal. I had to smack her to get her off me...."

"Specialist!"

"...she's nuts, Sarge. I tried to tell you but you wouldn't listen. Everybody knows she's nuts. Ask anybody. She never eats with us..."

"Specialist!"

He was red-faced and weeping and not listening. "...She wears black all the time like a damn witch. Wouldn't leave me alone. Always trying to lure me...."

"CRAFT! Were you born with this lying skill or did you have to work really hard to develop it? You really expect me to swallow all this shit?"

"It's the truth, Sarge. I swear it."

"Apparently your word is about as good as your magic rod." She watched his wet eyes set in anger and his mouth curl into a snarl. "Let's talk about nightly visits to a certain door to threaten, intimidate and harass a woman who only wants to be left alone. Let's talk about trashy things wrapped in brown paper and left at that same door, things like dildos, vibrators, blow-up dolls and an assortment of other obscene materials. Let's talk charges, Specialist, with all the necessary evidence to back it up. Let's talk stockade." To her astonishment he got down on his knees.

"I swear, Sarge. Tracer made me do it."

"Tracer?"

"He said if I spread enough shit about her she'd come running to me for comfort. When that didn't work he said there was only one thing left for me to do."

"Rape her?"

Still on his knees he nodded. "But I meant only good."

"Get up. Where was your brain during all this?" He stood but only stared at the floor. "No, don't answer. I know where it was. In your magic rod." She took her seat. It amazed her how sorry he had become now that he might be charged. Last night he would have raped, then probably sodomized and who knew what else. "Specialist Craft, you are accused of all the charges I've mentioned. I myself would have the MPs pick you up but I respect the wishes of Sturdivan. She's in no condition to press charges right now."

That's right! he remembered. Valez didn't press charges either. "She doesn't want to?"

"Clean your ears, Craft. I said she's in no condition to. You know from Tracer your new room is 102. Give me your key to 322."

He handed her the key while wiping away tears.

"You are restricted to room 102, this work office and the mess hall. You will go nowhere, I repeat, nowhere else. Your request for extension is disapproved. You no longer have the services of Papasan. In case you were not aware, Craft, that Papasan you call a half-head was a privilege bestowed on you. You no longer have it. You will stand personal and locker inspection every morning at 0645 hours. You will have the door open at that time. The dayroom as well as calling for snacks is off-limits. I will hand you your mail. Give me your mailbox key, your post pass and ration control card."

"I might as well be in the stockade!"

Folding her arms, she leaned back in her chair. "Would you prefer?"

He handed her the items.

"Every demerit you earn on your inspections will mean a day of extra duty. I want it like Basic. And be advised, I spent six years as a Drill. If you think for a moment I will weaken in

123

my resolve, then by all means *test me.* The crimes you have committed are hideous."

"I didn't fucking rape her! She put a goddamn hole in my leg!"

She squeezed her bat for patience. "To work off some of that bountiful energy you have you will pull chow duty every day, lunch and dinner, 1100 to 1330 and 1600 to 1830 beginning today. When Sturdivan is better and decides, we'll adjust. Be wise and heed my instructions. Any infraction will have severe consequences."

* * *

Huffing and puffing, sweat running down his face, Tracer stood before Barrett. "All moves completed, Sergeant."

She checked her watch. "You're two and a half minutes late."

"He had a lot of shit to move and three flights of stairs is no joke."

"Oh, no, Private. I am not joking. Did you think that maybe he had a lot of shit because you were feeding him a lot of shit?"

His jaw dropped.

"I remember our first talk together. I believe you said you wanted to have all the fun you could get while here. Is that correct?"

The rest of his face dropped to his jaw.

"Well, here's a really good funny. A young man just out to have a good time gets his buddy to terrorize an innocent woman for months, then gets him to try to rape her. All in fun. What's the harm in a little rape?"

"I ain't his mama, Sergeant. I didn't do shit."

"Tell me, Tracer. How many nights did you lay awake dreaming about her? How she'd feel on her back? Better still, on her knees?"

Tracer's jaw tightened.

"Too insecure to ask her out, you get your buddy to. Then when another specialist can't score, you know a private sure as hell won't."

"I ain't afraid to ask no...."

"So, feeling a bit pissed and maybe less than a man, you

get your buddy to wreak emotional revenge. That wasn't enough for your big appetite, so you get your same buddy to...rape."

"I didn't do nothing."

"You did, Private, quite the opposite. You guided him every step of the way. Helped formulate the plan."

"You ain't got shit on me."

"For starters, insubordination toward me and I don't take that lightly. But we're talking about someone else. Yes, try aiding and abetting in harassment and threats."

"I didn't twist his fucking arm, Sergeant."

"You didn't inform your First Sergeant of these crimes, either." Tracer shut up. "Then we move on to charges that'll win you stockade time. Try conspiracy to commit felonies. And if you're not aware, abduction and maiming and attempted rape are felonies." She watched his breathing harden. "You are subject to these charges. Craft was on his knees, spilling his guts. You are restricted...." She held his room and mail keys, his post pass and ration control card. "I'll give you a break. I won't consider the half minute. You will pull two days this weekend on Kitchen Patrol. Report to Sergeant Hart for the hours."

"Ain't you supposed to give me an Article 15?" He grinned, as if to say she had nothing solid to warrant an official report. He thought he was calling her bluff.

Standing, she leaned into him and grinned back, but with more pleasure than he was feeling. She called *his* bluff. "Soldiers aren't *given* Article 15s, they're punished *under* Article 15 of the military justice code, but for *minor* infractions. Apparently you aren't aware your offenses are *major* and you should be questioning Court Martial proceedings instead. If you prefer, that can be arranged. We'll formally charge you, then the MPs will pick you up, then—"

"Okay, okay! Two fucking weeks left."

"Remember what your inspections may bring you, too. We can do this my way or the formal way. I'll give you that choice for now."

"Your fucking way."

She sat down. "Well, Tracer, isn't this one helluva funny?"

Chapter Nine

Sunday's evening seemed even quieter than its day. Tory sat at Myra's desk, reading a used paperback, waiting for Myra to stir. The book was to pass the time but it was so eerily quiet that she found concentrating on the story difficult. It seemed the barracks itself was in mourning or paying its respects in silence.

Catching herself nodding off, she closed her book and stretched. At the same time Myra groaned. She looked over. Myra lay on her back, supported by three pillows. The fourth pillow Tory had earlier placed under her knees. Kneeling by the yo, she watched as Myra groaned again, struggling to open her good eye. The swelling had gone down some. Her lips looked only one and a half instead of twice their normal size. Good progress, she thought. This was only the third day of healing.

With cotton balls dunked in water she quenched Myra's dry lips. This time Myra moaned in pleasure. "Needed that, didn't you, babe?"

"Mm-hmph," Myra nodded, finally getting her eye open.

"Looks like the swelling's down some. How's it feel in there?"

Myra smiled through her eye. Reaching up, she ran her fingers through Tory's hair.

"Look like an angel."

"Well, I'm glad someone sees my true qualities. But how's it feel?"

"Beautiful, rich, silky...."

"Not my hair, silly! You! How's your insides feel?"

"Stiff. Achy." Myra stopped caressing her hair and stared

at the back of her own just-noticed hand. The knuckles were torn with thin scabs beginning to form, some fingernails broken.

Tory took her hand and kissed each knuckle. "A few days ago I don't think you were really aware of the extent of your injuries."

Myra raised the white sheet covering her and inspected her body.

"Sorry, babe. Had to use a military sheet. Yours was spotted with blood. Mamasan's trying to get the stains out." Tory saw her brows furrow and knew what Myra was thinking. She gently urged the sheet down.

"Bruised! Ugly!"

"Not ugly, babe. Bruised."

"Cuts! My breasts—"

"Are a bit of a mess, yes. But you're on the road to recovery. Just lie still. I'm going to heat a can of beef stew. I'd really like to feed you a fresh salad, pasta and garlic bread, but, considering where we are, not to mention the state of your mouth, stew will have to do."

Only half listening, Myra said, "Not hungry."

Tory went to the desk and opened the stew with a manual can opener. "Did I ask you if you were hungry? I have been force-feeding you chicken noodle soup. Now you advance to beef stew. And you will not fight me."

"Ask Mamasan to throw the sheets away and see me for money. I want her to buy some new ones."

"She bought your last ones?"

"She knows material. She'll get a better price, too. I pay her to make the run and let her keep the difference it would cost if I had made the purchase. It's a good deal. She makes out and I make out."

Having gotten the stew heating, Tory returned to Myra's side. "Consider it done. I'm not surprised you want to trash them."

Myra didn't want to talk about bloody sheets anymore. "Who doesn't see you as an angel? Everybody likes you."

"And you'd be surprised at how many like you. But I don't believe either Tracer or Craft are looking at me with stars in

127

their eyes."

"You didn't charge, did you?" Her voice held a note of panic.

"I wouldn't go against your wishes, Myra. But I had to take certain precautions. Neither lives in the room down the hall anymore. Both are restricted to the first floor...." The stew was ready by the time she finished. She patted at the pillow. "Let's get you sitting so you can eat." With much effort Myra accommodated her.

With the steaming pot on a towel Tory sat on the yo and held a spoonful to Myra's clamped lips. "Come on."

"I feel silly. Couldn't I feed myself?"

"Go ahead." She offered the spoon.

Myra tried to hold it but her fingers were too stiff and sore. Sheepishly, she surrendered.

"I don't mind. Anyway, Craft didn't have his door open for inspection Friday morning and his bunk wasn't tight, so he spent this weekend on KP with Tracer. He can't do much with his leg but that doesn't matter. Tracer was a minute late for KP on Saturday so he's earned another day next weekend. I told Sergeant Hart I don't want them talking to each other. At dinner neither was looking too happy. Hart was smiling with the help, though. And Top. You should see how he puffs up his chest and struts about with that cigar in his mouth every time he sees Craft on chow duty."

"No wonder you're a Sergeant. You know how to make troops weep."

"And think, I'm just warming up. KP from four in the morning to eight at night is going to feel like pleasure when I'm finished."

With the final spoonful gone Tory dabbed Myra's mouth with the corner of the towel. "I bet not just your tummy but your head feels better, too." Myra nodded. "And for dessert." Tory kissed the uninjured side of her mouth. "How's that?"

Myra put her arms around her neck. "More!?"

"As much as you want, sweetie, but duty calls." She came to her feet. "First, I wash the dishes and then I wash you."

After drying the pot and spoon, Tory pulled the sheet back. "Nice and easy, babe. Give me your hands."

"A shower!?"

"Yep! We're advancing. You're going to feel soooo good!"

Every movement caused agony. Her entire body including her head felt as if it had been beaten with a baseball bat. Still, she hobbled on with Tory supporting and guiding.

"You sure this is wise?"

"Trust your Sergeant, sweetie. The water will take some of that stiffness away. Now hang on to this wall while I turn the shower on."

Myra hung on to the half wall that divided her commode from the shower stall. Opposite the commode was the white sink with mirror above. She was lightheaded and wasn't sure of her own reality right now, let alone a shower that sounded hard and cruel.

"Temperature's almost just right," Tory called over her shoulder.

A wave of dizziness swept through Myra's head, seeming to go from left to right. Feeling pulled along, she turned with it then braced her back against the eight-inch thick wall. Once steady her good eye roamed and caught a glimpse of herself in the mirror. That surely wasn't her. She pushed herself away from the wall and used the sink as support. Then she braved the mirror. The side with her good eye was okay, but the other. She had thought her creases were ugly, but this was hideous. Her lips were split in three places, swollen and chapped, her cheek puffed like a chipmunk's, deep purple and blue, her eye swollen shut and bruised, her forehead like her cheek. Her face looked like something out of a horror movie.

"Okay! I believe we're ready!" Tory straightened herself and turned to find Myra staring at her reflection, touching it on the mirror in shock and disbelief. Gently she took hold of Myra's shoulders. "Come on, babe."

Myra wasn't budging. She took her fingers from the mirror and cautiously touched her own flesh. It was real. It was her.

Tory stepped behind her. "Babe, it's better. You're healing."

Myra settled her eye, shocked and incredulous, on Tory's reflection, then her head fell back and her body followed as she wailed, "Nooooooo!"

Tory seized Myra's elbows in her own and carried her away

from the mirror and into the shower. Weak and trembling, Myra wept while Tory, fully clothed and sopping, soothed her with a cleansing washcloth.

* * *

Top leaned both elbows on the counter to Supply and pulled his cigar out of his mouth. "Johnson!"

Pam jumped. She had been concentrating on issue forms for a Private Adkins. He had just arrived and would be replacing Tracer. Reluctantly she pushed herself up from Myra's throne. Since last Friday she and Guiterrez had kept it like a shrine awaiting her return. But today she had to sit at it since Myra kept the necessary forms in her desk drawer. Now she didn't want to part from it. Sitting there made her feel as if she were actually touching her. And touching, whether it involved Myra or a fantasy woman, haunted her since Friday when Barrett had told her her secret was safe. Magically, knowing that had somehow made her whole being feel safer. And now knowing Barrett and Sturdivan were just like her made her even stronger than she already was. To think that now she could possibly keep company with women like Barrett and Sturdivan gave her hope for all sorts of possibilities for herself.

"Yes, Top," she said, approaching him.

"You still got money in your budget?"

"Yes, Top. Anything special?"

"Paint." He stuck his cigar back into his mouth where he rolled it around, eyeing the walls and ceiling of supply. When he settled on her he pulled the cigar back out of his mouth. "Now don't get all bug-eyed on me, Johnson. If you were going to do the painting I'd have said so already."

Pam released her breath. "I'm a terrible painter, Top. If I had to I'd have everything but the walls painted."

He grinned. "Don't you fret none. I got me a volunteer."

She said nothing, though she did wonder who'd be crazy enough to do that. She looked at Top again. No. He had himself a volunteered volunteer.

"How much paint you think it'd take to do every room in this building? Maybe even the halls, too."

Guiterrez who had been stocking shelves behind them said

130

with his thick accent, "Ten gallons, Top. More if you want the halls done."

"Johnson, get me fifteen gallons. Check with the Captain and that young LT and Sergeant Barrett. See what colors they want their offices. Get white unless they say otherwise." He stuck his cigar back into his mouth and eyed the ceiling again, then grinned at her. "Yep, a coat of paint will do wonders for this place. I just love volunteers, don't you?" He turned to leave, then turned back. "And, Johnson, I want it by noon."

Pam checked the clock on the wall. It was ten. She looked at Guiterrez who was wearing the same panicked expression. "I'll start asking. You get the purchasing card and your hat."

* * *

Tory rapped four times, then unlocked Myra's door. Though she knew it wasn't necessary to knock, she thought the familiar code allowed Myra to breathe easier. "You'll never guess what I found," she cheered.

Dressed in a long, olive drab T-shirt, Myra was sitting up on her yo with her pillows behind her. A brown bag filled with what she knew was her dinner was in one of Tory's arms. There was nothing in the other. "What did you find?" she asked, watching her set the bag on the desk.

Tory raised a wait-a-minute finger and returned to the door. There she stooped and when she straightened carried a large, high-shined brass vase filled with flowers. "Somebody must like you!"

"Ooooh!" Myra intoned, coming to her knees.

"Get back down. Feeling better is no reason for all that activity."

Myra wiggled back down and reached out for the vase. Tory sat down and handed it over. Myra's surprised eyes absorbed the rainbow of assorted flowers and fern-like greenery. "It's beautiful! Thank you!"

Draping her side over Myra's ankles, Tory enjoyed the happiness on her face. "Oh, hey, don't thank me. I'm too military to think up something as pretty as this. But I've learned. Read the card."

Myra's smile dropped and her hands pushed the vase back

to Tory.

Tory pushed it back. "Just because you've had some bummer gifts before doesn't mean every one is. The handwriting is neither Craft's nor Tracer's. Besides, they're too crude to think this up."

After a wary check of the sincerity in Tory's eyes, Myra plucked the envelope from between the flowers. Seeing the "Specialist Sturdivan" written on it, she whispered, "Pam?" Inside was a half of a plain sheet of paper folded in half. A sad smiley face was drawn on its cover. Its caption read, "Heard you were feeling bad." On the inside was a note—"Did you really expect real flowers!? Remember where you are! Hope they brighten your day anyway—Spec 4 Johnson." Myra smiled as she handed the note to Tory and fingered the petals of a silk rose.

After reading it, Tory returned it to its envelope. Myra seemed lost in thought, gazing at the flowers, feeling their texture. It was Saturday night just one week after the attack, and Myra was healing quickly. All the bruises were taking on a yellowish tint. All the swelling was gone. The three slits on her lips were well scabbed as were the other cuts on her body. Her eye was open since yesterday but blood red.

"That eye still blurry?"

Without taking her eyes off the flowers, Myra nodded. "It'll get better though."

"Did you, uh, know Johnson liked you that way?"

Myra nodded again.

Unsure of what was going on in her mind, Tory raised up and fingered a path through the flowers. With a raised brow she asked, "Are we going to play fifty questions? That mouth of yours is better. Use it."

Myra looked at Tory, pursing her lips to prevent her smile from ripping her cuts open. "Yes! I couldn't help but know, the way those ice-blues follow my every move." She returned her attention to the flowers, rubbing their silky smoothness.

Wary now of what was going on in her mind, Tory said, "They are nice to look at. You have to admit that much."

"Oh, yes," she said without taking her eyes off the flowers. "And she's very nice; I'm very glad she works with me but..."

Afraid now of what was going on in her mind, Tory pushed. "But?" Uncertainty over Myra's relationship with Mamasan had worried her some but she hadn't expected to have to be concerned about Johnson, too.

Myra glanced at Tory, then settled back on the flowers. After a moment's pause she set the vase on the floor, eased herself into a reclining position and pulled Tory by her T-shirt down onto her. As she expected, Tory wouldn't let her body touch, thereby hurt, her own. "But." She held the front of Tory's shirt with one hand. The other she slid over and past Tory's breast to her groin where her fingers teased but a second then made their way back up to her breast. Caressing that lovely breast, Myra watched arousal take over Tory's cheeks and want deepen in her eyes, darkening them.

Tory's body tingled, then rushed, then tingled...but remained in a push-up position, using her elbows rather than her hands, over Myra. She stiffened yet more in her effort to hold herself off as she felt Myra's fingers squeeze her hard nipple. With a piercing rush her mouth fell open and a breathy shudder escaped her lips.

Myra squeezed that nipple again, enjoying what she saw, then released it to capture Tory's hot cheek in her hand.

Struggling to control herself, Tory kissed the palm of that hand and asked again, "But?"

Myra stroked her cheek, thumbed her brow, held her firm with a stronger hand then she thought she had. Anchoring her eyes on Tory's, she said, "But yours set me on fire."

That nearly dissolved all Tory's resolve. Still, she allowed her head to dive into Myra's neck, kissing, wishing she could kiss her lips. She kissed every inch of her incredibly soft throat to behind her ear where she whispered, "And yours light the match." She continued kissing, covering all the flesh she dared, keeping her body rigid over Myra's, until she found herself kissing her unharmed cheek, inching closer to the lips she didn't want to injure further. But Myra's strong hand on her own cheek urged her. With reluctance and hunger Tory kissed the uninjured side of Myra's mouth, taking her tongue, then freezing in motion as her body burned with a sharp, lingering rush.

"I love you, babe. Lower yourself to me."

"Oh, mama." Shuddering, Tory weakly shook her head. "I love you, too, but I can't. You're so bruised."

Myra brought that hand down to Tory's buttocks, inciting her. But Tory remained rigid, all muscles tight with control. "Come to me," she whispered and opened herself, bringing herself up and to Tory.

Even through her jeans Tory could feel Myra's nakedness, hot and moist. With a cry of pleasure and pain she pressed her groin into Myra's, undulating, giving as much as she dared, then suddenly rolled off and away. On weak knees she crawled the few feet over the rug to the desk. With one hand she held onto the desk's top as if it could help her. With the other she held her mound as if it could hold her excitement down.

Crouching behind, Myra embraced her, caressing her breasts, her belly. Nuzzling into Tory's neck, she unzipped her jeans and slipped into her wetness. "I remember so well your sweetness. I want to taste it again. I've been dreaming about you. If you run I'll only follow."

Tory's teeth sank into the desk, leaving their mark of her agony mixed with pleasure. "You're healing so well, baby. I'll hurt you."

Keeping one arm around Tory's waist, Myra took her hand into her own and kissed it. "It's your love that's healing me so quickly. Please." She brought Tory's hand to her cheek. "You have such beautiful hands. I want them. I need them. Unless...unless I'm too ugly right now."

Carefully Tory turned and took Myra's face in her hands. Too moved to voice the word, she shook her head, then tenderly kissed her fully on her injured lips, her injured cheek, her injured eye. With the same care she removed Myra's shirt, heedless of the ever-present dog tags that dangled under, not over, the shirt, and gently laid her down to begin hastening the healing process.

* * *

"One more." Tory held the bit of beef close to Myra's lips. "Come on." The lips were clamped shut, adamant in refusal. She brushed it along Myra's lips, the lips pursed tighter. Finally, Tory resorted to The Look. Myra's mouth opened and she stuffed the meat inside. "Bulgogi is very filling," Myra said after swallowing.

"That little bit of fried rice and beef?" Tory went to the desk and made their cups of coffee. "You've lost some weight in the last few days. It's time to get it back. Here." She handed Myra her own cup of coffee. "At least this is hot. I want you to know I rushed all the way from the NCO Club with that bulgogi, and you ended up eating it cold."

"It was your fault."

"My fault!? Who pulled whom on top of whom?"

"I had to do something! You were looking very nervous and...jealous."

"So now the truth comes out? You wanted only to make me feel better?"

"No," Myra said indignantly, then sipped her coffee. "But it sounds like a good excuse. And it was delicious anyway."

Tory wasn't sure if she was referring to the bulgogi or their lovemaking. "Well, since we're on the subject, you mind explaining all that deep thought over the flowers?"

"Ah! So you admit your jealousy."

"I'll up that to being out and out frightened. What was going through your mind?"

"Pam Johnson. I like her but I'm not attracted to her. Besides, she can't be more than twenty-one or so. I always felt she was a lesbian but I had no certainty."

"It's certain. We had a little talk after I saw those eyes nearly bleeding with the thought that someone hurt you. She knew exactly who."

"I'm sure Craft underestimates a lot of others. I'm flattered but...."

"But?"

Myra squinted in childlike delight. "That's what started the love."

"I like butts, especially yours." She quickly kissed Myra's cheek and retreated. "But?"

"It's hard to really appreciate her being like us. She never joined me at my table in the mess."

"She did defend you once, though. Very strongly, too."

"Did she? Maybe it's just that she's young and afraid."

"Maybe not so much that she's young. After all, we're still afraid. I think it's more that you're her superior and someone she's attracted to. Did you ever join her?"

Myra lowered her eyes. "No. But then Craft was always there." She left out how shortly after the alley incident she'd hear "dick" and "bull dyke" mumbled loud but low by others in the company as she passed by them. How others she had good working relations with suddenly started greeting her with cool cordialities. How she took her usual seat at the long table one day, determined to stop Craft from cutting off the few remaining friends she had, only to end up enduring the long, short while it took to force her meal down surrounded by cold, almost hostile silence.

"I see how he'd be a deterrent."

"Anyway, I was also thinking about a girl who just came in country about a month ago. She's young like Johnson and I think they'd make a good match. She works in supply for the infantry company next door."

"Myra! You're going to play matchmaker?"

"No, but she let me know in no uncertain terms that she was single and could use some company. I bet Johnson would like some, too. She's been here three months and holes up in her room a lot."

Tory smiled and patted Myra's knee. "We'll just see what we can work out. You should know Johnson and Guiterrez nearly had a fist fight."

"They get along great. Over what?"

"You. And Tracer."

The cup in Myra's hand started shaking. She placed it on her short side table. "You want to elaborate on that?"

"I swear. I had to intervene. It started when Johnson rushed into my office and asked me what color I wanted my walls. That was Monday. Not knowing what was up, I went to Top. Top was all puffed up with a shit-eating grin and he says, 'Now, Victoria, I know Craft's your baby but I didn't concede nothing with Tracer. You know I can't let you have all the fun.'"

"Fun!?"

"Top is feeling really bad that this happened to you. And

with your not pressing charges, he's been itching for some kind of justice. He also wants to make sure Tracer has no chance to do anything else."

"So he's got him painting the building!?"

"You got it. I've tied his weekend time up with KP and Top's got him painting all walls and ceilings every evening. Top told him he wanted it all done by the time he starts out-processing. You can bet he's been up late every night. If he gets it done by then Top will have him scrubbing and waxing all floors while out-processing."

"So what's the fight over?"

"Oh! Somebody's got to watch him every night in those offices. He was directed to start with your supply room. Guiterrez got the idea of what was up and Johnson knew ahead of time. Both wanted to help justice along where their superior was concerned. They started fighting over who would watch."

"Are you serious? They're willingly giving up their free time?"

Tory held up a pledging hand. "I swear! I settled it by having them take turns, starting with Pam. After all, she outranks him. Tracer was to neither talk nor do anything but work. Any problem was to be noted on paper and not addressed. Tracer has dark circles under his eyes and is starting to fall asleep during the day. And he's beginning to take on a scared look because he knows if he doesn't do it properly and on time, his visit in the Land of the Morning Calm is extended."

"It almost makes me feel bad."

Tory grabbed Myra's chin. "Don't you ever say that! Both of them deserve to be in the goddamn stockade! I'm sorry I have only one week and a half more to come down on his ass."

Chapter Ten

Thump! The dart hit a leg. He sat on his bunk and readjusted his headphones, though it wasn't necessary. The punk rock screamed loud and clear into his brain. He needed to hear it. He felt his brain was turning into silly putty. The music would bring it back to life.

Thump! The dart hit an arm. Goddamn Barrett. If she hadn't come along he'd have had Mikey by now. But, noooo! She had to come and put him in this cell she called a room. Five KATUSAs and him. All of them were gone to a movie right now. Just because they weren't paid for their services Uncle Sam let them in free while US soldiers had to pay. Fucking half-heads didn't deserve any pay.

Thump! The dart hit the same damn leg. Goddamn Barrett! Her image was on the dart board, arms and legs wide. "Gonna get your pussy," he mumbled, taking aim. Thump! He got her ankle. It was the room. It was the goddamn room throwing his aim off. He ripped the headphones off and threw them at the stereo.

Gotta think! Can't think, he thought, grabbing a fistful of imaginary hair. Need a drink! Can't drink. No fucking ration control card. Can't go to the club for Spec 4s and below. Can't even go down the hall to the fucking dayroom for a soda, let alone a beer. He lit a cigarette and watched the smoke. Big fucking deal. He'd had to beg to go to the PX for cigarettes and then goddamn Barrett walked him there and back. Sick. He was sick of the mess hall and the fucking smell of food. Sick of looking at everybody's meal tickets to make sure they were allowed to eat there. Sick of Top grinning at him. Sick of those he used to call friends giving him dirty looks and snubbing him. *He* was the one with the goddamn hole in his leg, not her. She was off resting for the last two weeks, but he had to work!

Tracer. He was restricted from talking to Tracer. He was glad of that. It was Tracer's doing anyway. "Follow her, ole buddy," he remembered Tracer saying. "Find out where she goes, what she does." No one had told him, but he was sure it was Tracer doing the painting. Good. Tracer deserved the extra duty. He didn't. Fuck, Mikey wouldn't even press charges. Mikey deserved what she got and she knew it. Just like Valez. Just like the ole lady. The ole lady sneaked out one day and was never seen again. But that was the ole man's fault. He didn't watch her close enough, too drunk all the time. He wouldn't make the same mistake the ole man made. Had to watch Barrett, too. Barrett was the one doing all these shitty things to him.

Snatching a dart, he whipped it at the board. Surprisingly, it hit her chest. "Fucking A!" he cheered. It was Barrett. He slung another dart. It hit her gut. "Yeah!" Gotta think. Gotta out-smart the bitch. How? Can't get *her.* That'd mean all sorts of extra duty. He rubbed the nearly-healed hole in his leg. Mikey. Mikey won't press charges. Mikey won't do anything to him. Mikey's keeping their little secret. Mikey can stop Barrett from giving him any more extra duty and get his pass and ration control card back. Thump! The dart hit her square in the fucking muff!

Yeah, Barrett will do what Mikey wants. But how? Can't leave the room. He grimaced at the return of the five KATUSAs. Or can he? He smirked.

* * *

One-two, one-two. Myra heard the four raps on her door and knew it was Tory. Since Tory had put Craft on restriction his nightly ritual had ceased. Myra was once again feeling safe in her own room. She turned on her yo and checked the clock on her side table—twenty-two hundred. Tory had left at nine to ensure Myra got a good night's rest before returning to work tomorrow. Maybe Tory forgot something.

She slipped her sheet aside and went to the door barefooted and wearing only her long, over-sized T-shirt. Reaching the door, she heard Tory rap the four-count again. Smiling, Myra flicked the light on and opened the door.

She hadn't expected what stood grinning on the other side of her door. It stunned her, stunned her long enough for him to grab the back of her hair and clamp a hard hand over her mouth.

"Ssssh," he said, smiling, pushing her back, kicking the door closed, then pinning her back to the door. "I'm not going to hurt you. You can trust me. I just want a little talk. Okay?"

Wide-eyed, Myra stared at him as her blood left her head. There was no panic rushing up her spine, no knotting of her stomach. This was it. She couldn't take any more. She felt herself giving up. She was passing out.

He saw the fluttering of her eyes and felt her body going limp. He shook her. "I just want to talk," he growled. "Just talk."

Unwilling, Myra returned but she felt dead. No one could help her. No one could stop him. No one but Tory and Mamasan gave a damn, but neither one could stop him. Her eyes went to her locker. The new switch blade Mamasan had gotten her was in there, so was the MP club, but they seemed so very far away.

Craft shook her again. "Listen to me." He lowered his eyes to hers, forcing himself on her.

Myra gave dead eyes to him.

"Now you listen good. Your friend Barrett is pushing it. I'm here so you see she can't stop me. Nothing can stop me. But I'm here in peace, to offer a truce. You willing to listen or do you want to be responsible for more blood?"

Myra said nothing. She had no energy. She didn't understand what he was saying either.

"You know you're to blame for what I did to that hole in the ville. I wouldn't've been out there if you hadn't gone there. And I warned you not to see Barrett again but you did. I told you I was watching you. How do you think I learned that little four-knock code? You got only yourself to thank for your little vacation." He laughed into her face. "So you see it's going to be up to you again. You can either go along with my truce or be to blame for what happens. Shake your head this way," he said, nodding his head up and down and grinning as if he were enjoying a childish prank.

Myra nodded but once, slowly.

"Good." He smiled. "Barrett seems to feel that taking my passes and ration control card and telling me to stay in my room will stop me. But you know different, don't you?"

Myra only stared at him.

"Shake your head this way," he said again, demonstrating.

Myra nodded as before.

"Good. In fact, you know that if she doesn't give me back my passes and back off I'm going to leave a trail of blood from her door all the way out to your sweet Mamasan's hooche. And you know my word is good. Didn't I tell you you'd regret it if you saw Barrett again?"

Myra nodded without his prompt.

"That's right. My word is good. So here's my truce. You get my fucking passes back." He pushed hard against her mouth. "You get them back and don't see Barrett again. She's a dyke. I don't want her defiling you. You're mine. You do what I say and everything'll be fine. You don't and there'll be a bloodbath. You understand?" He shook her.

Myra nodded.

"Good. And here's the other part of my truce." He grinned, laughing some as if he could hardly contain how good the part coming up felt. "You won't press charges, Mikey. We both know what happened to Valez just five months ago, don't we?"

As he laughed Myra remembered all too well what happened to Valez. Yes, she wanted to keep Craft away from Mamasan, and now she needed to keep him away from Tory as well, but what happened to Valez was the base of why, as Craft knew, she couldn't press charges. Beyond a doubt she knew what happened to Valez would happen to her, too.

"This man's Army is just wonderful, don't you think? And to prove you can trust me I'm going to leave quietly now like I never been here." He released her hair, pushed her head back against the door and brought his free hand down to between her legs.

141

Myra stiffened. Her eyes widened with fear.

He smiled. "This is very tempting, Mikey. No panties. Your fur's soft like a kitten's. And I bet what it covers is sweeter than candy."

She pushed herself back into the door but couldn't escape his touch. That familiar feel of helplessness was back. But accompanying it now was the sense that her lower body was crawling with roaches.

He grinned wider. "But I'm going to prove you can trust me. You scream and I'll snap your neck." He slowly released her mouth. When he saw she was frozen he smiled and gently took her by the shoulders, moving her away from the door. He said, "Sweet dreams," blew her a kiss and left.

* * *

The two week's vacation was up and Myra returned to her Supply Room the next morning, Monday, albeit nervously. Her cheekbone was still discolored and she hoped no one would say anything about it. Otherwise, she was healed—physically.

Welcoming her, Guiterrez and Pam clapped her on the back, though in her heart Pam wanted to hug her. And in her heart she also knew something was terribly wrong. It wasn't obvious. Myra smiled and did her work as usual, but she hadn't noticed the fresh coat of soft gray paint on the walls, the bright white ceiling, or even the shiny waxed floor that Craft had done just last night. Myra seemed preoccupied.

Actually, Pam had expected her to be. Barrett still wouldn't tell her what had happened. But she, as well as others, knew Craft and Tracer were responsible. And because Myra's cheek was still bruised after two weeks, she knew whatever they had done was nasty. Pam expected her to be preoccupied, but she hadn't expected what she saw in Myra's eyes—the look of defeat.

Concerned, she watched Myra all day. If Myra was going to be sick, she wanted to be ready for her. But Myra didn't get sick. Myra was watching the clock, and the later the day grew the more she fidgeted and the more a new look crept into her eyes, the look of terror. Pam suspected that what she had seen last night had a lot to do with her preoccupation.

At quarter to four Pam couldn't stand it anymore. Myra had let Guiterrez have the afternoon free for his time watching Tracer paint. They were alone and it looked as if Myra was breaking out in a sweat. It was a hot June day anyway. With no air conditioning there were three fans buzzing. They were allowed to take their fatigue shirts off and work in their olive drab T-shirts. But this was fear showing in Myra's sweat.

Crouching by Myra's desk, she rested an arm on it, facing Myra, glancing at the mess of scattered papers. Myra had always kept a neat desk, but right now Myra had her forehead in one hand and a poised pen in the other, doing nothing but sitting perfectly still.

"Sturdivan?"

Myra's head jerked. "Sorry. I didn't notice you."

"I know. It's almost quitting time. Can I do anything for you?"

Myra put a hand on Pam's forearm. "Thank you. No. Why don't you take off."

Pam didn't want to. She wanted to stay put and enjoy Myra's hand on her arm. "I'm really glad you're back."

"And I'm really glad you sent me those flowers. They did brighten my day."

Blushing, Pam looked away but felt Myra's hand suddenly squeezing her arm hard. She looked up to see Myra staring at the clock with a pained expression. "Is something wrong?"

"No! There is *one* thing you can do. Stay here for a few minutes while I go and talk to Sergeant Barrett, okay?" Before Pam could say "Sure," Myra had snatched her fatigue shirt from the back of her chair and was rushing out, then into the Admin office, heading straight to Tory's office, buttoning her shirt and looking at no one, especially not Craft who leered at her. Her dog tags collided outside her shirt as she came to an abrupt halt at the threshold of Tory's office.

Tory was pushing her chair to her desk, preparing to leave for the day when she noticed movement in front of her. "Specialist Sturdivan."

"Yes, Sergeant. I know it's the end of the day but I need to talk with you."

Tory leaned her hands on the back of her chair. "Henry, Walker, Adkins, Tracer, day's up. Craft, you know where to go." She watched them scoot out. Like the walking dead, Tracer lumbered out last. He'd be leaving Wednesday and had one last office to paint, Top's. Standing before her, Myra had her head hanging down. She was buttoning her last button but it was taking a long time to accomplish.

"Come on in, babe."

Grateful for something to do, Myra did as she was told, then, not having any more buttons, she crossed her arms tightly, holding herself.

Pulling her chair out, Tory gestured toward the extra one. "Have a seat."

Gluing her eyes to the desk, Myra shook her head no.

Tory stepped directly in front of her and gently laid her hands on Myra's elbows, ducking her head, trying to capture her eyes.

Myra stepped back out of Tory's hands and bumped into the door. There she stayed with her eyes down, hoping Tory wouldn't persist.

Stiffening with surprise and concern, Tory returned to the other side of her desk.

"You don't mind if I sit then?" When Myra shook her head Tory sat but on the edge of her seat and laced her fingers under her chin. After a moment she said, "I half expected this. At breakfast I thought there might be something wrong. At lunch I knew there was. Now there's only one question. Are you going to tell me or make me learn it on my own?"

The pain on Myra's face came out in her voice, barely above a whisper. "I put this off as long as I could. I had to talk with you now because I knew you'd be knocking on my door tonight."

"You make it sound like something dirty."

Myra shook her head again, then turned, leaning her shoulder and head against the door. "I don't mean to. It's just that if you knocked I'm not sure I could take it."

Tory took in Myra's stance. She was cringing, still holding herself tight. "You don't want me to knock so you don't want to see me."

"I, uh." Myra turned more into the door. "I think it's best we don't."

Tory stepped around her desk again and leaned back onto it. With a voice huskier than usual she said, "I won't come if you don't want to see me. Is that what you want?"

Closing her eyes, Myra put her forehead to the door and flinched when she felt Tory's hand sweep her hair.

"Last night you said you loved me. And I love you. We made love. What happened after I left?" She watched Myra purse her lips and shake her head.

"Nothing you need to know." Then, as if the words repulsed her sense of taste, she spat out, "Don't come to my room. Don't come to my table in the mess. Give Craft back his pass and ration card. It's over."

Tory folded her arms. "What has he done?"

Myra whimpered, pushing into the door as if her knees were giving out. "Can't you just do those things?"

"Baby, you know I'd do anything you asked, if I could."

"You can do this. Why do you have to be so hard?"

"Someone has to be strong. Now tell me what he did."

"Sergeant, you have no right. I'm not pressing charges."

Tory came to her two solid boots. "Specialist, I have *every* right. You also are one of my troops. I am responsible for you. I have been lenient with him because of your wishes. It's obvious you are scared to death over something that happened between the time I left you last night and this morning before breakfast. I can initiate an investigation with or without your approval."

Turning, Myra braced her back against the door and slowly raised her eyes. Tory's heart sank. Myra's eyes looked worse than the first day she saw them. There was only pain and hopelessness in them.

"Give him back his cards, Tory. Please."

Tory turned away and went back around her desk where she picked up her baseball bat and, enfolding it in her arms, squeezed it to her breasts. She didn't feel she ever had a lot to boast about. Her father had died in Vietnam. Her relationship with her mother had been poor. Her military career was her life and it more than once came before a woman. A month and

145

a half ago she found Myra and suddenly her world was filled with vibrant colors. Now, keeping her back to Myra, she rasped, "I'd do anything you asked, babe, but I won't do that. I won't."

Myra turned the doorknob and took one step out. There she hesitated, then pulled her case with the new switch blade off her belt, laid it on Tory's desk and left.

Closing her eyes, Tory listened to Myra's departing boot steps as the colors faded.

* * *

"SARGE!" Pam caught up to Tory who was making her way to the barracks. "Please don't think I'm poking my nose where it doesn't belong but I think you need to know something."

"Concerning what?"

"Sturdivan, Sarge. She's been acting funny all day and I think I know why. Or at least a little of why."

Staring at the mess hall, Tory took in a deep breath. Myra would be there for dinner but she couldn't approach her. Better not to be there at all.

"You doing anything important right now?"

"Just going to change and then the mess."

"Go change. You're going to be my guest at the NCO Club tonight. Meet me on the front steps of the barracks in fifteen minutes." Tory watched her race ahead. She herself didn't rush. Her energy had been sucked out of her by Myra's words.

Pam was waiting when Tory came through the door. "You want to walk, Sarge, or catch the bus?"

"For under a mile? We'd get there faster by walking. Let's go."

"This is great, Sarge. I've never been inside the NCO Club."

"Consider this training in advance. I've seen your file. Another three months you'll have enough points to be promoted."

"For real?"

"Guaranteed. You plan on staying in?"

"I just re-upped a year ago. So far so good. And I love it here. I guess because I got lucky with Sturdivan being my boss. But it's Top, too. I like the ole poot." She opened the door to the club for Tory.

It was dim inside. There was a big area with a stage up front, a bar in the back, tables scattered everywhere. At eight the entertainment would start, a Korean band playing either country or old rock'n roll. To the left of the bar the walkway led to a smaller room for those wanting only to eat or enjoy drinks. Tory led them to a table on a small, raised area to the left of the walkway. It held only five tables and was enclosed by a short, black metal rail fence.

"How about this one?" Tory chose the one in the back corner. "I always like to have a view of everything." They ordered coffee from the Korean waitress. "You know this is my first time here, too."

"For real? I'd be here all the time if I could. It's quiet. Our club for Spec 4s and below is always packed, mostly with infantry. Entertainment is a band and two Korean dancers wearing only pasties and G-strings. The guys hoot and whistle and throw money at them."

"Sounds interesting. I'll have to check it out sometime."

"No, Sarge. The dancers are drugged and it's not comfortable there."

"Well, I think they keep it quiet here so the NCOs can come down from their headaches. How old are you, Pam?"

"I'll be twenty three next month. You're not going to tell me I'm too young to hang with, are you?"

Tory smiled. "Now how old do you think I am?"

"You're thirty-six. Your supply paperwork has your birth date."

"Ah, yes. The Army tells all."

"When I make Spec 5 I'd like to hang with you to learn from you. I like the way you manage things. I mean, I like you, too. I'd like to learn from Sturdivan, too, but she won't let me get close. And I don't want you to be concerned about my liking her."

Amused, Tory cocked her head, then sipped her steaming coffee.

"I mean, I was in love with her, but I knew I wasn't lucky enough for anything to happen. And when you started hanging with her and she started looking happier I knew what was going on."

"Maybe you shouldn't take me on as a role model. I'm afraid I would've been jealous."

"Well, I was. A little. But—"

"But?"

"I'm glad we're having dinner because I know you're experienced and I could use some help."

Tory laughed. "Experience sure as hell doesn't mean wisdom."

"Well, it means more than what I got. The oddest thing happened today. It was about mid-morning. Sturdivan was kind of absent. You know, up here." She touched her forehead. "Then suddenly she took me aside and told me to take a pillowcase full of things like insect repellent, shovels, mosquito nets, and a case of MREs to the infantry supply next door and try to trade it all for any fans they had. You know, infantry needs that shit, being in the field so much, needing to dig latrines."

"So what was so odd about that?"

"Sarge, she always handles the wheeling and dealing with other companies herself. That's one. The other is we've got fans. I told her that but she snipped at me and told me to just do it."

Throwing her head back, Tory hee-hawed as the waitress laid their plates before them. "I'm sorry, Pam, but I know what she's up to. Did you get any fans?"

"I wish you'd explain it all to me because I was really worried. But, yeah, I got four plus more if I wanted to come back after them."

"Good. I want another. It's starting to get hot in my room."

"Sure thing. I'll get you one tonight. But, listen. This is where I need help. There was this Spec 5 there. Her name is Rose Connors. She shook my hand and introduced herself and said she's been here only a month."

"So?" Tory mouthed a forkful of fried rice.

"Sarge, she hung onto my hand and just stared at me."

"It's your eyes. They are beautiful, you know."

Pam blushed. "You think she likes me? Could I be that lucky?"

"That's the second time you mentioned luck. What has luck got to do with it?"

"Sarge, this woman is awesome. She's tall like me with a body that won't quit. Big green eyes. A beautiful mouth."

"And you're smitten."

Turning red, Pam dabbed her mouth with a napkin. "Problem, Sarge. When she held onto my hand I went blank. I swear I could only babble, 'uh, uh, uh.' I don't think I even told her my name."

Smiling wide, Tory asked, "Is this your first time?"

"Isn't it obvious? I think she thought I was retarded."

Tory patted her hand. "Oh, no. Tell you what. We'll work on that, but first there's a more pressing matter."

"Sturdivan, yeah." Pam finished her last mouthful and set her plate aside. "I swear, sometimes I think it's in the air, you know. The guys just dog the women. Poor Walker had so many guys after her she actually got scared and hooked up with Henry quick. I think for safety at first. Now she's in love with him, but I'm not so sure how Henry feels. You know, he's so mellow and I don't think he tells all. I had one guy constantly on my heels until I told him to back off. He must've had a real thing for tall women because he looked at me like he was worshipping at a shrine. It really gave me the willies. Anyway he got really pissed and called me a dyke and he said it right in the middle of the Admin hut hallway. Then I got pissed, mostly because Top's and the LT's and the Captain's heads poked out of their offices. I grabbed that sucker by the front of his shirt, lifted him clear off his feet and shoved him against the wall. Then I said loud enough for everyone to hear, 'If you ever call me that again I'm going to beat the holy fuck out of you, then pluck every hair out of those shriveled prunes you call balls.' The heads jerked back into their offices like they were afraid to be a part of it. I was satisfied with that so I dropped him. He left red-faced."

Under normal circumstances Tory would've found this tale hilariously funny but with the problems she was having with Myra and Craft she asked seriously, "And that stopped him?"

"Like a heart attack. I used to think my size was a curse but since I've been in the Army it's been a blessing. But Sturdivan can't do that. She's too little." Pam laced her fingers together and leaned closer to Tory. "Listen. You never told me what happened to her and, to tell you the truth, I'm not sure I want to know. But I roam the halls constantly. I guess I'm just restless. I came out of my room last night about ten, maybe a little after, going to get a soda from the dayroom. I heard a door close and when I turned in the direction of the sound I saw Craft rushing to the fire escape. His hand was sort of back and out like he just closed a door, and it had to be Sturdivan's."

Jaw tightening, Tory remembered she had left Myra around nine. "Craft? Are you sure?"

"Positive, Sarge. I went after him to see where he was headed but you know housing won't ever fix that damn light that's supposed to be lit over that escape. And he must've flown down those steps because I didn't see anything but dark."

"That bastard," Tory mumbled.

"Yeah. And after what happened to Sturdivan I got concerned and went to her door. I was going to knock to see if she was okay but, well, you know, you just don't knock on a superior's door unless you have damn good reason and I wasn't real certain. I mean I didn't hear any fighting or screaming or anything. So I put an ear to her door and I heard her footsteps and then water running, like the shower, but no crying or anything. I figured she was okay."

"He's on restriction. He's not supposed to leave his room."

"Oh, man! I'm sorry, Sarge. If I had known that I would've let you know right away."

Nauseated, Tory pushed her plate away. She blamed herself. Last night wouldn't't've happened if she'd had the MPs pick him up. But Myra refused to press charges. Right now she was running on the hope that Myra would change her mind. If she didn't Tory had no right to continue holding Craft on restriction. For a moment Tory stared at the cup in her hand, then raised it to her lips. The sight of it trembling startled her senses.

Pam seized the cup and Tory's wrist and eased both back down to the table, saying, "Sarge, I'll do anything I can to help." She looked at her Sergeant and was suddenly frightened. Holding onto both the cup and her wrist, she watched Tory stiffen with clenched fists and held breath, fighting to control her rage. When Tory began to raise both fists she released the cup and took hold of the other wrist. Having a good foot on her, Pam was stronger, much stronger, than Tory, and right now she was afraid that restraining those fists might mean breaking her wrists. To her relief Tory's fists finally uncurled.

"I'm okay," Tory rasped, taking in a deep breath. "Thank you."

Pam tentatively released her wrists and Tory pulled from her pocket the case Myra had left her. Staring down at it, she turned it in her hand while wondering who she was really mad at—herself for not reporting it, Myra for not pressing charges or Craft for...it all. Laying it on the table, she withdrew the blade from its home. "Myra came to my office this afternoon."

"I know, Sarge. I watched supply while she went."

"What we discuss here, Pam, must be kept secret."

"I understand, Sarge."

"She stayed in my office long enough to ask me to not try and see her again and to give Craft back his freedom. She told me I didn't need to know why. When I refused she left this on my desk."

"Sturdivan cut Craft with that. That was why he was limping."

Tory nodded. "She cut him, but not with this one. One that looked exactly like it. The one she used I have locked in the safe in my office."

"He raped her, didn't he, Sarge?"

Tory stared at her, then whispered, "No. She fought him off."

Pam blew out a heavy breath. "She healed okay from the attack and was acting fine up until today?"

Tory nodded again. "As fine as can be expected. Before I left her last night at nine we had made love. Now she refuses to see me."

She pushed a button on the white, mother-of-pearl handle and a razor-sharp blade, wicked looking and glistening, snapped out. Pam jumped with it. Tory pushed another button and the blade vanished back into the handle. Both jumped when the waitress suddenly appeared, asking if they wanted more coffee."

When the waitress left, Tory looked at Pam, then cocked her head in thought. "I just remembered. Myra told me she had stopped seeing Mamasan at her hooche because of him."

"And now she won't see you," Pam said, eyeballing the blade. "I don't know about you, Sarge, but I'll bet Craft threatened her last night."

Tory nodded, still thinking.

"I'll bet he threatened not her but you if she either sees you again or if she couldn't get you to back off."

"She left the blade for my protection. He is not happy seeing Myra happy, especially at my side."

"No, ma'am. I'd say he's got a serious case of big time angries."

"But what does Mamasan have to do with it? She's hiding something. Something that happened long before I came. She's staying away from Mamasan to protect her, too."

"I see it this way, Sarge. She told you about the attack on her but she won't tell you why she stays away from visiting Mamasan. That tells me that whatever she's hiding has to be even worse than the attack on her."

Tory tapped the blade in her hand, then returned it to its case, then to her pocket.

"Make no mistake," she said, controlling her anger as she picked up her cup of coffee. "He continues to pick on her because she's like an open wound, easy to hurt. All her energy is tied up trying to heal. I'm calling on your willingness to help but just for tonight. What I'm going to do is going to be very ugly."

Chapter Eleven

After dinner as Tory and Pam walked to their rooms they spotted Myra screwing something into the side of her door frame. Pam dropped the fan in front of Tory's door and, with forced calm, they approached her door, stopped and just watched. Myra was equipping her door with not one, not two, but five extra locks, including a three-foot, silver metal rod that was used to secure patio doors.

"Will you for godsake get away from here," Myra begged.

Tory looked at her. Her hair was pinned up as usual, but disheveled. She wore sweat pants, T-shirt, sneaks and socks, all black. She was sweating and appeared exhausted.

"You've had your look. You can have your laugh some place else."

"Yes. Of course." Tory turned. "Johnson, come with me. Myra," she called from her own door, "Pam's working special assignment for me tonight and will not be at work tomorrow." Without waiting for a response, she opened her door and walked in, followed by Pam.

Pam closed the door behind them. "She's freaking, Sarge."

"She'll be all right. You know what to do?"

"Maintain security on her. Follow her everywhere."

"But I don't think she'll be going anywhere. If she questions you?"

"Questions are to be directed to you. My guard duty ends when she enters the mess for breakfast tomorrow morning."

"Okay. I'll keep constant check with you until twenty-three hundred. At zero three hundred I'll give you a relief. Are you okay with this? This is dangerous."

Pam grinned wide. "This is great. I handled that other

twerp, I sure as hell will handle this one. I'll be carrying a blackjack and a knife that won't just put a hole in his leg, it'll cut it clean off."

Tory patted her arm. "Let's hope it won't come to that. And remember that report. I want what you saw last night, what you told me, and what you're doing for me tonight."

When Pam left, Tory changed into her fatigues, then banged on Craft's door. Jung, a KATUSA, answered. She called over him, "Specialist Craft, make yourself decent and get out here." She heard him zipping his pants and hurrying to the door where he braked to ramrod attention.

Barrett neared him, toe-to-toe. "Your little visit and threat last night was very effective, asshole. Congratulations."

A glint of victory replaced the fear in his eyes.

"But you overlooked one small detail."

His eyes started darting about.

"*I* am in charge, not Sturdivan and especially not you. Your threats will get you no freedoms, nor will they dictate who can or can not socialize with Sturdivan. However, your threats did earn you KP this weekend, both days. You will also pull KP every evening after chow duty. I will leave you with two bits of advice. One is don't try anything further. If you do you will, without hesitation, be immediately apprehended. From this moment on there is a guard watching you at all times. The second bit of advice, and heed this well, is rest. I am taking complete and unquestionable charge of you as of right now. I repeat. Rest. Crawl back into your hole. Mercy is a thing of the past." She walked away from his ashen face and wide eyes.

In front of her room's door was a paper bag.

"Sturdivan put it there, Sarge," Pam said, approaching Tory from her perch on the fire escape. She wore combat boots, jungle fatigue pants and T-shirt. She carried her blackjack in her left hand.

Inside the bag were five different kinds of locks and a note that said:

I'm sorry you're involved in this—Myra.

"Putting those up isn't a bad idea, even if Craft wasn't around."

"You room with Wilson, don't you?"

"Yeah, but she's in the ville most of the time. Her boyfriend from the engineering company has a hooche out there."

"We have three extra rooms in the women's section sitting vacant."

"Sergeant Gallo liked to keep those empty for any troops from other posts who had to stay overnight, like for boards."

"Nonsense. You take three locks for your own room and help me put up two tonight. See me first thing tomorrow. You're getting your own room."

"It's no big deal, Sarge. Like I said she's gone..."

"Pam! Think. Your getting Spec 5 in three months will be the official reason for your own room. But there's a better reason. Know what it is?"

Pam's brows creased.

"Where are you going to privately entertain a certain Rose Connors?"

"Oh!" Pam blushed, grinning.

* * *

The five KATUSAs from Craft's room stood in a line before Tory's desk the next morning. "Who speaks the best English?"

The one on the right, Jung, bowed. "Sergeant, I do."

Tory stood. "All of you are on special assignment." Jung translated for the others. "I will not tell you why. I will tell you only that Craft is to be guarded day and night. You five are in charge of that guard duty...Do you all understand?"

None of them liked Craft. He seemed sneaky and was always angry. They often wondered why he never left the room to go anywhere but work. Now they knew. All bowed and said, "Yes, Sergeant."

Jung said, "We will not fail."

Tory nodded. "Good, because if you do someone may lose a life."

"No, Sergeant. We will guard."

* * *

Shortly after Jung and the others left, Tory went into Top's office and discussed her next step with him.

"Victoria, I'd get a helluva lot more satisfaction if you'd concede to me hanging him up and skinning him. But I suppose that snot-nosed LT we have would be the first to notice Craft's blood on my floor.

"This will force her to take a stand, Alan. She has to do that."

"Yep," he said, picking up the phone. "Enough's enough. She can't stay terrified—Myra, come into my office." He hung the phone up and reached behind himself for his bat.

Myra came quickly, freezing on the threshold to his office when she saw Tory with her arms folded, leaning back against the windowsill and Top cradling his bat on his lap. "I'm not sure I want to come in."

Top pulled the cigar out of his mouth. "Gal, you got no enemies in here. Now, come in and close the door."

She did but stood in a guarded manner in front of it, her hands behind her using the door as support.

"Take a seat, Myra. We're going to have a little chat."

"I'd prefer to stand, Top."

"That's fine, too. There's a little dick in the other office we gotta do something with."

"Let it go, Top. I'm not asking you to do anything."

"Sergeant Barrett's already told me you don't want to press charges. But the dick's feeling good about that. Feeling so good that despite restrictions he's still managing to terrorize you."

"Leave it alone. I'll bide my time until he leaves."

"Staying holed up in your room?"

Myra threw hard eyes on Tory. "I told my piece yesterday. Why don't you stay out of it now."

Tory said, "So he could be free to begin a fresh reign of terror? Maybe the next time he'd actually succeed in the rape. No, Myra, I will not allow it."

"Gal, something's gotta be done. I've held off on pressing charges because Victoria said it was your request. I'll be damned if I know why. It's bad enough that punk Tracer, who was a part of it, is leaving tomorrow and all he got was a little tired from a little work. Now you want to let that Craft dick off scot free. No, ma'am! Charges will be pressed. Military justice requires—"

156

"Military justice be damned!" Standing tall, Myra wrapped her arms around herself and whipped blazing eyes on him. "What did you do when I came to you for help? No matter what I said, you said, 'It's only puppy love'."

Tory came to her two solid boots with her own arms folded in front of her. "I can tell you that was a mistake. A regrettable one. He can make..."

"You don't have to speak for me." Top laid his bat on his desk and leaned on it. "You're right. I fucked up. If I could do it again I'd do it differently, but I can't. I can do it right now, though. I can put him where he sure as hell won't get to you. I can make him suffer."

"By pressing charges!? Apparently I've given both of you more credit than you deserve in the common sense area. Suffer!? In this man's Army? Who would suffer more? *I'd* be put under public scrutiny. Everybody I ever slept with would be dug up. My going to a private place in the woods would be seen as a fucking invitation to him. And, oh, yes! Let's not forget the switch blade. Exhibit number one! Illegal to begin with, but to carry it in a concealed manner!? I'd be found guilty, not him. They'd hang me. And after the hanging they'd discharge me! And you know it, Top. You know it! You know what happened to Valez." Myra stopped, eyes bulging, breath hard.

Frozen in his spot, Top stared at her, jaw clamped on his cigar. Rocking back and forth on her boots, Tory glued her eyes to the floor.

After a moment Top slumped to his seat with his bat on his lap and stared out the window.

"If there's nothing else I'll leave now." Myra put her hand on the doorknob.

" Specialist Sturdivan, there is." Tory squared her boots on her. Glancing at Top, she made a mental note to ask him about this Valez, but later. "Justice, whether it be military or personal, must be served. If you don't press charges there must be an alternate discipline."

"I sincerely felt that you of all people would understand."

"I understand much more than you realize. I'm sure Top will agree. I'll allow you to handle it your way. It'll be your

157

choice, the military way or the personal."

"In other words, press charges or come up with a punishment."

"And I'll be more than fair. I'll give you until Monday to decide. Craft will be held in limbo until then."

"You'll initiate charges then if I don't do something else."

"That's right, Myra," Top said, still staring out the window. "Valez was different. The Captain couldn't get a firm ID on her assailant."

"Bullshit!"

Top chose to let her remark be. Half of him admitted she was right, the other half wished she weren't. His whole being cried silently for his daughter. Something went screwy with Valez and he couldn't help but feel the Captain had a lot to do with that. But this time he and Barrett were handling it, not the Captain. "I deeply regret not taking better action sooner. I ain't going to let this go by."

Myra's mouth opened, then slammed shut. She wouldn't win this one anymore than she'd win the charges issue. She snapped, "My, but aren't you both being so wonderfully gracious."

As soon as Top heard his door open then slam he said, "Victoria, you got that gal hating me and I don't like it."

"If she does it's evidence of your admirable performance, Alan. Did you see the anger in her eyes?"

"Yep. And I don't want to see it again."

"Alan, that anger is much better than what I saw in them yesterday. Besides, it won't be for long." She reached over his desk and jabbed his arm. "Guaranteed, you'll be her sweet Top again soon. I'll be back to get that story on Valez."

As she stepped out of his office, he said, "Victoria, I'd be proud to go into battle with you by my side."

Tory grinned. "That's because you know I'm the only one who'd want to save an 'ole poot' like you." To prove she was teasing she used Pam's name for him; the resulting twinkle in his eyes confirmed he loved it. Still, to punctuate her play she took off before he could respond.

* * *

The week passed dismally. Tracer's returning to the States was the only good thing that happened. Tory didn't dare approach Myra anywhere. And slipping love notes every evening under Myra's door gained her nothing. Myra wouldn't speak to her, wouldn't say good morning, wouldn't even acknowledge her. By Saturday Tory was beside herself.

Sitting on the threshold of the third floor fire escape, as she had done on her first Saturday in country, she waited for Myra to come out of her room for breakfast. She waited and waited, went to breakfast alone, returned to the threshold and waited. Lunch time came. She ate alone again, then came back to her perch. By dinner time her back ached, her butt ached, and her head ached. Believing she had missed Myra somehow, she was coming to her feet, ready to call it a day when she heard the click of a doorknob. Myra's doorknob was turning. Myra's door was opening. Myra herself was finally coming through the door, dressed entirely in black. Tory was glad to see her. She smiled. "Good afternoon. Or should I say, Good eve..."

Myra jumped. Though she recognized Tory's husky voice, she needed to look to confirm it. Or was it to draw comfort from?

"...ning," Tory finished, stunned. Myra's eyes were red, sore-looking, as if she had spent hours crying, her creases more pronounced.

Myra lowered her eyes, locked her door and, without returning the greeting, left in the direction of the inside stairs.

Tory scowled. She hadn't wasted all day, waiting, just to be ignored. Determined, encouraged by a bit of anger, Tory followed. Behind Myra in the chow line, she watched Craft take a long time checking Myra's meal ticket. "Specialist Craft, you are never to even look at Specialist Sturdivan's ticket again. Specialist Sturdivan, you will pass him without offering to show it."

Myra sat at her usual table. Tory sat at a separate one. Henry, Walker, Pam, and Guiterrez, sitting at the long one, watched the goings-on at the two tables and caught Craft smiling. When Myra left Tory followed.

As Tory and Myra left the mess Guiterrez shifted his eyes from them to Craft, then to Henry, Walker and Johnson. "You," he said, addressing the group, "thinking what I'm thinking?"

Henry rubbed a helpless hand across his brow and down his cheek. "Something's up. I feel like something's going to explode."

"He's smiling real good," Guiterrez said, looking at Craft. "Like he's planning something that won't fail."

"He did something to her. We know it. So why doesn't she press charges on the sorry bastard?" Henry asked.

No one said anything, especially not Pam. Walker cast a wary eye at Henry, then brought her long-fingered, black hand to her lips. Behind that hand she spoke quickly and timidly. "My daddy beat on my momma until she saved enough to move her children and herself to another state. Years of beatings she took. She called the cops on him a lot and he'd be taken away for awhile, but he always came back. And when he did the beatings got worse. Sturdivan's scared. Like my momma was scared."

Henry, sitting beside her, took her hand from her mouth and held it in his two, smiling at her. "You remember Valez?"

Guiterrez as well as Walker nodded in serious concern. Pam's back jerked straighter as her brows creased. "I don't."

"I don't really," Walker corrected. "Henry told me about her."

"You two came a couple of months after Valez had gone," Henry said. "But Guiterrez remembers."

Shaking his head, Guiterrez said, "Valez worked in Supply. You replaced her, Pam. It was just me and Sturdivan for a while until you came. Valez was a gorgeous woman. Mexican. Gorgeous. Long, wavy black hair, dancing black eyes, sexy."

"And just about every guy was after her," Henry continued. "She had gifts coming from everywhere. Some even begged her. She was always kind and always smiling but returned everything."

"Man!" Guiterrez said. "You should've seen the supply room then. It stayed full with flowers, stuffed animals, all kinds of brass things. Anything to hook her."

"But that was from mainly four guys." Henry raised four fingers. "By then most guys after they were refused once didn't have the guts to try again. But four guys couldn't take no. Valez was starting to show wear by then, too. She went to Sturdivan, using the chain of command you know, to help her with her problem."

Guiterrez snickered. "Sturdivan called the guys in one at a time, told them they'd be standing before the First Sergeant if they didn't stop their nonsense and made them take their gifts back. They were red-faced but wouldn't stop. Sturdivan didn't trust Gallo anymore than she trusted the Captain, but she had to go through Gallo to get to Top so she requested permission from him to talk with Top. After Top talked with them that supply room started looking like a supply room again. And Valez started breathing easier."

"Until," Henry broke in, "one of the guys spotted Valez coming out of the theater one day with a woman from another company."

"The beginning of the end," Guiterrez said.

"Accidents started happening," Henry went on. "That half door to Supply used to be unlocked until Valez got slammed good by it. One of the four guys just happened to be on the other side of it, apologizing big time. Sturdivan didn't see it as no accident and kept it locked from then on."

"Another of those four came to exchange his helmet one day," Guiterrez said. "He claimed it was cracked but Valez couldn't find no crack. He took it from her to show her and suddenly that helmet jumped up and smacked her in the face. Broke her nose. She bled and he apologized. Sturdivan took her off the counter."

"Accidents, you see," Henry sneered. "Got accidentally bumped in a doorway, spraining her shoulder and banging her head. Got accidentally hit by a whipped softball, slugging her in the back. Accidentally fell down stairs, spraining a wrist. Accidents, all of them. Accident, too, that one of those four was always near when she had one of those accidents."

Guiterrez and Henry both went silent at the same time.

"Well, what happened?" Pam demanded.

Henry looked sheepishly at Guiterrez, then shrugged. "Not long after, she came to work one morning with a swollen face and stitches on both cheeks and across her lips. That same day she went to the Captain's office to press charges. At least I thought so. But she disappeared."

"Disappeared!?" Pam asked, incredulous. "You don't just disappear."

This time Guiterrez shrugged, staring down at the table. "Sturdivan's probably the only one who knows what happened. Besides Top and the brass."

Walker locked hard eyes on Henry. "You didn't tell me nothing about no stitches. You just said she disappeared."

Lowering his eyes, Henry shook his head. "Didn't think you needed to know that part. And I didn't think you'd care. You don't want anything to do with Sturdivan because everybody says she's a lesbian."

"Craft started that shit!" Pam had to say it, couldn't keep quiet anymore. "And you all know it. He got pissed because she wouldn't go out with him. He used it to turn everybody against her. Tracer wanted her, too. That's why he helped Craft. Craft terrorized her every night. That's why she hid herself at night. That's why she stayed away from this table."

"All this time," Walker said in remorse. "All this time I thought she was crazy and now I find out he's been making her crazy." She felt Henry squeezing her hand in support, encouraging her. "We shouldn't have listened to Craft. We shouldn't have excluded her. No wonder she went to be with Koreans instead of us. Even if she was crazy or a lesbian we shouldn't have excluded her. We all like her. She's a good supervisor. She don't bother nobody and she gets the work done. Craft kept saying I'd look like a lesbian, too, if I was friendly to her. And after you," she nodded to Henry, "told me what happened to Valez, I didn't want to disappear, too."

The others nodded solemnly, though none of them knew what exactly they were feeling—whether it was guilt or embarrassment or regrets or...the beginnings of understanding.

"Craft tried to rape her," Pam blurted, trying to decide if she was betraying Barrett's confidence.

All eyes widened on her.

"Yeah." She nodded. "He was always watching her and followed her one night out to a hiding place of hers. He attacked her and they fought. He beat her face good. She had lots of cuts all over her body, too, because there was glass on the ground. But he didn't get to rape her. She stabbed him."

"That's why his face was messed up and he was limping," Guiterrez said, his teeth gnashing.

"We got to do something," Walker said, fear in her eyes. "Craft has no right to force himself on her just because she don't want no part of him. If he gets away with it, what will happen next?"

"Why won't she press charges?" Henry asked again.

Walker slapped at his chest though she wasn't directing anger at him. "You two just get through telling us how Valez disappeared with a slashed face, and you wonder why she won't press charges! She's scared. She's afraid she'll disappear, too. She ain't got nobody backing her up."

Henry turned to Johnson. "How'd you find all this out? Who told you?"

"Barrett."

"Why'd she tell you and nobody else?"

"She doesn't want anybody to know until Sturdivan presses charges. I think, too, because I caught Craft last Sunday running away from Sturdivan's room and I told her. He was on restriction but he broke it and went to Sturdivan's room and threatened her. He threatened to do something to Barrett if she couldn't get Barrett to back off. And I think he threatened to do something to Mamasan, too, but I don't know why, except maybe because she likes Mamasan."

"That's why she stopped going to Mamasan's hooche," Henry said. "But that was a while back."

"Barrett thinks something else happened before Sturdivan was attacked. Something that made her stop visiting Mamasan. And now, well, you just saw Barrett and her eat at separate tables."

"So," Guiterrez said, "Sturdivan's staying away from everybody to protect them..."

"From that bastard," Henry finished.

163

"Barrett put a guard on him," Pam continued, "but it looks like Sturdivan doesn't trust a guard to keep him in his room."

"Can't blame her," Henry said.

"He beat the hell out of her," Guiterrez added.

"Then he broke restriction." Walker stared wide-eyed at the others. They returned her look.

"Something's going to explode," Henry said.

"We got to do something," Walker repeated. "We're soldiers."

* * *

Tory followed Myra out of the mess and onto a bus going to the gate. They sat on separate seats. In the ville Myra boarded a Korean bus going South to Osan some thirty minutes of bumpy, winding road away. Tory sat in the seat directly in front of her and about half-way into the ride she suddenly turned around and snapped Myra's picture.

"Gotcha!"

Looking hopeless, not so much as flinching, Myra asked, "You don't get it, do you?"

Despite her knotting stomach, Tory smiled wide. "I know I'd like to get you."

"I don't know how you found out about his coming to my room, but I suspect Pam had something to do with it. Her guarding me that night gave her away."

"He threatened to do me bodily harm, didn't he?"

"What you don't realize is that his threats are warnings. He told me there'd be a bloodbath if I either saw you again or didn't get you to back off."

"So to protect me you won't see me. Very gallant."

"It's not just you, Tory. It's Mama—" She stopped but not soon enough.

"What's Mamasan got to do with it?"

"Nothing."

"Bullshit! What are you hiding?"

Myra closed her eyes. She didn't want to see the humping form in the alley but she saw it just the same. Only now it humped over Mamasan, making the pain worse.

Myra raised lifeless eyes. "He threatened once before that

164

I'd be sorry if I saw you again. That threat came just a few minutes before you came to my room that first time. That very same night he attacked me. Do you think he's playing? Do you really think a guard will stop him? Did your restriction stop him?"

"A guard is different from a simple restriction."

Myra wearily shook her head. "Then say a prayer for that guard. He won't be vicious enough to stop him."

"You're frightened, babe. That interferes with proper judgment. Tell me what you're hiding and I'll handle it from here."

Myra hung her head down and closed her eyes.

"Don't let him get away with it, babe. You're a soldier. Pick up your weapon and fight."

In Osan, half dazed, not knowing where she wanted to go or do, Myra got off the bus, then got on the next one back to Seoul. Tory followed. In Seoul Myra suddenly stopped in her tracks and said, "It's getting dark."

"That's what happens at night. So?" Tory asked.

Myra looked sadly at her. "Go back to the barracks, Tory. You'll be safe there."

"Like you were?"

"I wasn't raped. Yes. He knew one scream would get help and fast."

"Then come with me."

Myra didn't answer. She went down the right side of the road in front of the gate, the direction she had never taken Tory. It led to hooche after hooche where hooker after hooker was picked up by GI after GI. Half-naked children played on packed, dirt ground. There was no grass, no trees, no toys, no pets. The very air seemed more oppressive in this section.

Myra knocked lightly on a door to a hooche. It was like a sliding glass patio door, except it was made only of heavy paper. To Tory's surprise Mamasan answered.

"Stuuurdi! In, in," she waved. She was about to close the door when she spotted Tory. "Baarrett, too. Come, come. So happy!" she said when they both were inside. She introduced her sister Chong-kil to Tory, then said, "Stuurdi, I get."

While Mamasan was gone Tory put a hand on Myra's forearm. "You said it was Mamasan, too. You told me you stayed away from here because of him. Why come here now?"

"I told you, Tory. His threats are warnings. You're here. Safe. You'll be safe in the barracks, too. Those barracks are quiet but not empty. He knows that. But he's pissed, Tory. He wants his passes back and he wants you to stay away from me. He hasn't gotten his passes back and this evening he saw you right behind me all the way. By now he's probably frothing at the mouth. And a guard? He's going to laugh at his guard, then show up here, Tory. I don't want Mamasan facing him alone."

"Press charges and he'll be out of the way."

"'For godsake, be real! All he has to do is say one word!" she said, raising an angry index finger. "One word—lesbian. And they'll forget whatever charges I'm pressing and focus on that one word."

"Craft never mentioned it when I came down on him."

"Not to you he won't, and he won't to Top. But to the Captain and the LT he will. He knows what happened to Valez. He doesn't know exactly what happened to her but he knows she didn't win. And because he knows that we're going to need a fucking M16 to stop him."

"Top told me about Valez. He said she didn't press charges because she couldn't, without a doubt, say who did it to her, so they sent her to another post for her own safety."

"The part about her safety is right." Myra sneered as Mamasan returned from a smaller back room, carrying a set of yellow sheets and pillowcases like the ones Myra had before the blood stains.

Having Myra at her home again gladdened Mamasan. Surprised her as well since only a couple of days ago Myra had snapped at her, saying she wouldn't come again until Craft was gone. Mamasan hadn't taken offense. She knew Myra had really snapped at the Army as well as Craft, and she just happened to be in the line of fire.

"Maybe it's time to speak of what happened to Eun Lee," Mamasan had said. Seeing Myra despondent hurt her and Myra's keeping distance from Tory was heartbreaking. She hadn't waited for Myra to answer but had said, hoping to make

166

Myra smile, "You remember Sun-he, the woman in the fish market? We are lovers."

"Really!? That's wonderful! Will you live together?"

"Yes, yes. We will move out of the Alley, too, so you will not get a bad name for visiting. We will do things together, you and your friend and me and mine. We can be happy but we must get rid of this problem with Craft. It's not right that all of us suffer for what he does."

"Eun Lee won't talk and I'd end up gone. We wouldn't be able to do things together." Myra had shaken her head, sadly.

Mamasan had insisted, "We can. We must tell—"

Now Myra took the sheets from Mamasan, then withdrew a ten dollar bill from her wallet. "Can I get?"

Bowing, Mamasan smiled wide. "Yes, yes."

"Myra!" Tory cried, laying a stopping hand on her elbow. "Don't. You don't need to buy it. I can give you that!"

"I'm sure you can. But she's good at it."

"And I'm not!?"

"You, too," Mamasan said. "I give you free. You Stuurdi's friend."

"No!"

Hurt by Tory's rejection, Mamasan turned. Myra shrugged a 'Your loss' and stepped into the back room, pulling her shirt up and over her head as she disappeared behind the blue curtain following Mamasan.

Steamed beyond words that Myra could even think of sex, let alone buy it, while this problem with Craft was going on, Tory turned her back, crossed her arms and bit at her top lip. And with Mamasan. She'd never be able to look at Mamasan the same way again. And Myra had lied to her. They had had, and still did have a sexual relationship.

Chong-kil touched her arm. "I give. You like. You feel good."

Tory stared at her a moment, then thought, I'll be damned before I let her go without a fight. Turning on her sneakered heels, she tossed the curtain aside and stormed into the back room.

And just as briskly came to a screeching halt. Belly down, Myra was lying on a thin mat on the floor with her shirt off and

Mamasan was kneeling over her, giving her a back massage. Suddenly Tory felt very embarrassed and very relieved as she watched Mamasan whisper into Myra's ear.

Myra lifted her head from the crook of her elbow. "Mamasan says you're very tense today and need this."

"I didn't know you understood Korean."

"A little. Speak a little, too. Nothing to boast about." She slid to the edge of the mat and Mamasan, no longer hurt since Myra had explained what Tory probably thought was going on, patted the extra space. "Chong-kil's just as good. She'll give you a full body massage if you want."

Tory knelt on the mat and removed her shirt. "Just a back will do."

Smiling, Mamasan continued on Myra as Chong-kil knelt over Tory.

"Quite a treat you've kept secret."

"I would've introduced you to it when I thought you were ready. You can get it at the post's beauty salon, too. But I like Mamasan more."

"Oooh!" Tory crooned, enjoying the warm lotion being rubbed into her back. "Very stimulating," she grinned, nose-to-nose with Myra. "When we get back to your room I'll give you a full massage—free."

Exasperated, Myra closed her eyes.

"Babe, look at me. I love you. Do you really think I'd do anything to hurt you?"

Myra kept her eyes closed. "Pushing me to face that asshole?"

"You have to stand up to him to stop him."

"Piss him off is more like it. You're not in my shoes, Tory. You're not being haunted. You're not the one scared to death that someone will get hurt because of you. You're not the one thought of as the crazy lesbian that won't go out with him. You're not terrified like me that any day you'll be called in to the Captain's office and humiliated, degraded and investigated like you're a piece of slime."

"If you're so damned worried about being thought a lesbian why did you go to Top and tell him you wanted to get out of the company?"

"I was desperate. I knew he wouldn't believe me. I figured he'd arrange for me to go to another company, that's all."

"Well, it failed. And Craft failed, too. He's destroyed his own credibility. Nobody believes it."

"Big fucking deal." Myra couldn't decide which was worse, the feeling of betrayal in keeping her secret safe or being ostracized for it.

"I should think it would be. Myra, I'm beside you all the way. I can make it so he'll think seriously before ever doing something like that to you or any other woman again." When Myra didn't answer, Tory elbowed her. "Hey! I'm talking to you! You might want to consider that I took a risk, too. Despite everybody thinking you were a lesbian, I went ahead and became your friend anyway. And you know in the Army guilt by association is the same as guilt."

"Bullshit! You have a cover. I know damn well Top put you on me to help my state of mind. Word gets around damn fast in a company."

"Maybe he did, but I didn't fall in love with you at his request."

Myra's teeth clamped tight. Tory was right. Still, she was fed up. Wishing it would all go away, Myra opened angry eyes. "Get off your cloud, Ms. Macho. You think you're going to make a difference? Go ahead and press charges. Within a week we'll both be under investigation for the criminal act of lesbianism. With the help of a smiling boot *we'll* go flying out the door hand in hand. And him! Hell, he'll be patted on the back for his valiant effort in trying to save a Godless pervert, an abomination in the eyes of the military."

"I can see your mind is set."

"And I can see that right now you're being just as rotten as him."

Shock and anger burned through Tory. "What!?"

"Against my wishes you're following me just like he follows me."

Pushing herself to her knees, Tory snatched her shirt and harshly pulled it on. "I'll tell you one damn thing, Ms. Know-it-all! I saw your picture of what you looked like when you first came here. And to see what you look like now! Craft scratched every one of those creases into your face and you let him by not taking a stand." She reached into Myra's hair and yanked out one of the pins. "I often wondered why you never let your hair down, beautiful as it is. I know now. You started growing it, thinking it would stop others from talking about you. Dykes, after all, don't keep long hair! You don't like it long but you suffer it, and to counter your suffering you pin it up. Well, let me tell you something. People are going to think what they want regardless of what you do to sway them otherwise."

She tossed the pin on the mat in front of Myra's nose. Then she dived into her hair, pulling out all the pins, freeing it. "Your picture showed you are beautiful inside as well as out. If you think long hair will camouflage you, think about this. Your failure to act firmly against an asshole who beat you and tried to rape you is going to make others think you *are* trying to hide something. That maybe you are a dyke and you yourself feel you deserved what you got." She threw down all the pins, paid Chong-kil and left.

"Stuuurdi!" Mamasan cried. "Baarrett good. You love her. You her." She crossed her index and middle fingers in serious concern.

Myra's head fell to her hands, her hair cascading over her shoulders, making her feel like a stranger to herself. "I know, Mamasan. I know."

Chapter Twelve

While Tory was tearing pins out of Myra's hair, Craft was blowing smoke at the window of his room. He lay on his bunk, watching the dark of night settle in and waiting for the KATUSAs to leave for the free movie at the theater. Jung would be his guard while the rest were gone.

His wait was only a few minutes. He thought he could smell the air freshen as they left his room. He waited another couple of minutes to make sure they had time to leave the barracks and be on their way up the road. When he felt his way was clear he pinched the spent cigarette between his middle finger and thumb, squinted as he sucked a last drag from it, then crushed its burning ash between his fingers. He looked at the mangled butt in his hand and whispered to himself, "I warned you, Mikey. Now you got only yourself to blame for what happens. I didn't let no woman's restriction stop me and I sure as hell ain't letting no half-head."

He raised himself to a sitting position and cocked his head as if he had heard something. "You going to answer that?" he asked Jung who was sitting opposite him on his own bunk, polishing his boots.

Jung looked at him as if he was nuts. "Answer what?"

"The door, you fucking half-head. Somebody's knocking on the door."

Jung laughed at him and twirled his index finger by his forehead. "You loco, GI. No knock."

"No loco, half-head. Somebody knocked. If you don't answer, I will."

Jung waved his hand, saying, "No knock."

"All right," Craft said, pushing himself to his feet. "Just

remember I asked you to answer it." He went to the door and Jung was on his own feet and right behind him. Craft opened the door and no one was there.

Jung peeked around from behind the door and, seeing no one, laughed again at Craft and twirled his finger by his temple. "Loco GI."

Craft threw his head back and laughed with him. "Yeah, half-head. I guess I was hearing things." He laughed again and kept laughing as he shoved the door fast and hard into Jung's face. Jung staggered. Blood ran down from his nose. Closing the door, Craft grabbed Jung by the back of his head and smashed him into the door again. Jung dropped to the floor. Craft tore a strip of sheet and tied Jung's hands in back.

Before closing the door as he left, Craft blew Jung's unconscious body a kiss and said, "Sweet dreams, half-head." He smiled wide, locking the door behind him.

* * *

Myra pounded the mat once with her fist, then pushed herself up. She pulled her shirt over her head and pinned her hair up. "You said Sun-he comes here. Where is she?"

Confused and frightened by Myra's anger, Mamasan said, "She leaves the market at nine. Stuurdi, what is so wrong? Why are you fighting?"

Myra hugged her. "We're not really fighting, Mamasan. It's okay. I'll be back," she said and went out to find Tory, to stop her.

She found Tory a few feet from Mamasan's door, standing still. "Tory?"

Tory turned hard eyes on her. "I don't know which damn alley leads back to the gate."

"This place is like a maze if you don't know it. That alley, straight up." Myra pointed. "Come on. I'll walk you if you promise to stay in the barracks where it's safe."

Tory raised a hand, warding her off, heading towards the alley at a rushed pace. Myra hurried, keeping up with her. "Tory, wait."

"Wait, hell! I've waited too long. I'll be damned before I allow him to dictate where I go or who I go with. I should've had him arrested at the very beginning."

"No, Tory. You don't understand."

"You're right I don't understand. I don't understand why you continue to refuse to press charges."

"I can't win, Tory. There's more to it. I can't win."

They were at the gate. Myra's eyes were pleading as they darted from the MP checking their IDs to Tory. Tory saw it and didn't alert the MPs then. She walked through the gate. She'd call them when she got back to the barracks. She hurried on.

"Tory, please," Myra begged, half running to keep pace with her. "I got to get back to Mamasan. Promise you won't do anything."

"Then go back to her. Stay scared. Stay on alert. Let the creases on your face get even deeper. Let the nightmares eat you up. Let—"

Myra stopped in her tracks some twenty yards from Admin. "No, Tory, I can't win. You can't win. She won't testify and it's all my fault."

Tory stopped and turned to see Myra holding herself with one hand about the waist, the other covering her mouth. She clenched her dog tags in a tight fist, looking as if she was going to be sick.

Tory walked back to her. "Your fault? Who won't testify? Mamasan?"

Myra shook her head, trying to hold back the tears, too many of which she had already shed during the day. "Eun Lee."

"Who's Eun Lee? Is that Mamasan's name?"

Myra shook her head again, weeping.

"Talk to me, dammit!"

"October," Myra managed, then took in a deep breath. "I was at Mamasan's hooche. It was her birthday and I stayed late. When I left I heard sobbing coming from the same alley we just went through. It was so dark and I couldn't see well, but I knew a woman was being raped. God, Tory," she said, holding her fists to her temples, the dog tag chain appearing like a noose around her neck. "I can still see him. I see him in my sleep, humping. Hard. Fast. I still hear her sobbing. Muf-

173

fled. Like he had his hand over her mouth. I was so scared. I slung a rock at him. He stopped and she ran. I ran, too. He caught me and pulled me back into the same alley. It was Craft, Tory." She brought the back of her hand holding her dog tags to her mouth. "It was Craft."

Tory could only stare for the moment.

Myra bent over as if she had crippling stomach pains. "He said he wasn't finished when I assaulted him. Called her his 'hole' for the night, bought on the 'buy now, pay later' plan. He said it was my fault. If I'd gone out with him he wouldn't have followed me, and if he hadn't followed me he wouldn't have been in the alley waiting for me, and if he hadn't been in the alley Eun Lee wouldn't have been.... It's my fault, Tory. He was mad at me and took it out on her. He was going to force me to help him finish, and if I said anything about it he'd tell them I was lying to cover up my being in Thousand Won Alley buying pussy. I bashed his head with another rock and ran."

"That was Thousand Won Alley?"

"I wasn't buying any pussy, Tory! But nobody will believe me once he says something like that. You know the Army. Once they get wind of something like that it's all hooks and no let up. And Eun Lee won't testify."

"Why wouldn't she? How do you know?"

"Mamasan asked her for me."

Tory waited but Myra wasn't saying anything more. "Well! Why?"

"She was in Thousand Won Alley. She's a college student and has a friend there. But her parents had forbidden her to ever go there to see her friend. If she testified her parents would know she went there against their will. I tried to get her to. Mamasan tried. She's terrified. She won't, and if I tell I won't have anyone to back me up. Craft would be freed from charges and he said he'd get Mamasan if I told. And last week he said he'd get Mamasan or you if I didn't get his passes back. You'll be okay in the barracks, but I've got to get back to Mamasan, Tory. This is all my fault. He's mad at me but he takes it out on others."

Teeth clenched, Tory said, "When Pam told me she caught Craft leaving your room I was so pissed. I blamed Craft for it all. Then I blamed you for not pressing charges. Then, I blamed myself for not calling the MPs." She closed her eyes momentarily. When she opened them she said, "None of this would've happened if we didn't have to hide. You could've laughed in his face when he threatened to say you were buying pussy. You could've laughed and reported it and stopped it right there. But you couldn't because the military already had you under threat. Baby, don't fall for that. You're not to blame."

Myra straightened. "I know that, Tory. I mean my head knows that but my gut doesn't. I feel like I'm to blame. Just like he attacked me after I didn't do what he wanted me to."

Tory reached out and took hold of Myra's hand, the one squeezing the life out of the tags. "No, baby. You're not to blame. But I would be if I didn't report it after all you just told me."

"No, Tory. Don't. He'll be freed. Eun Lee won't testify. And in the end we'll be under investigation for loving each other. Please, don't."

"She'll testify. I'll have a talk with Mamasan and then Eun Lee. If need be she'll be court-ordered."

"A court order won't make her tell the truth. She'll deny it in the face of her parents."

"That's a risk I'll have to take."

Myra got down on a knee, clutching her dog tags in one hand and Tory's wrist in the other. "Don't, Tory. Please. Top didn't tell you everything about Valez. I'm not sure he even knows the whole truth and even if he did he couldn't have changed it.

"She wanted to press charges. I was with her in the dispensary when she was having her face sewn up. I was her boss. The medics called me. She said she was going to the Captain and press charges. I knew what the Captain was like. I told her not to go to him, to go to Top, but she was in pain and screaming and weeping and not listening.

"I was with her the next day in the Captain's office. She told him who the two guys were that threw a blanket over her head and dragged her behind the barracks. They slashed her face so quick she never got to see their faces but she knew their voices. They called her 'dyke' and 'whore' and 'worthless piece of shit' while they slashed and spit on her and kicked her. The Captain looked at her like she was the 'worthless piece of shit' they called her. He told her he had heard she was a lesbian but would've let it slide since she was in Korea. But not now. She was causing too much trouble for boys who already had it hard enough here. He would take action against her.

"I couldn't believe what was happening. She couldn't either. In the end he told her she had a choice. She could either take a transfer to another camp and forget it happened or press charges and be dishonorably discharged. And he made it clear the charges wouldn't hold because identifying only a voice wasn't good enough. One of the guys did his year and is gone Stateside. The other is our LT.

"Please, Tory. I got you here. I got Mamasan. I'll take the beating just like Valez took it. I don't want to be transferred now and I don't want to be discharged. I've got sixteen years I don't want to lose."

Though Tory wasn't angry with Myra, she whipped wet, blazing eyes on her. "I got eighteen and, by God, I won't lose them either!"

* * *

"HEEEENRYYY!" Walker screamed, running the hallway from her post at the side door of the barracks to the exit door on the other side.

Henry turned in time to catch her, stopping her run.

"Henry," she said, trying to catch her breath. "I didn't try to stop him. I did what you told us to do. I watched him go. He was rushing in the direction of the gate."

"Okay, okay. You did good, sweetheart." He kissed her on her forehead. "Go get Pam and Guiterrez and meet me in front of the barracks."

She took off for the rear of the building and he went to the front.

"His guard, Henry," Pam said as the group met. "What happened to him?"

"Guiterrez, go check his room," Henry said.

In less than a minute Guiterrez was back. "The room's locked. I knocked. No answer, no sound from inside."

The group exchanged worried looks. "Shouldn't we bust the door down?" Pam asked. "I mean, he had a guard. He had to do something to get away."

Henry put his fingers to his lips, thinking. "No. I can't do that on my own. Walker said he was heading for the gate. Anybody know...."

"Mamasan," Pam blurted. "He's headed for Mama...."

"EH!" Guiterrez cried. "Look," he said, pointing to the right of Admin in the distance. "There's Sarge and Sturdivan. Sturdivan's kneeling."

The group didn't pause to wonder why, they went running to them.

"SARGE!" Pam called.

Tory turned from Myra to Pam, Henry, Walker and Guiterrez.

"Sarge," Pam said again, "Craft's gone."

A whimper of pain escaped Myra's lips. She sprang to her feet and took off running for the gate. There was no need to hear the rest. She knew where she'd find Craft.

Tory caught Pam's arm as she tried to run after Myra. "No. He has no pass. He can't get off post."

"Sarge," Henry said, "Craft hardly ever showed his pass. He knows the MPs. "

Tory's teeth clamped. "First things first. Come with me."

At Craft's room Tory tried the knob. Locked. The master key was secured in her locker in her room.

"Pam, Henry, break it down." Without hesitation, they reared back together and slammed two powerful feet into the door. It was a little awkward. They stumbled into each other but the door flew open. Inside, Jung lay on the floor with his hands tied in back, groaning, moving as if trying to regain consciousness.

"Walker," Tory said, "you stay here. Untie him, call medical and call the CO to alert Top. The rest of you come with me."

Pam took off, her long legs carrying her twice as fast as Myra's had.

"Johnson!" Tory yelled, but Pam didn't slow. "Dammit! I don't know my way back into that maze where Mamasan lives."

"No sweat," Guiterrez said, grinning. "Come on. I know."

* * *

Craft raised a hand and smiled wide, greeting the MPs at the gate. "How's it going tonight, gentlemen?"

"Hey, m'man!" one of the MPs greeted back as he continued to check a bag in front of Craft. "Life sucks in the world of endless search."

Craft laughed. "Tough break, man. Tell you what. I'll have one in your name tonight," he said, reaching in his back pocket as if for his pass.

"Yeah," the MP laughed. "Better make it two or three. Go on." He waved Craft through without checking his pass.

Craft waved a thank you, mumbling, "Stupid bastard," and lit a cigarette as he rushed to Thousand Won Alley, gulping down huge breaths of the sweet scent of freedom. At Mamasan's hooche he smiled as he looked at the door. Squinting, he took a last drag on his half-spent cigarette, then flicked it to the dirt.

"You are going to be so sweet," he whispered to the door, knocking.

When Mamasan answered Craft grabbed her by the throat and mouth, backing her inside. "Close the door," he snarled, gesturing with his head.

* * *

Sweating, pausing to catch her breath, Myra stood in front of Mamasan's hooche. The children that were playing in the dirt earlier were no longer outside. An American soldier came out of the hooche three down, smiling, adjusting his belt.

Myra wiped her palms on her jeans, then checked her belt. But of course her switch was gone. She had given it to Tory. All for the best, she said to herself. If he saw it he could probably take it from her anyway. She grabbed two rocks from the ground, one for each hand, then tested the door, hoping it wasn't locked. It slid silently to the side.

Craft had his back to the door, holding Mamasan against a wall, a hand over her mouth. Her skirt was still down and he was trying to unzip his pants. By the other wall in the corner, Chong-kil was crouched, cowering. Myra caught

Mamasan's eyes and brought a finger to her lips, telling her to be quiet. But too late. Mamasan spotted Myra and cried, "Stuuurdi!" into Craft's hand.

Craft swung around, propping Mamasan in front of him. He reached into his back pocket and pulled a switch blade from it. He snapped the blade free and touched it to Mamasan's throat. He laughed. "See, Mikey? You taught me something. This," he said, twirling the blade in his fingers, "is a nice little tool. Now close the door behind you like there ain't nothing wrong in the world."

Hiding her rocks behind her back, Myra did.

"That's a good girl."

* * *

"Who's Barrett?" an MP with Sergeant rank asked the group at the gate.

"I am," Tory said. "Is there a problem?"

"Your company CO called. Per your First Sergeant, me and a KNP are to meet you here and escort you to wherever you're going."

Tory glanced at the Korean National Police standing beside him, then down at the weapons on their hips. "Yes, please. Follow Guiterrez."

* * *

Pam was in the alley opposite Mamasan's hooche. Her heart was pounding hard in her chest. She had just watched Sturdivan close the door, had seen Craft holding Mamasan hostage. Gripping tight the slapjack in her hand, she approached the door and put an ear to it.

Craft laughed. "Mikey, you must think I'm really stupid. Bring your pretty little hands out from behind your back. I saw those rocks and I remember when you used one on me. Drop them."

After a moment one thud reached Pam's ears, then another.

"Oh," he said, laughing. "This is going to be one nice night, don't you think?"

The door slammed open. Pam ducked her head and stepped inside, looking like a giant. "I don't know, Craft," she said, slapping her jack against her thigh. "Am I invited?"

179

Myra's heart danced almost drunkenly to the beat of hope as Craft's jaw dropped. He turned pale. He stepped back, bumping the wall, pulling his hostage with him. He twisted Mamasan's head to the side to show the blade at her neck better. "You come any closer and I'll slice her throat." The point of the blade broke skin. A trickle of blood escaped.

Myra's hands bolted up, showing earnest palms. "Okay! Okay! Nobody's going to move. Chung-ja," Myra called Mamasan by her name to secure her attention. "Ga-man-he-kye-sae-yo. Um-jik-i ji ma-sip-si-o. Na-nun-ku sa i yam i tang-sin-sul-da-chi-ge-ha-got-sul won-ha-ji-an-sum-ni-da. Sin-yong ha-da." which meant—Be still. Don't move. I won't let him hurt you. Trust. With her index and middle fingers she motioned the drawing of a small cross over her own heart, then tapped a loose fist to it, saying, "Sa-rang-he." —I love you.

Chung-ja didn't grow calm but she did believe her American friend who had saved her job, opened her heart, helped her find herself and then Sun-he.

Pam was suddenly shoved to the side, slamming into Myra. The MP put a hand to the weapon on his hip, warning, "Drop it, soldier."

Stunned, Craft stared wide-eyed at him. He couldn't move.

The KNP slipped to the side of the MP and drew his weapon. He spoke in Korean but his message was clear in any language. He wasn't warning. He crouched in a defensive position and demanded Craft drop the knife. Craft was frozen in fear. The KNP crept closer, put the muzzle of his weapon to Craft's head and cocked it. Craft still couldn't move. Tears ran down his cheeks. The MP reached out, took the blade, then laid him down on the floor and cuffed him as Chung-ja flung herself into Myra's arms.

Chapter Thirteen

At their table in the mess, Tory, Pam, Walker, Henry and Guiterrez were eating breakfast, or trying to. They were unusually quiet, thinking about all that happened last night—Craft's arrest and all his charges, so many they overwhelmed the mind; calming Mamasan down; comforting Chong-kil, Eun Lee and her parents; the translators, the KNPs, the statements, the hours. So much it made the head heavy.

Henry broke the silence though he sounded numb and worn. "Me, Walker, and Guiterrez finished about midnight, Sarge. When did you?" he asked, meaning her, Myra and Pam.

Tory picked up her cup and sipped some coffee. "Half hour ago."

Henry turned questioning eyes on Pam. "You had to stay that long too?"

Pam shook her head. "I stayed as body guard."

"In the MP station?"

Everyone chuckled, albeit wearily. "No!" Pam defended, blushing. "I made sure they got back to the barracks all right."

Walker jabbed Henry's side, making him grunt. "How come you didn't do that?"

Henry draped an arm along the back of Walker's chair. "Because, sweetheart, I was already assigned to guarding you. And don't ask Guiterrez because he was assigned to guarding me."

Everyone laughed again. Tory rubbed tired eyes, smiling. "Keep up the humor, gang. We're going to need it for a long time."

"How long you think it'll take, Sarge?" Guiterrez asked.

Tory shrugged. "A couple of months? A couple of years? The complicated fact is that he has Korean National charges against him as well as military. Of course, Tracer will be brought back."

Guiterrez stood to leave. "I guess if I'm going to have to be here a couple of years I'm happy I'll be with all of you." He left the table, leaving all of them momentarily silent.

Walker clasped her hands together on her lap and, looking down at them, said, "I'm happy, too."

Henry squeezed her shoulder and nodded, agreeing.

Pam and Tory exchanged smiles.

"Sarge," she continued, "none of us slept much last night. And Sturdivan has to be more tired than us. And maybe with the way we treated her before, well, couldn't you ask her to come back to our table?"

Tory smiled over Walker's turnaround from the first day Tory had sat with them. "I think it'd mean more if you asked her. But," she glanced at Myra sitting at her private table, "I think she needs a little time. You know, to sort things out and come around."

After Henry and Walker left, Pam asked, "You're waiting for her, huh?"

Tory nodded as if to say the wait would be long.

Pam pushed her chair back. "If you need me, call. I'm gone."

Tory waited ten minutes, then went to Myra. Over the table she leaned into Myra and whispered, "Craft's no longer with us, baby."

"He's not?" She pivoted her sight at the long table. "They were good, weren't they, Tory? Coming to save, to defend."

"Yeah," Tory said softly. "The colossal, protective shield."

Myra looked at Tory, then dropped her eyes. "It's going to be a long, hard trial."

"Maybe not as bad as you think. Eun Lee didn't lie. Her parents were upset but not with her and they thanked you."

After a moment Myra said, "I think, Tory, I need to be alone."

Tory glanced at the dog tags that lay on her breast, reassured her with a squeeze to her hand and left.

* * *

A week had passed since Tory left Myra at her table. She had been good to her promise, had left Myra alone, but she had to share this. "MYRA! MYRA!" Her call pierced the hall and into the supply room where Myra and Pam exchanged questioning looks.

"Myra!" Tory caught hold of the counter to Supply, halting her run. Breath hard, she wore an ear-to-ear grin as she waved an open envelope and letter at her. "Come on. You're not going to believe this."

Tory stormed Top's office and closed the door after Myra entered.

"Gal," he said, standing. "I've had about all the excitement I want in the last week. I was hoping this week would start out kinda calm and dull if you know what I mean."

Tory poked his shoulder. "Sit down, you' ole poot.'"

Top looked to Myra for help but she could only shrug.

"Sit," she ordered. Hesitantly, he did and Tory waved the letter in front of his nose. "This is to inform you you are again a proud papa."

"What in the hell are you talking about?"

"Four years ago you lost a daughter. Today," again she waved the letter in front of his nose, "you get a second chance."

Top snapped at the letter but Tory was quicker. "No, no." She wagged a teasing finger. "You have a bouncing baby girl named Cassandra, twenty-two years of age and doing fine."

Top stood. "Victoria, I ain't never hit a woman before, but I swear to all that's holy if you're fucking with me I'm going to hit you. I'm going to hit you hard."

"Cassandra respected and loved her father very much and was crushed when she had to leave him. Terrified of him as well for a long time. She's grown and apparently got some smarts from where I can't begin to guess. She's working as a computer repair technician and, yes, would like to get in touch with her father. You have Myra to thank."

Top leaned into Myra. "You know her?" he snarled. "And

didn't tell me?"

Wide-eyed, Myra reared back, then her eyes squinted in childlike delight. "I didn't know she was your daughter."

Tory slipped a picture between their two noses. "Cass," he whispered, taking the picture and slumping to his seat.

"The letter is yours, of course. But she asked me not to give you her whereabouts until she's established peace with you and has received your blessing on who she is and where she's coming from. I'll be more than glad to address any letter you want to send."

Staring at the picture in his hand, Top turned his back and sniffled. Quickly wiping his eyes with his hand, he turned back around. "Victoria, Myra, I know you gals are dedicated and all that shit, but I'm ordering you to take the rest of the week off."

Both stood still, shocked by his generosity.

He looked up at them with wet eyes. "What d'you want me to do, plan your route of travel? Get outta here!"

Tory placed the letter in his hand. "I'll leave after I address that letter for you." She squeezed his hand and left.

"You up to going anywhere yet? Doing anything?" she asked Myra, walking her back to Supply. "It's been a long week for me."

Myra cocked her head as if listening and grabbed her dog tags, but she didn't squeeze them in her usual death grip. Instead, she held them to view in the palm of her hand and, looking down at them, said, "You know, what happened in there with Top." She stopped, bounced the tags once in her hand, clenched them in a victory fist, then dropped them. Fists on hips, she leaned her head back and inhaled deeply as if she were breathing fresh air for the first time. "What happened with Top makes me almost believe I really might win this one. His love for his child gives me hope."

"You gave him back his daughter. He'll put up one helluva fight before he lets you fall, babe. And so will I."

Myra looked at Tory and mouthed, "I love you."

"I love you, too," Tory mouthed back.

Speaking to Tory while glancing over the Supply counter at Pam, Myra asked, "How about we go to the NCO Club tonight?

184

I'm going to visit a certain Rose Connors." She turned her back to the counter and lifted both elbows back onto it. "You know, Tory, there aren't a lot of women here but there are some. Back in the States I could count on eventually finding my way into a group from the post. We'd meet at somebody's house off post or at a women's bar. It's not so easy here. And of course there's the fear. Some of us were either sent here or requested transfer here because of being suspected. There aren't any groups that I know of here but..." She stopped, looking intently at Tory. "...that's not to say we couldn't start our own."

Tory raised a surprised but pleased brow.

"And I don't know of any women's bars here either but...."

"But?" Tory asked.

Myra smiled impishly. "We can't do it here in public, Tory. Don't start no 'buts'."

Tory pinched her arm and gave her The Look.

Myra grunted with the pain. "But Mama—. No. Chung-ja. We're going to force her to take her name back. Chung-ja has a hooche off post."

"Is she, Myra!?"

"Yep. Just came out to me this past week."

"AH!" Tory squealed. "That's great! We could—"

"Be discreet. Maybe we could if we're very, very discreet."

"First you tell me about this 'sa-rang-he' you said to Chung-ja."

Myra's brows creased. "Oh! Pam told on me again, huh?"

"Uh-huh," Tory nodded. "Said she remembered it from a song that's popular here."

Myra smiled. "Okay. First lesson. Sa-rang-he means 'I love you' between friends. Just friends," she emphasized. "But from me to you it'd be sa-rang-hap-ni-da." And she said it into Tory's ear, then she yelled "PAM!" over her shoulder. When Pam came to the counter Myra threw her head back, looking up at her, saying, "How about joining us for dinner tonight?"

"For real? Yeah. Are we celebrating something?"

Myra and Tory traded conspiratorial grins, then Tory said to Pam across Myra, "Let's just say we're breaking you in."

Myra turned and patted Pam's arm. "Supply's yours the

rest of this week per Top. Be at the club nineteen-hundred."

At Tory's room door, Myra asked, "It's ten. Would you like to have coffee at, oh, one? My room?"

"One, hell! We're going now!"

Myra raised halting hands, backing toward her room. "One, okay?"

Tory watched her squeezing the bill of her cap in her hand. "Okay."

* * *

Apprehensive, Tory stood at Myra's door. Because Myra had appeared so nervous a couple of hours ago she herself was now nervous, wondering what had made Myra that way. At the same time her groin was hot and excited with expectation. Though the need was gone, she knocked the four raps.

Myra opened the door.

One look at Myra froze Tory to her spot.

Myra quickly pulled her in by an arm and locked the door behind her. Seeing Tory still just staring, she scurried to the coffee pot, poured her a cup and brought it back to her. Tory was still staring, making no move to take the offered cup. Myra picked up her hand and put the cup into it, hurried to the opposite end of the room, eyes darting about. Finding nothing to lean against, she turned in front of her plant table and faced Tory, arms holding herself.

"You don't, uh, like it?"

Shocked, Tory absorbed the new Myra standing ten feet away in stonewashed jeans, a rose silk blouse and—beautiful, short, layered hair that flowed softly back. She looked like her picture of a year ago but for the creases. But even those had lightened. Like they were healing. She looked like the proud, beautiful dyke that she was.

With no answer from Tory, Myra ran a defeated hand through her hair.

"Yes!" Tory blurted, finally finding her voice, and took a sip of coffee as well as a step closer. "You did that yourself?"

Uncertain, Myra nodded. "I always cut my own hair. Chung-ja was here. She was so excited and more nervous than I was. Almost made me cut a hole in back. Said she now had her 'true American' friend back."

Tory cocked her head and took another step closer. "I'm sorry. I was taken aback. You look so different."

"But not, uh, better."

"Better?" Tory took another step. "Mama! Gorgeous!" she took another step.

Myra raised a nervous, halting hand. "You were right. I prefer my hair short but grew it to hide. Now I figure if I'm going to go through with this anyway, I might as well go all the way. I didn't want to tell you about the problem with Craft. I wanted to keep it all underground. I didn't want what happened to Valez to happen to me and I didn't want it to happen to you either. I was afraid to involve you and I suppose I was afraid you'd think less of me for not handling it all better."

She took her dog tags in her hand. "These things. My crutch. It got so bad for me around here that I was doubting myself. I was beginning to feel ashamed for being what I am. So, whenever I grabbed them, I reminded myself of who and what I am and that I was OK." She lifted the tags up and over her head and dropped them onto the short table behind her. Eyes misting, she looked directly into Tory's, smiled shyly but smugly and confirmed, "I'm OK."

"Oh, babe," Tory said, placing her cup on the desk. Taking Myra's cheeks in hand, she rasped, "You were always OK. But right now it's me that's not. I got a body begging for your immediate attention."

Enfolding her in her arms, Myra brought Tory's lips to her own. "You're my Sergeant and duty calls." Smoothly, she guided Tory down to the yo.

The author, born and raised in New England, now resides in Tidewater, Virginia. Three years of her life were devoted to the Army's Military Police Corps. She left service as a Sergeant. Two of those three long years were spent in South Korea. Her reality now focuses on the creatures and plant life of the earth which include her beloved cats and parakeet, fruit and nut trees and garden. She owes eternal gratitude to her lover, also an ex-MP, now a mental health clinician, for nothing short of her own mental health. Thank you and love.